BOOKS BY MACDONALD HARRIS

The Treasure of Sainte Foy   1980

Pandora's Galley   1979

Yukiko   1977

The Balloonist   1976

Bull Fire   1973

Trepleff   1968

Mortal Leap   1964

Private Demons   1961

THE
TREASURE
OF
SAINTE
FOY

THE
TREASURE
OF
SAINTE
FOY

MacDonald Harris

NEW YORK   ATHENEUM   1980

Library of Congress Cataloging in Publication Data

The treasure of Sainte Foy.

I. Title.
PZ4.H4687Tq 1980 [PS3558.E458] 813'.5'4 79–23242
ISBN 0–689–11025–1

Published simultaneously in Canada by McClelland and Stewart Ltd.
Manufactured by American Book–Stratford Press, Saddle Brook,
New Jersey
Designed by Harry Ford
First Edition

FOR ANN *Remembering Room 9*

*There really is a town called Conques, and the
hotel there is really called the Hôtel Sainte-Foy.
Except for that, this story is a fiction.*

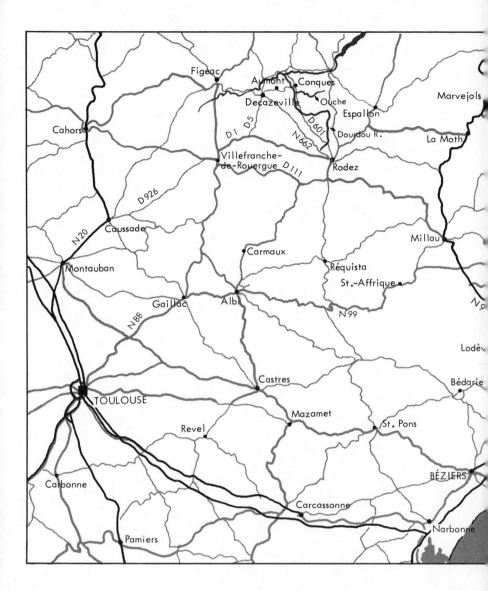

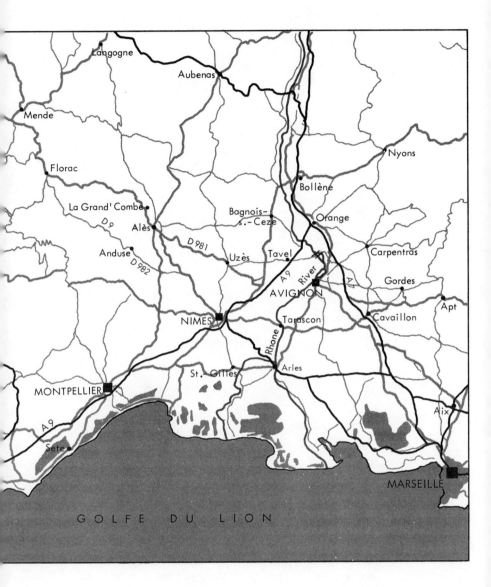

Langogne

Aubenas

Mende

Nyons

Florac

Bollène

La Grand'Combe

Bagnois-
s.-Ceze

Orange

D 9

Alès

D 981

Carpentras

Anduse

D 982

Uzès

Tavel

Gordes

A 9

River

A 7

AVIGNON

Apt

NIMES

Tarascon

Cavaillon

Rhone

St. Gilles

Arles

MONTPELLIER

Aix

A 9

Sète

MARSEILLE

G O L F E   D U   L I O N

THE
TREASURE
OF
SAINTE
FOY

ONE

Patrick comes out of the apartment into the hallway, bringing with him a camera bag, a medium-sized suitcase, and a cardboard carton full of photographic equipment. It takes him two trips to get all these things out the door. He locks the door behind him and carries everything over to the elevator. He pushes the button, there is a hum in the innards of the building, and after a while the small door slides open. He gets in with the camera bag and the suitcase. But the elevator is tiny, only the size of a phone booth, and there is no room in it for the cardboard carton. He leaves it in the hallway, planning to make a second trip back up to get it. But at the bottom he realizes that he is reenacting the fable of the peasant who wished to cross a river carrying a goose, a fox, and a bag of grain. He can't go up again without leaving the suitcase unguarded in the entryway, which he doesn't care to do. After considering for a moment he takes the elevator back up to the fourth floor with the suitcase. When the door opens he puts all the baggage in, reaches in to push the down button, and withdraws his arm quickly as the door shuts. The elevator descends with a hum, and he dashes down the stairs to keep up with it. At each floor he catches a glimpse of the elevator

3

in its glass shaft, going down at about the same rate he is. He reaches the street floor just as the door opens and takes out the baggage, only a little out of breath.

The car is parked under the plane trees in front of the building. It is a Renault 6 which he rented the day before at an agency on the Boulevard Matabiau. He has given a considerable amount of thought to the model of the car and even to its color. The small Renault is underpowered and rather cheaply built, but he has selected it precisely because it is one of the most popular cars in Europe and will not attract attention. It has a hatchback, and the rear seat folds down so that heavy or awkward cargoes can be loaded into it with ease. Its color is a pale neutral green, rather drab. He opens the hatchback, loads in the suitcase and the carton, and locks it again. Then he opens the front door and gets in behind the wheel, setting the camera bag on the seat beside him.

First he fastens his seat belt. Then he adjusts the rear vision mirror, focusing it exactly on a piece of medieval wall in the grassy field across the street. He takes out his sunglasses, puts them on, and adjusts them too. They are the kind that are a smoky gray in the daylight and turn clear at night. In this way he only has to possess one pair of glasses, an economy that pleases him. They are slightly loose, and he reminds himself that he ought to go to an optometrist and get them tightened. Next he fastens to the dashboard a device consisting of a rubber suction cup with a clip attached to it. Into the clip he puts a Michelin map. Then he inserts the key, starts up the Renault, and backs out of the parking place.

Toulouse, like many French cities, is built on the plan left behind by the concentric medieval walls that are still preserved here and there in places. He drives down to the river and along the quays to the circle of boulevards that follows the line of these old walls, crosses the Canal du Midi, and leaves the city by the Boulevard des Minimes. In only a short while he is in the open country, on Route Nationale 20, the main highway from Toulouse north to Paris.

At this hour of the day, just after lunch, there is not much traffic. When the city is behind him he reaches into his shirt pocket for the pack of Silk-Cut Filters, slips one out, and lights it without taking his eyes from the road. It is mild, with hardly any taste at all except for a faint flavor of menthol, and anyhow Patrick doesn't inhale. He expects to live a long time yet if he goes on smoking Silk-Cuts. When it is finished he extinguishes it carefully into the ashtray of the car, which he shuts. For about an hour he drives on over a broad plain, with dairyland and pastures on both sides separated by rows of poplars. It is a fresh April day and the sun is shining brightly. He glances at his watch : two thirty.

A little beyond Montauban he turns right onto a secondary road which leaves the plain and begins mounting up into the high stony plateau of the Rouergue. In only a few kilometers the aspect of the country changes abruptly; from a flat plain it is transformed into a complex and broken terrain of hills and ravines. Because of the low-powered engine he has to shift constantly on the grades, down to third and even to second. He likes driving on these winding back-country roads and enjoys doing this, even though the Renault's shift is wobbly and uncertain. Climbing constantly, the road curves its way through maize fields and tiny orchards fitted into the spaces between the hills. The peasants in this part of the world raise geese. They feed them on the maize until their livers are so enlarged they can't walk, then they sell the livers for cash, to be turned into pâté de foie gras for the expensive shops of Paris. The rest of the goose they preserve in its own fat, and in the winter they use this along with beans and onions to make cassoulet, the specialty of the region. These are a frugal people. They are independent, like all highlanders, and in the Middle Ages many of them were heretics. The Albigensians came from this part of France. Patrick has studied the guide before he left Toulouse and has all these facts in mind in orderly fashion. He feels good to be out of the city and mounting up into the hill country where the air is crisp and clear. This is good country, he thinks.

At Villefranche-de-Rouergue he glances at the map clipped to the dashboard. It is Carte Michelin 80, opened to folds 1 and 2. On it the major roads are printed in red, the secondary ones in yellow. The logical route from this point would be to continue on Départmentale 111, a red road, to Rodez, and then go on up the valley of the Dourdou to Conques on D601. But after some thought he turns off toward Decazeville on Départmentale 5, a smaller secondary road printed in yellow on the map. It occurs to him now that it would be a good idea to have a look at the hilly country north of Decazeville, since it is difficult to get a complete impression of the terrain from a map. A second reason is that he has made better time than he expected, and he doesn't want to arrive at his destination too early. If he checks in at the hotel at four o'clock there will be nothing to do except take a walk, or stay in his room waiting for dinner, and either might be conspicuous. Whereas, if he arrives at five thirty, it will be perfectly natural for him to stay in his room unpacking for an hour or so until dinner is called, which at such hotels is usually seven or seven thirty. The impression he wishes to give is that of an ordinary tourist, or more precisely a serious visitor with cultural aims in mind. Five thirty, he decides, will be exactly the time to arrive.

Decazeville is a small town; he is through it and out the other side in only a few minutes. To the north now there are no more towns of any size for a long way. This is a remote part of southern France, difficult of access and thinly populated. It is three hours' drive to the nearest city in any direction: Clermont-Ferrand to the northeast, Limoges to the northwest, and Toulouse to the south. In an emergency, for example if a patient has to be taken out to a hospital, the best access to this part of the world is by helicopter. Even the farms are thinly scattered, and there are large stretches of primitive country, thinly forested with pines. The road goes on through a tiny hamlet: Aumont. The church has a curious steeple, with a slate roof like an old-fashioned pointed hat. Patrick knows a good deal about romanesque churches, but he has never seen a steeple like this before except in photographs. He slows down a little to take a look at it. A woman is standing in the churchyard with a pail in her hand, her face turned in his direction. At first he took her for an old woman, but now he sees she is not as old as all that. She has the usual peasant stolidity about her and goes on staring at him without a sign of expression on her face. He puts the car back in gear and drives on up the twisting road.

Aumont is the last village. After another forty-five minutes of winding through the hills on a road hardly wider than his car, he comes out abruptly and unexpectedly onto the valley of the Dourdou. It is a steep ravine, heavily forested on the west side from which he is approaching, and rising up on the other side in a series of broken hills. Conques is visible across the valley. The town is small, self-contained, and perfect, almost exactly as it was in the Middle Ages. It is built not on a hilltop but in a kind of bowl nestling in the steep slope falling away toward the Ouche, a tributary that joins the Dourdou at this point. There are perhaps a hundred houses. Dominating them is the immense bulk of the church, far too large for such a small town. This is because the church was an abbey, originally, and the town grew up to serve the needs of the monks.

He stops the car for a moment to look. He still has plenty of time. In the afternoon sunlight the peach-colored stones of the town and church glow richly. The town shines out as though it were golden—a treasure scattered for some unknown reason on the rocky and arid slopes of these hills. There is almost no sound. He can hear the river purling far below him, and a distant metallic clunk from across the valley, perhaps a goat bell. When this town was built, he thinks, Paris was only a village. A shadow creeps across the valley toward the town. In a few minutes it will reach the base of the church. Patrick starts the car again and continues down the road, which descends sharply into the ravine and then turns in a switchback toward the river.

The bridge across the Dourdou dates from the fourteenth century. When he first catches sight of it he imagines that, although the map shows the road going over it, he is not going to be able to negotiate it. It was built for oxcarts, not for cars. It seems too narrow even for the small Renault. It tilts to one side, and there are weeds growing out of the cracks in the stones. He puts the car into gear and creeps gingerly across. On the other side he comes out onto Départmentale 601, which comes up the valley from Rodez. A short distance down this road a small lane turns off up the hill. There is a sign: CONQUES 1 KM.

It is almost exactly five thirty as he enters the town past the Mairie with its tricolor flag. There is only one street, with some steep cobbled lanes climbing at right angles to it up the hill on the left. On the other side of the street, to the right, a precipice falls away into the valley of the Ouche. At first he has trouble finding the Hôtel Sainte-Foy, because the vines have grown over the sign on the front, almost concealing it. Turning around and driving back down the street, he catches sight of it. The sign is inconspicuous, only a small blue-enameled plate. It is a three-star hotel, which is surprising in such a small town.

Leaving the car blocking the narrow street, he goes in and searches for some time through the hotel, which seems to be entirely empty. On the street floor there is only a corridor. Upstairs on the first floor there is a reception desk, and beyond it a dining room and an en-closed garden. All these rooms are deserted. Finally he finds a kitchen boy in a white apron and asks him what to do with the car. You put it in the garage. Fine, where is the garage? Là-bas. Below, where? Just there, in the street. Patrick persuades him to come down and show. There is really no garage. Dug into the hillside next to the hotel is a kind of cave, with walls of heavy stone, deep enough to hold three cars end-to-end. He pulls in behind a Citroën with a Paris license, takes out his bag-gage, and locks the car. The boy requests politely that Patrick should give him the keys. How, give him the keys? It is, the boy explains, that someone might want to make the Citroën go out. He speaks a slightly stilted French suitable for foreigners. Patrick gives him the keys. Then he goes up to register.

This time the patronne is at the reception desk, stand-ing as though she were waiting for him. She is a woman

8

in early middle age, formally and even elegantly dressed, in a tailored suit and linen blouse. Her hair is fastened at the back in a barrette. Her eyes are shadowy and thoughtful, set in a fine pattern of wrinkles.

"I reserved by telephone from Toulouse. Adrian Proutey."

For a moment she doesn't reply. Then she says, "Bon."

There is the typical French inflection, rising slightly at the end. There is no implication of *good* in the word. Simply *I understand*. She continues to regard him. After another interval she begins speaking again in a brisk but even voice, with a hint of Parisian accent.

"I can give you a large room facing inward, on the garden, or a smaller one on the street. It is only a dormer, but it has a view of the church."

"The room on the street."

"Number 9 then." She glances at the suitcase and the cardboard carton on the floor, and the camera bag over his shoulder. "You have more baggage?"

"This is all."

"Dinner is at seven thirty, and breakfast at any time after seven. You may take it in your room. I am Mme Greffulhe," she adds at the end, almost as an afterthought. Then she turns and leaves the room. She doesn't ask him for the British passport. This is too bad, because it is an excellent one.

The room is very small. He puts the carton in the bathroom, and the camera bag on the small table. With the suitcase on the floor there is almost no room to stand, so he sits down on the bed. The heavy roof beams pitch down on one side so that there is barely headroom even when he is sitting. Everything is whitewashed and clean. There is a small bath and it even has a W.C. and a bidet in it, which is surprising. But after all it is a three-star hotel. There is a slightly musty, old-maidish sort of odor to the cleanliness, perhaps because the room hasn't been occupied for a while. It is still April, and the season won't begin for another two months. On the single dormer window is a pair of heavy shutters, tightly closed, with a crack of light showing between them. The hardware on the shutters is rusty and massive. In addition to the bed the furniture consists of a bureau, an armoire, and a table and chair, all in the heavy dark-wood style of the early eighteen hundreds. There is an English print on the wall. The hotel gives the impression, somehow, that it has been arranged by women and is maintained by women. Women of a special sort. It gives the impression, precisely, that it has been arranged by Mme Greffulhe.

After sitting on the bed for a while he gets up and goes to the window, unfastening the heavy hardware and pushing out the shutters. The town is very quiet. He hears the creak of footsteps passing in the street below; except for that, silence. It is a little after six. The sun has gone down behind the hills to the west, but there is still a good deal of light. A kind of burnished yellow glow hangs in the air, as though the atmosphere itself were impregnated with tiny particles of gold.

The church is directly across the street. The massive wall of pinkish-yellow sandstone almost fills the opening of the window. Patrick already knows a great deal about this church, although he has never seen it before except in photographs. It is in the classic romanesque style, with rounded arches, solidly rectangular buttresses, and walls two meters thick. If it is unusual in any respect, it is that it was built on the side of a slope, on a broad terrace cut into the hillside below the street, so that Patrick's eye, as he looks out the second-story window, strikes almost halfway up the immense nave. It was built in this remote place because the track of the medieval pilgrims, on their way from Flanders and the Lowlands to the shrine of Santiago de Compostela in Spain, passed through these hills. Relics, holy jewels, and other objects of veneration were collected, over a period of several hundred years, to attract and awe the pilgrims. The church is sacred to Sainte Foy, a child-virgin martyred by the Romans in the reign of Diocletian, in the fourth century. Compared to other romanesque churches of the Midi, for example Saint-Sernin in Toulouse, Sainte-Foy is rather stark. It is not

10

particularly celebrated among art historians, except for the rather unusual bas-reliefs in the tympanum, and for its Treasure.

Patrick can't see very much of the town from his window. A few rooftops are visible to the right of the church. The cemetery, built on another terrace below the church, is out of sight from his vantage point. Beyond that the hillside falls away steeply to the bed of the Ouche a hundred meters below. The hills on the other side of the river are featureless. There is nothing particularly French about the landscape; it might be Montana or South Dakota.

From somewhere a bell rings: even, burnished spheres of sound expanding one after the other in the quiet air. It goes on for some time, in groups of three. Then it stops, and another and heavier bell begins, leaden rather than brazen. The notes come more slowly, at even intervals. Mechanically and passively, simply because there is nothing else to do, he counts. It is seven o'clock.

It is not necessary for Patrick to dress for dinner. In any case he always wears the same thing: faded khaki pants, a shirt, a loosely fitting gray sweater, and moccasins without socks. From long habit he does not wear underwear. In the bathroom he runs cold water over his hands and dampens his face. Then he dries it with a towel, regarding the image looking back at him out of the mirror set into the wall. The glass is rather tarnished and lends a grayish cast to everything. Even in the seeking light of the bathroom he looks younger than his age, which is thirty-nine. But it is not a vigorous or aggressive kind of youth; there is something scholarly about him. It is perhaps in the eyes, which are watchful and intelligent but passive. They record everything in exact detail, quietly, but look away if another glance meets them directly. A clear complexion, with dark-brown straight hair, cut rather long, falling over the rather high forehead. A thin straight nose. He is slightly over six feet tall. Or, since he has been living in France now for almost two years, he thinks: one meter eighty-four. His frame is rather slight, and the bluish-gray sweater, which is too large anyhow, hangs in folds from his shoulders. There is a tiny brown dot, a birthmark or mole, below one eye. And on the sweater, to correspond, a small stain of something the size of a coin, perhaps oil. He thinks: your disguise is excellent. You look like an art historian.

The brown camera bag on the table is plastic and made in Korea, but exactly resembles leather. In it he keeps his cigarettes, his glasses, his Pentax 35 SLR with its spare lenses and equipment, his maps and guides, and his kleenex. (He owns no handkerchiefs either, so that, lacking underwear and socks, he has no washing to do in the hotel rooms in which he customarily lives.) He takes the bag, hangs it over his shoulder, and goes out, locking the room behind him. The key he slips into the small side pocket of the bag, where he also keeps his money. He has about a thousand francs in cash, as well as some travelers checks made out to Adrian Proutey. If he pays Mme Greffulhe with the checks, he now thinks, she will be obliged to ask for his passport, and so she will get a good look at it.

His accent in English is international, neither British nor American, and his French is grammatically precise although obviously that of an English-speaker. In the dining room he is seated at the table and provided with a menu without having to engage in any conversation at all. But it is Madame, and not the waiter, who comes to take his order.

There is a prix-fixe at twenty-eight francs. He decides on cold salmon, médaillon of veal, and salad.

"And to drink?"

"What do you recommend?"

"As you will. A wine of the region. A Cahors perhaps. Or a Corbières rouge."

"Is there a house wine?"

"Very well." She writes out the order and tucks the slip under the edge of the tablecloth. He has fallen somewhat in her esteem, this is clear. It would have been better to take the Cahors, if only to be inconspicuous. She remains for some time after taking the order, as though she wishes to say something else to him; except that she never has the air of wishing or lacking anything. She is self-sufficient, composed, and slightly glacial, although not unfriendly.

"Do you plan to stay with us for some time, Monsieur Proutey?"

"Several days. I plan to do some—researches—on the church."

"Ah, our church. You are a scholar then?" This last, perhaps, with slight irony.

"Comme ça."

With this noncommittal and idiomatic term he seems to regain a little of the esteem he has lost. She admires, perhaps, people who don't reveal themselves too much. Continuing in this tactic, he says nothing more. "Still," she adds, lingering a moment longer, "several days is hardly long enough for researches. If they are serious."

"Very serious," breaking his bread. He rises again in her esteem. She leaves, still showing no expression.

The waiter comes with the wine in a carafe, and Patrick eats his dinner. There are only two other guests, a middle-aged couple who are perhaps Belgian or Dutch, with a guidebook on the table between them. A little later another diner comes in and takes his seat at a small table by the wall. He has the air of being completely at home in the place and is perhaps a resident of Conques who only comes to the hotel for his dinner. He is a bison-shaped individual who looks like Johannes Brahms; he has a large paunch, a protuberant white goatee, and conservative black clothes. A Jewish scholar? No, Patrick decides he is echt deutsch. His face is rather lumpy. His eyes have difficulty in seeing out from the lumps, and must roll about in a slightly wild way in order to find a path of vision. Because of his paunch, he is obliged to sit bolt upright at the table, with his back straight and his arms extending out with unbent elbows, like Brahms at the piano. Only the cigar is missing. Becoming aware of Patrick in the room, he stares at him over his glasses with a glance that is not so much suspicious as piercing and authoritarian. Patrick looks away.

The salmon is excellent, the médaillon also very good,

and as for the wine Patrick could hardly tell the difference between the Cahors and a house wine anyhow. If he prefers to stay in good hotels it is because he likes comfort, and not because he is a dedicated gourmet. It is a good meal, but he would be almost as happy with steak and french fries. In any case he cultivates a certain austerity, in his sensual life as well as in his clothing. He has a cheese, a local Chèvres (Madame seems to approve), and finishes off his bread. At this point the waiter comes.

"Professor Proutey?"

"Yes."

"There is a telephone from Toulouse."

He has been expecting this call. Flecker was to check with him, about dinnertime, by calling from a pay phone. It would be impossible for him to call Flecker without revealing the telephone number of the Toulouse apartment to the hotel, and in any case the phone in the apartment has been dead for several weeks because no one has paid the bill. Then too there are other advantages, quite unplanned, to his taking the call from Flecker. The waiter is impressed, and Madame too has observed the small drama. He is firmly established, not only as Proutey, but also as a professor. He picks up the phone feeling a distinct sense of well-being; partly, no doubt, from the wine he has had with dinner.

"Professor Proutey?"

"Yes."

They speak English, which Madame probably understands, even if the waiter doesn't.

"This is Gabriel. You've arrived safely?"

"Yes."

"And the hotel is satisfactory?"

"Quite."

"Have you begun your studies yet?"

"No. I only got here an hour ago."

"I understand. I imagine you got a look at the surrounding countryside. Is there a place for birds to light?"

"I imagine so. I haven't had a chance to check on that either."

14

"For tomorrow then. I'll call again. What's your room number?"

"Nine."

"Is there a phone in the room?"

"I believe it works. I haven't tried it."

"It sounds as though you haven't done much."

"I told you I just got here."

"It's all right, Professor Proutey. Don't concern yourself about it. I'll call again tomorrow when you have more facts. Is there anything special you need for your research?"

"What for example?"

"Anything at all. Materials, or any kind of help we can give you."

"I'll be able to tell more tomorrow."

"Until tomorrow then. About the same time."

"That would be best."

They end it at this point, without any farewells on either side. Patrick hangs up. Madame is nowhere in sight. He goes back to the table, not because his dinner is unfinished, but because he had left his bag there. This is an error on his part; he makes it a practice never to be separated from the bag, which not only has his money in it but also his camera and passport. It is exactly where he left it. He doesn't open it to see if anything is missing. The Belgian tourists are gone now, but Johannes Brahms is still there. Laying down his fork, he gives Patrick another long and slightly apoplectic glance over the top of his glasses.

Patrick, who had only come back for his bag, doesn't sit down. But Madame comes, nevertheless, to see if he wants anything.

"Coffee, monsieur?"

He shakes his head.

"A liqueur?"

"No. I never take liqueur. I seldom even take wine, as a matter of fact."

Madame smiles faintly, to show that she understands.

T W O

The next morning at eight thirty, after breakfast, he goes out with his camera bag. In the doorway of the hotel he stops to polish his glasses, then puts them on and adjusts them carefully. They are still loose, but probably there isn't an optometrist in Conques. He sets off down the street.

The spring morning is crisp. It is colder here than in Toulouse, even though the altitude is only about two hundred and fifty meters. There is a mountain feel to the air. With a kind of exhilaration, the traveler's pleasure in being in a new and unexplored place, he looks down the street to fix the location of things in his mind. He decides to inspect the church itself first, although this is not what he is ultimately interested in. It appears that nobody in Conques gets up very early. In the hotel only the waiter was up, and the streets are absolutely deserted.

In order to reach the church, which is ten meters or more below the level of the street, he has to walk around several houses and then descend a stone stairway, shady and covered with lichen. At the bottom of the stairs he reaches the terrace on which the church has been built. There is no filled land; the church rests entirely on a

16

cut made into the solid rock of the hill. On one side is the high retaining wall with the street above it. Although the terrace is broad, the church seems too large for it. To the left, along the retaining wall, it almost touches the shoulder of the hill. There is a passage between the church and the wall, so narrow it seems almost dark.

He stops to unlimber the Pentax, insert the wide-angle lens, and photograph the general layout of the church and the approaches to it. The Pentax, like the Renault, is a very ordinary piece of equipment that doesn't call attention to itself, but it is of excellent quality. The exposure is automatic; he lines up the scene in the viewfinder, rotates the focus ring slightly, and presses the shutter. There is a complex little sound, a click with a soft chunk superimposed on it, almost inaudible. He rewinds and shoots again: *ka-chunk*. In about a minute he has photographed the stairway leading down to the terrace, the curve of the street above the church, and a wide-angle view of the whole position of the church on the terrace.

The door to the church is locked. Probably it opens at nine—a few minutes yet. He walks around to the north side of the nave, in the narrow cobbled passage between the nave itself and the retaining wall, and around the north transept. The choir, which faces east, is a rather elaborate pile of towers, turrets, and buttresses, giving the impression that it hasn't been particularly planned but has simply accumulated as various architects felt the impulse to add their bit. On the south side, still on the level of the terrace cut into the hill, is a small cloister with a covered porch. Various pieces of romanesque junk are on display here, or simply stored: some fragments of sculpture, a broken capital or two, a grotesque figure that was perhaps part of a gargoyle. Even these broken fragments date from the twelfth century and are valuable, but they don't seem to be guarded and there isn't even a fence around them. Anyone could back a truck down from the street and carry them off, especially since the inhabitants of Conques seem to sleep so late in the morning. Although now, as Patrick inspects the fragments under the porch, he sees someone looking down at him from the street above : an old woman with a milk can. Since he is familiar with the habits of the Midi, he knows that she very likely keeps a pair of cows and has brought in her milk to sell it to the crémerie before it opens. Probably she was up at five or earlier. She regards him indifferently out of her creased face. He stares back at her, since he doesn't care to go on with his inspection of the church while she is watching. Finally she turns and goes on up the street with her can.

Patrick continues on around, circling the church entirely. To his left, on the edge of the terrace, is the presbytery : a solid-looking building of square blocks of sandstone. There is a small open area between the presbytery and the church. Coming around to the front of the church again, he now sees that there is another way to get down from the street to the level of the terrace. It is not necessary to go down the stairs; there is a steep little lane, wide enough for a small car, coming down from the street behind the houses, where it was invisible from the hotel above. He takes out the Pentax again and photographs this. There is no barrier or chain to bar the lane, nor does there seem to be any provision for one; he walks casually up the lane a short distance to look for eyebolts or hardware in the walls. There is nothing. Anyone could drive down the lane and back a car right up to the door of the presbytery.

The door to the church is still locked, although it is after nine now. He climbs back up to the street, turns to the right, and continues on up through the town past the hotel. There is a boulangerie-pâtisserie, a tabac, and the milk bar where the old woman was taking the can. After only a few hundred meters he has left the houses behind. The street continues along the side of the hill, with a stone balustrade and the cliff falling away on the right. Then it widens out into a broad asphalt surface, perhaps a hundred meters long and half as wide. There is a sign : a blue square with a large white P. It is here that the tourists park in the summer, since the street in the town is only wide enough for a pair of cars to pass. He gets out the camera again and takes several shots of the parking lot, including one with the wide-angle lens to take in the entire lot and its approaches. There are no trees or other obstructions around the edges of the lot. There is a steep hill on the north side, of course, and on another terrace higher up is a building that he doesn't identify. Although it is built of the same pinkish-yellow stone as the rest of the town, and in a style that attempts to imitate the older houses, it seems to be modern. There is an elaborate antenna on the roof, perhaps for television. He sits on the stone balustrade and studies this building for a while. It is perhaps another hotel, although the guidebook didn't mention another hotel. Because of the angle of the cliff the lower half of the building is hidden. Patrick can see only the windows of the upper floor, and the slate roof with its dormers above them. The camera is still hanging around his neck on its strap. He changes to the standard 55-millimeter lens, frames the building in the viewfinder, and presses the shutter. *Ka-chunk.* He gets up and walks back down the street toward the town.

A few more people are out now : a boy on a bicycle, a woman with a long loaf of bread, the postman with a leather bag. No one pays any attention to him. With the camera bag and his foreign clothes he is taken for an ordinary tourist. When he reaches a point on the street opposite the hotel he goes down the stairs again to the church. Standing on the parvis in front of the façade, he takes the guidebook out of his bag. Directly in front of him is the large semicircular tympanum over the doorway. It is an extraordinary piece of bas-relief. It is made of a different stone than the rest of the church, harder and finer-grained, and it is far less weathered than the other parts of the façade even though it is exposed to the storms from the west. The eye is struck by the exuberant richness of the tympanum and the extreme poverty—the nudity almost—of the rest of the façade. Balsan and Surchamp, who have published a monograph on the tympanum, contend that it is of a later date than the rest of the structure and was probably made for another church. They mention traces of polychrome;

19

Patrick makes out a tiny spot of color here and there. The bas-relief represents a Last Judgment, with Christ enthroned in the center and hundreds of carefully wrought figures filling the rest of the space. In the guidebook there is a sketch in blank with numbers to identify the figures. The Elect are to the left, the condemned to the right. Or more correctly, from the viewpoint of the figures themselves, the Elect stand on the right hand of the Savior. Patrick identifies Sainte Foy receiving the Divine blessing, Satan enthroned amid imps, the angels contemplating the torments of the damned. Three monks are caught in a net pulled energetically by a devil with a paunch; one of them holds a crozier. This, according to the key in the guidebook, is Etienne, Bishop of Clermont and governor of the Abbey of Conques in the tenth century, who, conniving with two nephews, looted the Treasure of the church. The bishop lacks contrition; he only looks embarrassed and out of sorts at being caught.

Patrick becomes aware that for some time there has been someone standing behind him and slightly to the right. He turns. It is a young woman in neatly fitting jeans, a white shirt, and a blue rebozo around her shoulders. She is tall, with a long, slightly equine face and a grave manner; a lock of hair has fallen across her forehead. She is watching him in an intent way and yet calmly. Even with a trace of amusement.

"You are interested in the church?"

There is something odd about her French. But perhaps it is only the accent of the Midi, with its rolled *r*'s that are almost like Spanish. She also touches slightly on the silent final e of église.

He explains that he is sorry the church isn't open. He has hoped to see the interior.

Without replying to this she looks past him at the bas-relief over the door. Her manner is prim.

"I've noticed that your attention was caught mainly by the right-hand side of the tympanum. You seem to be interested in the various varieties of sin."

He says, "Sin is always more interesting than virtue,"

20

feeling that this is a banal remark.

She smiles faintly. Yes, she does think it is banal, her expression says.

He asks, "You have been watching me for long?"

"A few moments."

"Why?"

"There's nothing much else to do in Conques."

"Do you live here?"

"In a manner of speaking."

He turns away from the church now and studies her more carefully. She seems an odd creature. She has somehow the air of an educated person, in her assurance and the precision of her language. Yet there is something simple about her, almost primitive. She has large hands with long narrow fingers. Her feet are large too. His eyes wander around to the other parts of her body. She is not disconcerted by his glance. She goes on looking past his shoulder at the tympanum of the church. Reluctantly he transfers his glance back to the tympanum again.

"Some of them are really sinners, but not all," she says. "I'm afraid the monks who commissioned the sculptures were rather vindictive. You see the knight in chain mail, who is being pushed by the demons with pitchforks? His only sin was that he was an ambitious neighbor of the abbey who disputed with them over some land."

The knight, in fact, is upside down, and the demon is prodding him in a very delicate part of his anatomy. Other figures are nude and bound : the adulterers.

"And there"—she points farther to the right—"are a lot of poachers who have hunted in the woods of the Abbey. They are being roasted on spits, and the rabbit they hoped to catch is helping with the job."

"You seem to know the tympanum very well."

"I am a guide to the church."

She says this quite matter-of-factly, without seeming to wish to provoke any response, but he is disappointed. She only wants a little money to show me around the church, he thinks. Reflecting on this little twinge, he realizes that he has been attracted to her.

"Sinners," she reads in a slightly theatrical tone from

the inscription in the stone, "if you do not reform your ways, know that you will have a dreadful fate."

The Latin in its archaic script, and its medieval turns of language, would be difficult even for an expert. Patrick, who has studied epigraphy in graduate school, could hardly have deciphered it himself. He is on the point of asking her more. But, without commenting further on sin, or on poachers, she goes quite simply to the heavy door of the church, takes out a key, and unlocks it.

"You are coming?"

She has turned in the doorway and is looking back at him in her calm, slightly distant way.

He follows her into the cool, dark, and deserted interior of the church.

She has none of the manners of a guide. She doesn't lecture him, neither does she conduct him on a fixed itinerary from one thing to another. It is he who goes ahead, slowly, while she follows at his elbow and a little behind. She herself looks about with something of the air of a tourist, raising her eyes to the carved capitals of the columns, glancing at the stained-glass windows. Now and then she makes a comment on something. But just as often the comment is his. She seems to accept that he knows something about romanesque churches and, in some matters, is more expert than she is.

The interior of the church, although sober and austere, is very fine. There is a great impression of height, of lightness and air, of fragility; it is almost gothic. She points out the iron grilles of the chancel, which, she says, were forged from the chains of prisoners who won their freedom by praying to Sainte Foy.

"Really?"

She glances at him, and offers a trace of a smile. "No, not really. These are modern copies. Iron could hardly last so long. In any case it would take a good many chains to make all these grilles. There's a good deal of legend in this church. If you prefer you can call it fraud."

Her manner is grave and yet light, and underneath

it is something like a trace of mockery. He wonders if she is a Catholic. He has known a certain number of Catholics who permitted themselves to be sarcastic about the pretensions of the Church, while retaining their faith. She gives the impression that she is a person capable of great faith, in something. Perhaps not in the Church. His curiosity is provoked. He feels a vague and latent, but rather strong urge to know this odd creature better.

He inquires why the grilles were built around the chancel, although he already has an idea what they were for. She points out the ambulatory, a tall somber passageway circling around the choir. It was through the ambulatory that the pilgrims circulated to behold the relics of the Saint, which were displayed on the high altar. Many of the relics were enclosed in gold or silver receptacles. The grilles closed off the chancel to protect the relics from thieves.

"Are the relics still here in the church?"

She glances at him oddly. He has perhaps carried his simulated naïveté too far. A person who knows as much about the church as he does would hardly imagine that the relics were still in the church.

"No. They're not here anymore."

"They're in the presbytery?"

She nods. But she seems more wary of him now, or perhaps it would be more precise to call it disapproving. She is still friendly, but there is a slight distance that was not there before.

After a moment she says, "You don't want to take pictures?"

"Is it permitted?"

"Of course."

It occurs to him only a moment later to wonder how she knew he had a camera. It is true he is carrying a camera bag, but many people use them for other things. Probably, he decides, she has seen him earlier in the morning photographing the outside of the church.

He gets out the camera, cocks it, and glances through the viewfinder to adjust for the light.

"What I would like is a picture of you."

She smiles.

"I'm not very holy."

"Neither are parts of the church. As you explained."

"Where do you want me?"

"Against the grille."

"Like Saint Lawrence?"

"Like a liberated prisoner."

"Saint Lawrence was liberated into Eternity."

"That may be. What is certain is that he was roasted alive."

"Are you a Catholic?" she inquires with her little smile.

It is the question he was going to ask her. "I'm an art historian."

"You could be both."

"And what are you?"

"A guide."

He isn't certain whether to offer her money. Finally, as they approach the oblong of sunlight at the end of the nave, he reaches in his pocket for a five-franc piece.

"I don't know whether . . ."

She takes it quite simply. But, instead of keeping it for herself, she drops it in a box by the doorway, marked "Pour les guides." Again he has not done the right thing, and again she has subtly corrected him, always with her air of perfect composure in which a trace of irony is detectable. Outside in the sunlight she removes the rebozo, holding it in one hand, and he is able to get an idea of her figure for the first time. The lower part of her body in the jeans is neat and lean, although it gives the impression of being slightly elongated, like an El Greco figure. The upper part of her body has this same stretched-out quality. The shoulders are narrow and the breasts small. The neck is long, and above it is the large oblong face with its grave manner and calm dark eyes. For a half an hour, from the time they entered the church together, he has been trying to recall where he has seen her before. Finally he remembers: she looks like photographs of Virginia Woolf. She locks the door of the church, puts the key away in the pocket of her jeans, and turns back to him.

For a moment neither of them says anything. Like any schoolboy who has met a pretty girl, he doesn't want to lose her. He is mildly surprised at this reaction in himself, even slightly amused. At the same time he finds himself casting about for some way of staying with her a little longer, or of finding out where she lives.

"Do you have to—stay on duty here?"

"Stay on duty?"

"Can you leave and go somewhere?"

"Of course."

"Is there a café in Conques?"

Nothing seems to surprise her; she accepts everything with aplomb and there is no false modesty or coyness about her. It seems perfectly natural to her that he, a man who is still young, should want to become better acquainted with a young and attractive girl. At the same time her manner offers no promise that she plans to grant him anything in particular, other than a half hour over a cup of coffee. They go together up the stone stairway to the street, and she points out the café. It is just down the street a little from the hotel. Because there are no signs in the town, or only very inconspicuous ones, he hasn't noticed it before, although he has passed it several times. It is called the Café de la Terrasse. The street isn't wide enough for tables on the sidewalk, so the terrasse is a tiny balcony on the first floor, overlooking a corner of the street. The terrasse isn't used at this time of the year; the umbrellas are folded and the chairs inverted on the tables. The café proper is a small room on the street floor below. She opens and enters. There is no one in sight. There are a few tables, a zinc counter, and a red-and-blue Cinzano sign.

She calls "Sylvie" in a conversational tone. They sit down at a table by the window. The girl comes out from the back room, and they order two cafés crèmes.

Again there is a silence. They sit with the two cups of coffee in front of them. He lights a Silk-Cut, and she watches with a kind of detached curiosity, as though she has never seen anyone smoking a cigarette before.

"You're from Toulouse?" she inquires.

"Why do you say that?"

"The license number of your car ends in thirty-one."

"You've seen my car?"

"It's a very small town."

After a moment he says, "No, I'm not exactly from Toulouse."

She doesn't pursue this. Instead she says, "I ask because I'm a Toulousaine myself. Or at least I went to the University there."

"What did you study there?"

It's a very conventional conversation, he thinks. But, like all conversations between a man and a woman who have just met, it has the air of really being about something else.

"Letters."

"And you became a guide?"

"There aren't very many jobs for graduates in letters."

She sips her coffee, still without taking her eyes from him. The silences that occur now and then have a curious quality. They aren't embarrassing or awkward. They are like the silences between old friends, or between married couples who speak only when they have something to say to each other. If there is a way in which she doesn't behave like an old friend it is that she continues to watch him in her grave and detached manner, as though she were studying him.

He would still like to know whether she is a Catholic. He notices now she is wearing a cross on a chain around her neck. It is visible in the opening of the shirt, the top button of which is unbuttoned. The cross is heavy; it is silver or perhaps polished pewter. The form is that of a Greek cross, with all four arms the same length. Each arm expands into a broad triangular blade, and on the three points of each blade are small silver balls or beads: twelve beads in all. Although Patrick has seen crosses of many forms he has never seen one like this before.

"What is that?"

Mechanically, still with her Virginia Woolf–like calm, she performs the gesture that all women do when their necklaces are mentioned: she looks down and

26

touches the cross with her fingers, a gesture that also calls attention to the opening of her shirt, and to her breasts. A necklace, Patrick thinks, is an arrow pointing to a part of a woman that she ostensibly wishes to conceal.

"It's called the Cross of Twelve Pearls. It's the Cross of Occitania."

"Occitania?"

"Originally it was the cross of the Counts of Toulouse. Then it was the symbol of the Cathars, and today it's used as the sign of a—kind of movement."

"What sort of movement?"

"People in the Midi—we call it Occitania—are struggling to preserve their culture. They resent the domination of Paris over the South. We would like to revive the original language that was spoken before the Franks from the north imposed their culture on us. It's called Occitan."

Patrick goes on playing the game he has fallen into with her; the game of false naïveté, of pretending to know less than he knows.

"That's an odd term."

"It comes from *oc*, the old southern way of saying yes. In the Middle Ages the southerners spoke the Langue d'Oc, the northerners the Langue d'Oïl. The *oïl* became *oui*, and when the Franks conquered us the northern language was imposed on everybody. But Occitan isn't dead. It is still spoken."

"What kind of language is it?" asks Patrick, although he knows a little about this too.

"It's a form of the old Provençal of the troubadours— the language of Arnaut Daniel and Bertran de Born. But," she says, "our Occitan is different. It's a modern language. People speak it every day."

"Who speaks it? Peasants?"

"No. Not only peasants. Students. Workers. Poets. Young people, mostly."

"Is it taught in the schools?"

"No. We want it to be. That's one of our goals."

"You say *our*. Then is it really a movement? With an organization, and leaders?"

But she is reticent about this. "There are many people who are interested in it. They have different ideas. We aren't all agreed."

"What are the other goals? Besides the language."

"As I say, some people have one idea and some another. Some say that Occitania is for the Palestinians, or against American imperialism. That's nonsense. Some would like the South to secede from France, to be an independent country. Others just want more autonomy. The Occitan language in the schools, and in public documents. More self-government. The freedom to preserve our culture. And economic help. The South is poor. There are no jobs. The government tells us to emigrate to the north if we want jobs, to lose our identity and become Parisians like everybody else. But we say: *Vòlem viure al païs.*"

He translates: "We want to live in our own country."

She gazes at him curiously for a moment. Then she says with her slight irony, "Bravo."

"It's not very difficult. It's something like Catalan."

"You know Catalan?"

Instead of answering he parries with another question. "Who were the Cathars?"

"Surely you know that."

He says nothing and waits for her to go on.

"They were medieval heretics, here in the south of France. Some people call them Albigensians. They took this cross as their sign." She touches the necklace in the opening of her shirt. This feminine gesture contrasts curiously with the tourist-guide tone of her lecture. She goes on, a touch of color in her face. "They were ascetics. They renounced the sensual world as the invention of Satan. They were opposed to the corruption of the clergy. They refused to take oaths or acknowledge any monarch. They would not bear arms. They wouldn't kill any living thing. They abstained from meat, and even from milk, cheese, and eggs."

"Why milk, cheese, and eggs?"

"Because, like meat, they are produced *per viam generationis seu coitus.* Everything that is sexually begotten is impure. They lived lives of total chastity."

28

"All of them?"

She smiles a little at his skeptical expression.

"No, not all. They were divided into two classes. the Believers and the Perfects. The Believers were the ordinary adherents of the sect. They kept the fast, and refused military service. But they could be married and have children. When you became a Perfect," she explains, "you renounced marriage and all the things of this world, and you could own no possessions. The Perfects were a kind of priesthood. But both men and women might be Perfects. The Cathars," she says, "practiced total equality of the sexes. They were modern in many other ways. They were totally democratic. They believed that everybody was equal before God; for them there were no nobles or monarchs."

"Was it a movement of the common people against the nobles, then?"

She glances at him. "You ask all the right questions. You know more about this than you are saying."

He says nothing.

After a moment she goes on. "No, it was not a movement of the common people against the nobles. Many Cathars were noble. The Duke of Aquitaine was a Cathar, and so was Raymond VI, the Count of Toulouse in the thirteenth century. In fact the movement was strongest among the nobility, those who spoke the Langue d'Oc. The Cathar movement was the center of the struggle of the South to be independent—to be free of Paris."

"They failed."

"Yes. Saint Dominic came from Spain to preach against the Cathars. The Dominican order was founded to suppress Catharism. Saint Bernard preached a Crusade against it. Armies came from the north; the Cathars were tried by the Inquisition and put to death. The city of Toulouse was besieged by the Crusaders. Finally it surrendered, and Raymond had to recant. The citadel of Montségur was the last stronghold of the Cathars. When it fell, two hundred Cathars were burned by the Inquisition in one day. Paris won. Provençal civilization was destroyed. No more troubadours. The language was stamped out. The nobles became vassals of the French king."

She is still calm, but a note of asperity creeps into her voice as she speaks these clipped sentences.

"And now you wear the same cross."

She takes the rebozo from the chair beside her, and drapes it around her shoulders. "That's really an accident. It isn't the same thing. We wear the cross because it's the Cross of Toulouse."

"I was going to ask you if you were a Catholic. Now I know the answer."

"No. The Church is our enemy. So is the State," she adds.

"Is the movement secret?"

"If it were I would hardly tell you about it, would I?"

"Have you ever heard of the Front de la Jeunesse?"

She is silent for a moment. Then she says, "What do you know about it?"

"Nothing much. I saw some graffiti on the walls in Toulouse, that's all."

She has nothing to say to this.

"Is it connected?"

"Some people belong to both. But they use violence. Or they say they will—mostly they talk."

"Would you?"

"What?"

"Use violence."

"I don't know. I might if a thing were important enough. I'd rather not."

After a while she adds, "Anyhow, I'm not very strong."

"You don't have to be very strong. All you have to do is pull a trigger, or light a fuse."

She is silent. Then after a while she says, almost as an afterthought, "I could do that, I think. I have nothing against it, really."

"You're not Perfect, then."

"No I'm not."

THREE

Her name is Marie-Ange. She is twenty-seven years old and she comes from the small town of Castres, near Toulouse. In Castres, she says, there are old half-timbered houses built over the river that were formerly the dwellings of tanners and dyers. The river water was necessary for their trade, and they lived over their shops. There are no more tanners and dyers now; the industry in France is all in the north. But the old houses over the river are still there, and Marie-Ange grew up in one. She went to the lycée in Castres. She was the only girl in her class. Then she went away to the university in Toulouse. Now, here in Conques, she shares a room with another guide, a girl named Erica.

And is she content to be a guide here in this small town? Doesn't she have ambitions to do something else?

She doesn't know. There aren't many jobs for graduates in letters, as she has already explained. At least not in the South. She could go to Paris and be a typist, perhaps, in the Ministry of Fine Arts.

There is no rancor in all this, nor any sarcasm. She explains all these things in a voice that is almost indifferent.

Are her parents still living?

Yes. But she doesn't see them much any more. They don't approve of her ideas.

What ideas?

At this she only lifts her shoulders slightly and smiles.

Her family name is Duplexis. But among the people she knows everybody goes mostly by first names. Patrick hasn't told her his name; or rather he has simply told her that his name is Adrian and that he is an art historian who has come to do research on the church.

"And especially on the Treasure?"

"Why do you say that?"

"You didn't seem very interested in the church."

"There are a lot of romanesque churches. Sainte-Foy isn't very different from the others. When will the Treasure be open?"

"I can show it to you now if you like."

"It isn't necessary. When are the regular hours?"

"From two until five, every day except Tuesday."

Today is Tuesday. He has the continual impression that she is playing games with him, in spite of her grave manner and her precise and factual, measured way of speaking.

"It's closed today, then."

"Yes. The church, you see, is always more or less open. But the Treasure is under the Monuments Historiques, which is part of the Ministry of Fine Arts. All museums in France are closed on Tuesdays."

"I'll wait until tomorrow."

"It's closed, you see, by order of the Ministry. But the Ministry is in Paris. That's a long way from here." Still staring straight at him in her mocking way, she reaches into her shirt pocket and takes something out, with the ceremonious, slightly theatrical gesture of a conjurer. "This is the key," she says. "It belongs to me."

The so-called Treasure of Sainte-Foy is displayed in the strong room of the former presbytery, the abbatial residence immediately adjoining the church. The heavy stone walls of this building are more than two meters thick. There are no windows in the strong room. The corridor leads past a small office, then it turns to the left and descends a short flight of stairs. The floor of the strong room is evidently below the level of the terrace outside. The door to the strong room is steel, and is fastened with a deadbolt lock.

Actually, the key in her pocket is not the key to the strong room. She explains that on ordinary days, when the Treasure is open, there is a Dominican father in the office, from whom one buys tickets. The key in her pocket is to the office. She unlocks the door, switches on the light (the office too is windowless), and crosses to the desk. From the drawer she takes out a bundle of keys, and a small pad of pink slips of paper.

"I have to ask you for four francs."

He gives her a five-franc piece, and she returns the change from the loose coins in the drawer. She passes him a ticket and puts the others away in the drawer. He examines it, amused at the primly formal way she conducts all this business.

VISITE DU TRÉSOR DE CONQUES

№ 15398   Fr.: 4,00

Ce ticket doit être présenté à toute réquisition

ENTRÉE

"And who gets the four francs?"

"The Ministry."

"Is one allowed to offer gratuities to the guides?"

"No." She isn't amused.

She is careful to lock the office door behind her. They go on down the corridor, turn to the left, and descend a pair of stairs. Patrick notes that the ceiling of the corridor too is made of solid blocks of stone, probably weighing tons. Marie-Ange inserts a large key into the door and turns it two full turns. The bolt grates, and the door opens.

Just inside the door is a switch. She touches it, and the room is illuminated by an indirect yellowish light from the glass cases along the wall, and from the free-standing glass cabinet at the end. There is perhaps other lighting; a pale white phosphorescence seems to glow from the ceiling.

While he is standing in the doorway Patrick is struck by the object in the glass cabinet at the other end of the room: the Majesté d'Or de Sainte Foy, a statue-reliquary in heavy gold constructed over a wooden frame. He has seen photographs of this before, some of them in color, but the sight still strikes him with a little shock, a kind of shimmer of the nerves. The figure is that of a young woman with short proportions and an oversized head; a naïve, somehow oriental style. The crown on the head resembles a turban. The throne on which the figure is seated is solid gold, with crystal ornaments on the arms and back. The pose of the figure is hieratic and cere-monial: bolt upright on the throne, the head tilted slightly upward, the short arms extended to hold out a pair of odd golden tubes like cigarette holders. Yet in some way the impression given is not that of a statue but that of a *person*. The photographs haven't prepared him for this. It is perhaps an effect of the eyes, which are alabaster ovals with inset pupils of ebony. As in many medieval statues, the eyes are depicted with an odd real-ism, contrasting with the stiff and ornate artificiality of the figure itself. They are wide open, and seem to stare directly at him from the other end of the room. She—it —*is* looking at him. He feels a warmth in his face, and a prickle of perspiration. Probably Marie-Ange has noticed nothing.

She precedes him into the strong room, leaving the door open behind her. But once inside she allows him to go around the room and look at things in the order that happens to strike him. He deliberately turns away from the statue of the Saint for the moment. Instead he begins examining the objects in the glass cases along the walls.

He has seen photographs of most of these things too in the Zodiac volume edited by Gaillard. But a photograph can show things only from one angle and always omits the finer details. Besides he is as much interested in the way the objects are displayed, in their position in the room and the construction of the glass cases, as he is in the objects themselves.

He stops before a heavy triangle of massive gold, perhaps twenty centimeters on a side, with a large crystal lens mounted at the top. Like the statue of the Saint, the triangle is encrusted with gems. In spite of its luxury there is something naïve about it. It has the look of a triangle to be played in an inferior and rather odd orchestra.

She says in her guidebook tone, "The A of Charlemagne."

"Why is it called that?"

She points out the two golden bars fixed vertically at the bottom of the triangle. If they are taken out and fitted into notches on the legs, they form the crossbar of the letter A. The attribution to Charlemagne is apocryphal. The Emperor, according to legend, distributed to each of the abbeys in his realm a golden letter of the alphabet, reserving the first for Sainte-Foy as a sign of his preference. In actual fact the object dates from at least two centuries after the Carolingian period.

"If it isn't a letter A, then what is it?"

"Just a reliquary."

She presses a button under the glass case, and the triangle revolves on its pedestal with a faint hum. When it is turned around she reads for him the minute inscription in archaic Latin on the back. *"Abbas formavit Bego reliquiasque locavit.* The Abbot Begon fashioned this and placed relics in it."

"My eyes aren't good enough to read that."

"I know what it says. Begon the Third was Abbot in the twelfth century. The relics are fragments of the True Cross, or so they say."

"If all the fragments of the True Cross were added up," he says, "they would weigh several tons."

She ignores all his attempts at jokes, or levity.

"The gold is applied over a wooden base, as in the case of the statue. X-rays have shown that the wood is hollow. But it's not even certain that there are any relics in it. No one has taken it apart."

"How much does the whole thing weigh?"

"Perhaps a kilo."

"And then there's the value of the stones."

She offers a silent examining look, for perhaps a second. Then they pass on to other things. A small golden coffer, known as the Reliquary of Pepin. A silver reliquary in the form of an arm, containing, it is said, the humerus of Saint George. A portable altar, in silver and porphyry inset with gems. An odd object, a reliquary-monstrance in gold with embossed miniatures, called the Lantern of Begon. A processional cross in which the gold is practically hidden under a thick incrustation of jewels. There are perhaps thirty objects in the glass cases in the room. All are gold or silver, and all are inset with gems. Their weight ranges from half a kilo or so to two kilos. But the medieval craftwork, of course, and the relics contained, make the objects priceless.

Now Patrick turns back to the Majesté at the end of the room. The statue is enclosed in a heavy glass cabinet, evidently of the kind of tempered glass used for automobile windshields; it has a faint grayish cast. There is a lock at the bottom, but it is not clear how the cabinet opens; perhaps one of the glass sheets slides upward or to the side. The illumination is from below. The throne on which the figure is seated rests on a sheet of frosted glass, or plastic, with lights in the pedestal below. This accounts for at least a part of the uncanny effect of the figure; the light from below illuminates the eyes and accentuates the calm, hieratic expression of the face. Perhaps because the eyes are set in slightly behind the rims of their sockets, there is an impression that there is a living person enclosed in the hollow metal statue. The gold, from all indications, is heavy and massive. Probably it weighs fifty or more kilos. In addition the figure is covered with jewels, so thickly encrusted in places that the gold is hardly visible. Some of the cameos and intaglios are Hellenistic, others date from the Roman or Gallo-Roman periods. The medieval gems are cruder, but some of them are of an astounding size. There are only a few diamonds; most of the gems are sapphires, rubies, opals, emeralds, amethysts, tourmalines, and carbuncles of garnet. There is a large rock-crystal intaglio on the back of the throne. The odd tubes held in the fingers of the figure, says Marie-Ange, are for flowers. A hollow in the head is said to contain part of the cranium of Sainte Foy.

Patrick gets out his camera, checks the light, and sets it for f.11 at a fiftieth. He stands in front of the Majesté looking at it. He remembers Flecker asking him if there was anything he needed for his research. "I wish I had a tape measure."

She goes off to the office and comes back with a meter stick. She holds this by the side of the cabinet while he fine-adjusts the focus and turns the camera sideways for a vertical. "No, a little higher. No. lower. That's it. Hold it." He presses the shutter, and the camera makes its small feathery clunk. Then he also photographs the statue from the two sides and from the rear, while she moves around to hold the meter stick next to it. As measured by the stick, the statue including the throne is about eighty-five centimeters high.

"Is that all?"

"No."

Without explaining to her what he is doing, he changes to the wide-angle lens and takes the shots he really wants: several general views of the room, including one from the far end behind the Majesté, showing the layout of the place and the position of the door at the other end.

Marie-Ange shuts the steel door and turns the key in the lock twice. The bundle of keys she replaces in the desk in the office. Then she locks the office door with her own key. All this takes some time. Patrick watches her, without a word. When the office is locked she turns toward him, expecting that he will turn and lead the way out of the corridor. But he stands in the narrow corridor, blocking it. She waits for him to move out of the way, with her usual composed expression, not at all curious about his behavior.

"When will I see you again?"

"I'm here every afternoon when the Treasure is open, from two to five, except Tuesday."

"That isn't what I mean."

"Your meanings are sometimes not very clear."

"Perhaps we could go somewhere—for lunch."

"Where?"

"I don't know. Perhaps the hotel. Is that all right?"

"It's very nice. If you can afford it."

"I can afford it."

They are so close, in the narrow corridor, that by stretching out a hand he could touch her. It is absolutely silent. He is aware of her odor: the freshness of a healthy young woman, a touch perhaps of lavender, and something else that in some way evokes a ghost out of his past. It is the odor, he realizes, of the high-school girls of his American youth, the scent of half-bloomed flowers enclosed in the faded and tightly fitting denim of the jeans. His adolescence was not a happy time for him. He was thin and studious and not very popular. Now, in the nostalgia evoked by the subtle mélange of odors, there is a melancholy mingled with a vague promise of happiness, of the recovery of youth.

"Well, have you had enough of looking at me?"

He realizes that he has been staring at her for some time. The slightly amused expression still plays at the corner of her mouth. He says nothing. It is the first time, he thinks, that she has spoken to him in the familiar second person: *Tu en as assez de me regarder?* He turns and leads the way out of the corridor onto the terrace.

At the hotel he opens the door and then stands aside for her to enter. She precedes him across the vestibule and up the stairs. He follows behind her, contemplating the cluster of soft hair at the back of her neck, the blue rebozo, and below it the slim legs in blue denim. Her ankles in the faded blue espadrilles are bare. On the stairway his eyes are exactly on the level of the long thin tendons rising out of the espadrilles, each tightening

38

rhythmically as she mounts the stairs. At the top, at the door to the dining room, she turns and waits.

Madame appears in her dark tailored suit, the memo book in hand. Two? Very well. She shows no surprise. But Marie-Ange must go down the hall to refresh herself before lunch. She reappears, with the same imperturbable expression. Madame seats them by a window overlooking the street. The two Belgian tourists nibble quietly at their food at the other end of the room, and Johannes Brahms is missing. They have the place almost to themselves.

Marie-Ange sits opposite him, placidly toying with the knife and fork. It strikes him now that she oddly resembles the golden statue in the strong room, even though she is narrow and elongated and the Saint is short and somewhat squat. It is because she is sitting down now, he thinks. She sits with her back straight, not quite touching the chair, looking across at him with her large head held just a fraction of an inch high. She even holds the knife and fork in the same way that the Saint holds the small flower tubes, delicately, with the ends of her fingers, but more or less upright. But part of it is her facial expression: the imperturbable and imperial calm. She might simply have modeled herself on the statue, he thinks, consciously or unconsciously, from the long hours she has spent in the strong room showing it to visitors. There is nothing extraordinary about this. Some girls, he thinks, model themselves on movie stars.

The lunch is very simple: a sole in white sauce, cold chicken, a salad, fruit, and cheese. There is a little difficulty about the milk. Marie-Ange has a carafe of the white house wine, but Patrick has found that it doesn't agree with him to have wine twice a day, and usually he has milk with his lunch. This is sometimes not easy in France. As it happens, there is in fact milk in the hotel, but it is some time before it appears on the table. The reason is that the milk is used only for café au lait and for cooking, and it is boiled before use. Thus it has to be cooled before a glass can be brought to Patrick. It tastes, precisely, like milk that has been boiled and then cooled. But he doesn't drink milk because he likes the taste. He drinks it because it is an old habit, and because it is good for the digestion. Marie-Ange contemplates this little drama with interest, but Patrick offers no explanation.

He attempts to get the conversation going again, in another direction. "You don't have to work this afternoon?"

"No. As I told you, the Treasure is closed on Tuesday."

"What do you usually do on your day off?"

"Various things. Sometimes I just stay in my room and read. Or I may drive around the countryside, to look at a church or a ruin of some sort. Sometimes I go to Toulouse."

"You have a car?"

"Yes. A small one. A Mini-Cooper."

"You do all these things alone?"

"Sometimes. I have friends in Toulouse."

Des amis and *des amies* in French are pronounced the same. The friends may be of either sex.

A thought occurs to him. "It's your day off today. And yet you stayed in Conques. In fact you even came to the church."

She permits herself a little smile, and lifts her shoulders. "It was because you had come. Somebody different, who was interested in the church. You see, it's a very small town, and everybody knows everything."

"What did Madame tell you about me?"

"Mme Greffulhe? I hardly know her."

This doesn't entirely answer the question.

"So you were curious about me?"

There is no coyness about her, and no false reticence. She reflects over the right term, and after a while says, "Interested," in a matter-of-fact way.

They have finished lunch and sit for some time without speaking. The plates with fruit peelings and scraps of cheese are on the table in front of them. There is still a little wine in Marie-Ange's glass. When his eyes turn to her, each time, he finds her watching him with her usual calm, although it seems to him that the color in her face is a little higher than usual. Probably it is just the

40

wine. Slightly disconcerted at this steady glance, he lowers his eyes and finds himself staring at the Cross of Twelve Pearls in the opening of her shirt. She seems to notice the direction of his glance; she smiles faintly.

"Where can we go?"

"It's a little difficult. Not to my room. Erica is there. We could go out in my car if you like. Or in yours."

"Where?"

"There are places. The woods up beyond the campground, for example. It's a traditional place," she says, "with the local youth."

Patrick doesn't find this very attractive.

"Why not here?"

She says without surprise, "If you like."

With a kind of balletlike formality, almost in slow motion, they rise from the table. The Belgian tourists watch them. They cross the hallway, Marie-Ange preceding. She has already started up the stairs when Patrick perceives that Madame is standing below at one side of the stairway, almost invisible in the gloom, watching them with a kind of sibylline and faintly arch calm that seems to be her specialty. His first impulse is to ignore her, then he changes his mind and confronts her rather assertively.

"Is it permitted to have guests in the rooms?"

She says nothing. Her chin perhaps descends a millimeter, and he decides to take this as an affirmative. He goes on up the stairs behind Marie-Ange. "After all it isn't," she says from above him, "a monastery. It's a hotel." They go on down the corridor and into the room. Patrick shuts the door and turns the key in the lock.

"She's a countess. Would you believe that?"

"I would if you told me."

"Her name is really Mme de Greffulhe, with the particle."

"Why would she want to conceal that she is a countess?"

"Everybody tells lies about themselves. Some want to make themselves seem more than they are, some less."

"And you?"

"And I what?"

"What lies do you tell about yourself?"

"If I tell lies about myself," she says, "it is about my body. For example, I wear a shawl because my breasts are not very good. Also I am too thin."

"Don't worry about it."

She does not, in fact, seem to worry very much. She drops the rebozo on the floor almost absent-mindedly. She kicks off the espadrilles, removes the silver cross on its chain, and hangs it on the chair. Then, standing with her side to him, she unbuttons the shirt. It too she drops on the floor. The jeans and underwear she removes almost in a single gesture. Seen from the side, her body is even narrower; it is a kind of stretched-out ectoplasm with a dark tumble of hair at the top. Waiting for him, she turns to look out the window. The shutters are almost closed. A thin vertical bar of light is visible between them. Over her shoulder and under her arm is a narrow fragment of the church, like a strip cut out of a magazine.

"Close the shutters."

She pulls them shut and fastens the heavy iron fitting. Now the light is cool and obscure, with a faint tint of mauve. She turns away from the window and faces him, her legs slightly apart like a fashion model, or a young giraffe. It is true she is very thin. The breasts seem half formed; there is no discernible line or crease at the lower edge where they join the rest of the body. From breasts to waist, where the faint knobs of the pelvic bones are visible, the body might be that of a boy. The long legs are perfectly formed. The tuft of hair between them is a small neat triangle, hardly noticeable. Her body is pristine, adolescent, sparse, provoking an emotion of the protective rather than the voluptuous. But there is no appeal to the protective in her manner. She is self-sufficient and calm, always with a slight suggestion of irony. Patrick tries to imagine Virginia Woolf unclothed, but this is unsatisfactory. She resembles a Cranach nude, he decides.

It is always an awkward moment turning back the covers of the bed. It is too domestic, and too explicit. The

white bed linen, when revealed, is almost more sugges-
tive than a naked body. Patrick is self-conscious about
his own thinness, and about the quite evident visible
signal of his desire. He displaces himself sideways to the
far side of the bed, where the sheet covers him to the
waist. The light in the room is dim and violet, sub-
aqueous. Everything ripples slightly; it is the light of an
aquarium.

For her part she gets into bed quite naturally, as
though it is usual for her to take a nap after lunch. The
bed is narrow. She pulls the sheet up and flops it over
them both. Her head descends; he feels the brush of
hair against his chest. He is motionless, the desire between his parallel legs straining like a clenched knot.

Through the wall, slow and measured, the brazen bell
rings in groups of three. Then, after a pause, the larger
one: a heavier clang expanding over the rooftops and
across the hills.

BONG.
BONG.

He has dozed, and is awakened only by an awareness
of motion beside him. She gets out of bed, trailing part
of the sheet after her. He is left to protect his modesty
with the blanket. When she sees he is awake she offers
one of her perfunctory smiles, then turns away almost
indifferently to the window. She tries to peer out through
the crack in the shutter. He contemplates her back, which
is straight and so thin that a tiny row of dimples is
visible to mark the vertebrae. Below them a dagger-
shaped cleft of shadow, faintly mauve it seems to him,
leads downward into the separation between the legs.
With a stir of desire he recalls the particular lemon-
flavored quality of her body. He had expected that after
their intimacy things would be different in some way,
that she would have surrendered something of herself
or that he would know something about her that had
previously been hidden. But she is exactly the same as
before. It is clear that what has happened has given him
no particular power over her, or claim on her emotions.
In fact, it was she for the most part who took the active

role and he the passive, although she did so in a quite detached way, fully conscious, watching him all the while out of her large gray eyes. His penetration of her has been purely mechanical, and he has reached nothing in her that is essential or private.

She turns from the window and regards him for some time with an air of consideration, as though he were a picture in a gallery.

"You're very nice. Although," she adds, "another time you should try having wine for lunch instead of milk."

"It makes me sleepy."

"You're sleepy now anyhow."

"That's because . . ." Not knowing quite what he is trying to say, he trails off.

"You mean—that making love makes you sleepy? Then why don't you say so?" She is amused. "Are all Anglo-Saxons like you?"

"You haven't known any others?"

She is serious again, or at least the smile disappears.

"I haven't known very many—people. In that way."

Turning away from him, she unfastens the heavy iron fittings and pushes the shutters open a little. From violet the light in the room changes to a subdued and shadowy bronze.

"Then people—as you put it—are making a mistake."

"My breasts aren't very good, as I told you. And I'm too thin."

"I'm thin too."

"Yes, you're very thin," she agrees, turning around again. "You should drink wine for lunch, and that will give you an appetite and you will gain weight."

"You don't like me thin?"

"I like you perfectly, just as you are."

This zigzagging and paradoxical manner is difficult to seize. He gets out of bed and pulls on his faded khaki pants. She is still by the window, looking out through the crack in the shutters or pretending to. He stands up and fastens the zipper over the now somewhat languid remnants of his desire.

44

"Aren't you afraid somebody will see you from the street?"

"It's dark in the room. Anyhow," she says, "they know how a woman is constructed. There are sculptures in the church."

"Nude?"

"Some of them. Didn't you notice?"

"It isn't common in the romanesque."

"No," she agrees, "more in the gothic."

"Cranach, for example."

"More in the gothic," she goes on, so that he never has a chance to tell her she looks like a Cranach nude. "But this is the Languedoc. There was no northern puritanism here in the Middle Ages. People were franker about bodies. It was the influence of the troubadours perhaps."

"Yes, the bishops had mistresses."

"Why shouldn't they?"

"It's not exactly in accordance with Christian doctrine."

She turns from the window, picks up her shirt, and slowly and almost dreamily begins putting it on. Her long legs, diverging at an angle, stick out from underneath it.

"Well, I'm not a Christian. I believe," she says, "there is a spiritual world, but we don't know anything about it and we can never go there. It has been made for somebody else. Another race of beings. For angels perhaps." All this in a contemplative, slightly forlorn tone, as though she were talking to herself. "We aren't angels. We have to live in this world. I don't like angels."

"But you like churches."

"I like beauty, and old things. But medieval art has nothing to do with Christianity. It was made by artists. It belongs to us; to the people. It belongs to Occitania."

"It was made by artists," he argues, "but it was paid for by the monks. It's the expression of a religious impulse. You can't," he tells her, "divest something of its origins just by changing the names of things. You don't want the Church to be Christian, and perhaps I don't want to be Anglo-Saxon. I might say to you, look, I'm just Patrick and you're Marie-Ange, we're just two human beings, I'm Mediterranean like you and your friends, so don't make jokes about my inhibitions. It wouldn't do any good, because I'm still Anglo-Saxon."

"I don't make jokes about your inhibitions." And after a pause, "Why should you call yourself Patrick?"

"It's just a family name." He feels himself blushing. "A nickname."

"A nickname?"

"It's what they used to call me in the family, when I was a child."

"You don't seem to me," she says, "like the kind of a person who would have a family."

"Well I did."

"Shall I call you Patrick then?"

"Call me whatever you like."

He comes to her and passes his hands about her waist. The thought occurs to him that it is the first time he has really touched her body. Before, in bed, it was she who touched him. Her waist is unexpectedly firm and solid, except for the softness at the front. He attempts to kiss her. She raises her head and turns away slightly, and his lips bump her jaw at the corner of the throat. It is another firm place : the hardness of the bone under the skin, and the firm line of the tendon just below it.

He turns her head around and kisses her firmly on the lips, which part slightly. From the waist his hands move up under her shirt.

She turns and slips away, the corners of her mouth lifted in the little smile that he no longer understands very well.

"Patrick, you are doing this in your sleep."

FOUR

After dinner Patrick carefully closes the shutters and locks the door of the room. He switches off the light by the bedside. Then he goes into the bathroom, shuts this door too, and sets the cardboard carton of photographic equipment on the seat of the toilet. The canister of film he sets on the edge of the wash basin. He checks to remind himself where everything is, then he turns off the bathroom light. It seems perfectly dark. To be sure he takes the towel and stuffs it into the crack at the bottom of the door.

Then, in absolute darkness, he feels in the carton for his equipment. Each item is stowed in its proper place in the carton, so he is able to find everything quickly. The Paterson quick-fill tank, the bottles of developer and fixer, the funnel. He pries off the end of the film canister with a bottle opener, and pulls out the film. Holding it carefully by the edge in order not to touch the emulsion, he bows it slightly with his fingers and feeds it into the reel. He is skillful at this from long practice, and he has no difficulty doing it in the dark. He slips the reel into the tank, fits on the lid, and turns the light back on. Then he pours in the proper amount of developer and begins agitating the tank.

In a half hour the film is developed, fixed, and rinsed. He takes it out and hangs it in the bathtub. It will take a while for it to dry, but he has nothing else to do until bedtime anyhow. He goes out for a walk, spends a half hour prowling through the lanes in the upper town where he hasn't gone before, and smokes a Silk-Cut on the parapet overlooking the church. When he comes back to the room the film is dry. He cuts it into short lengths with a pair of scissors. Then he plugs the safelight into the fitting provided for an electric razor, and turns the other light off. In the red glow he arranges his trays in the bathtub and fills them with developer, stop-bath, fixer, and wash. He lays the negatives in the contact frame and fits a piece of print paper over them. Then he turns the bathroom light on for exactly four seconds.

Touching the paper only by its edges, he slips it into the developer. Then, in the red glow coming from over his shoulder, he rocks the fluid from side to side. For a while there is nothing. A few shadowy lines begin to take form in the tray. The dark places spread and co-agulate, then more quickly, with a silent snap so to speak, the images spring out on the paper. The twenty small rectangles are sharp and clear, and all the exposures are correct. He fixes and washes the sheet and turns the light back on.

The light in the bathroom is only a small one. He takes the still wet proof-sheet into the other room and arranges it on the bedside table on a towel, directly under the light of the lamp. Then he examines it.

Every body in its natural state is made of a series of ghostly images, films of light that conceal the true nature of whatever is inside. These husks and shells, being only a dance of photons, are shifting and elusive; they are as ephemeral as time itself. Photography, capturing these outer semblances and bringing them to a standstill, permits them to be examined at leisure; that is, it steals their power and leaves them disarmed and naked. Patrick, by turning from one photograph to an-other, can cause time to go backward or forward, or remain fixed in the single moment. He is master of time. In this world he is immortal.

Furthermore, photographs can not look back at you. They are therefore free of another of the disadvantages of the real world: its tendency to regard *you* as an object to be examined, and therefore penetrated and disarmed. This is particularly noticeable in nudes and other erotic photographs. They are superior in at least one respect to the objects they represent: they are unable to look back at you, perhaps with faint irony, and note your own curiosity and desire as you examine them at your leisure. Patrick's first interest in photography, in fact, began with a boyhood collection of indecent photographs. This led him to become, first of all, a connoisseur of solitary vice, second, a keen but passive observer of the external world, then an amateur photographer, and finally an art historian; that is, one who spends his life examining the images created by artists, which are themselves imitations of those other ephemeral films enclosing the objects of the real world.

Patrick understands clearly the reluctance of some primitive peoples to be photographed or portrayed in pictures, in the fear that something essential will be stripped away from them in the process, that their souls will be stolen. Because, when an object is photographed, it always *gives up* something of itself. For, if a photograph of a woman's body, even in a childish game, can bring the beholder to the point of orgasm, has not that woman, even though unknowingly, surrendered something of herself? So Patrick reasoned in his boyhood, and so in a sense he still believes. He always examines newly developed photographs, therefore, with curiosity, even with a keen desire touching on the sensual, knowing that something will be revealed in the tiny silver particles held in the emulsion that was not apparent to the ordinary eye.

He first examines the shots of the outside of the church and the rest of the town, including the odd building above the parking lot. The wide-angle shots are most useful. An expert would even be able to estimate the dimensions of the lot, knowing the inclusion angle of the 28-millimeter lens. The shots of the interior of the church confirm something he didn't notice at the time but which Marie-Ange has already told him : that some of the sculptures are nude. He gets out a magnifying glass to study one of them in more detail. It is a figure in the capital of a column, depicting a Blessed Soul being elevated, into Paradise. In characteristic medieval style the figure is emaciated and without prominent sexual features; the small breasts resemble buttons. Behind it are male figures, their private parts concealed by angels. There is very little evidence of Marie-Ange's theory that this art is influenced by the troubadours. There is nothing sensual in it, and it seems merely to illustrate the doctrine that you must cast off all earthly raiment before entering Heaven.

At the end of this strip is Marie-Ange herself, standing against the iron grille of the chancel with her fixed little smile. It is in all respects, he now sees, a photographic smile, contrived and a little artificial. It is the smile of someone who has *decided* to smile for some reason, and not of someone who is amused. Her hands are behind her and she is standing with her legs slightly apart. This pose, in combination with the iron grillework behind her, in some way suggests the role of prisoner or martyr. But it was she herself, when he asked her to stand against the grille, who jokingly compared herself to Saint Lawrence. Patrick recognizes, after a moment, what the pose reminds him of : his boyhood collection of erotica. He feels a stir of desire. But it was not to look at this picture, he reminds himself, that he developed the roll.

The shots of the Treasure are more successful than he expected. There is only a little reflection from the glass cabinets, and the exposure—f.11 at a fiftieth, he never forgets an exposure—is perfect. The principle of revealed secrets is demonstrated in almost every photograph. The two small angels on the A of Charlemagne, one male and one female, are thurifers; they bear incense burners which they swing, perhaps, to perfume the holy relics, or to cover the odor of flesh. According to doctrine angels are supposed to be sexless. But perhaps this is Marie-Ange's influence of the troubadours. The angels are fully clothed and the only sign of concupiscence is that they seem to be glancing covertly at each other. In the Reliquary of Pepin there is a ruby the size of a bicycle reflector; he hadn't noticed this before either.

The four photographs of the Majesté d'Or, perhaps because they are posed so diagrammatically from front, back, and two sides, resemble anthropological materials, or shots taken in a morgue or police station. Especially from the sides the outstretched arms—holding nothing, since the flower tubes are empty—suggest the pose of a drowned body, with the arms held stiffly in floating position. This impression of rigor mortis, in fact, is apparent even from the front—except for the eyes, which give the impression of something living enclosed or imprisoned in the lifeless shell of gold. When Patrick gets out the magnifying glass, and stares straight into these eyes in their calm and gnomic face, he becomes aware to his mild surprise of the same slight stirring in his trousers that he felt, only five minutes ago, at the photo of Marie-Ange against the grille. He shifts the position of his legs in order to allow this phenomenon room to operate, and reflects that it is probably only because the statue is so valuable. He goes on to the other pictures.

These 35-millimeter contacts are very tiny; they are intended not to be viewed in their raw state but to be enlarged. They are hardly larger than postage stamps. But Patrick is practiced at analyzing them and noting their finer details. He uses the magnifying glass only occasionally, when he wishes to verify something he has already caught with the naked eye. His attention is now drawn again to the photograph taken up the hill from the parking lot, and showing the top half of the building with the four dormers and the elaborate antenna on the roof. It strikes him now that the antenna is not for television but for some kind of communications equipment, although he doesn't know enough about electronics to tell what sort. There are four windows in the upper story of the building, exactly symmetrical with the four dormers higher up on the roof. In the second window from the left he now catches sight of something odd. Although he didn't notice it when he took the picture, there seems to be a figure standing in the window. Because of some peculiarity about the lighting in the window it is visible only in silhouette. The picture was taken at a five-hundredth of a second, and records only a tiny instant in the passing of time. But something about the stance or outline of the figure suggests that it has been standing there for a long time. There are other peculiar things about it. The figure is unmistakably human, but the top of the head is square, and there are what appear to be tufts of something growing on the points of the shoulders.

Patrick studies it for some time in the magnifying glass, moving the proof sheet around to get a better light from the lamp. He can't tell very much about it. There is something to one side that is perhaps an arm, perhaps only a shadow. It is not even clear that it is human at all. Nothing human has a flat head like that, and the *fixity* (this is the only way he can put it) suggests a cardboard figure or something out of a scare movie. Honest voyeurs conceal themselves. They don't stand in open windows, staring straight at you. He feels the hair standing up a little on the back of his neck. That thing was watching me, Patrick thinks.

FIVE

The apartment in Toulouse, in Boulevard Armand Duportal, is in a new building, on a broad avenue lined with plane trees in the university quarter. Everything is modern and clean, and there are expensive cars parked under the trees in front of the buildings. The street lamps cast a dull yellowish glow on the pavement every few hundred yards; in between them it is dark. Across the street are some irregular shadowy shapes, fragments of the old medieval walls of the city. Beyond them is the Faculty of Social Sciences, and from there it is only five minutes to Place du Capitole in the heart of the old city. Now, after midnight, it is quiet except for an occasional motorcyclist racketing his way down the boulevard toward the river.

The apartment is on the fourth floor, with balconies front and rear. The shutters on the windows are solid, without louvers, and when they are closed not even a crack of light is visible from the outside. The walls are solid masonry and soundproof. Inside there is a small salon, a kitchen, a bedroom, and a study. There is almost no furniture in the apartment, and the light comes from bare bulbs screwed into the fixtures. In the salon which also serves as dining room there is an unpainted wooden table, stacked with dirty dishes. For sleeping there are mattresses on the floor in the bedroom and in the study. In the bedroom there are khaki duffel bags, a cheap imitation-leather suitcase, and items of loose shaving gear on the floor by the mattress. The room is almost bare. The study, by contrast, is crammed so full of things that there is almost no clear floor space. A mattress occupies one corner. Across from it, against the wall, are two large wooden packing cases with UNIVERSITE DE TOULOUSE-MIRAIL. INSTITUT DE GEOPHYSIQUE stenciled on the sides. The tops of the cases are heavy plywood fastened with wing nuts. There are cardboard boxes with government topographical maps and aviation charts, a pair of 8×50 binoculars, a drafting machine, a pair of surplus American paratroop boots, a miniaturized UHF transceiver with telescoping antenna, stacks of military field rations in khaki cans, coils of dirty nylon rope, a photo enlarger, and bottles of developer and fixer. A pile of soiled clothing has been thrown into one corner of the room, along with a sleeping bag which has not been properly rolled up but only piled in a heap. A small study lamp on the floor casts a circle of light a meter or so in diameter. The dead telephone is sitting on the floor just at the edge of this circle of light. In the lamplight Gaspar and Flecker are studying an aviation chart, NA 1209, including the area from Albi north to Clermont-Ferrand. They are sitting on the edge of the mattress, which has a rumpled blanket on it but no sheets.

Serge Gaspar is a Toulousain, dark, with a Spanish look to him. He has the body of an acrobat or a tumbler, agile and slightly simian. His shirt is unbuttoned to the waist, showing a thick mat of black hair on his chest. He is wearing tight-fitting jeans with bell bottoms and patent-leather shoes. To look at the chart he wears Franklin half-glasses with horn frames, a scholarly touch that contrasts oddly with the rest of him. From time to time he raises his hand to scratch at his chest with a jabbing, animal-like gesture. But the glasses are the correct clue; he is a university professor.

Martin Flecker is different from Gaspar in almost every external way. American is written all over him.

He is large and square, built like a barn door, with reddish hair and a mottled complexion. His shoulders are broad and he has a thick neck with a scar at one side of it. There are deep crow's-feet at the corners of his eyes, and a crease in his forehead that gives him a watchful and skeptical expression. He is always aware of what is going on around him. His clothes contrast sharply with Gaspar's too: a nylon turtleneck jersey, a hand-woven linen shirt over it which he leaves hanging out, and Levi's. He is smoking a cigarillo and from time to time he knocks out the ash into a tin can on the floor near him.

Across the room Sara is sitting against the wall with her knees up, bored. She is the same Toulousain type as Gaspar, with dark hair, a neat compact body with somewhat short legs, and a clear olive complexion. She wears an olive-green military shirt with the sleeves rolled up to her elbows, trousers of the same color, a wide belt with a heavy brass buckle, and polished leather boots. All this clothing comes from an American surplus store in rue Saint-Rome, the rich-hippie quarter of Toulouse. The only English she knows is "Okay." She stretches out her hands in the shadowy light and examines her nails; she is meticulous about her manicure. The fingers are shapely and graceful, if somewhat short. The nails are finished in silver lacquer with a faint cast of violet. There is a touch of the same violet in her eye shadow. The eye shadow and the fingernail lacquer are her only cosmetics. Her hair is cut short, in a kind of glossy mop.

Gaspar scratches his chest. "The approach to the north is over high terrain. It's good. There's nothing up there. It's mountain country."

"It's too far out of the way. You'll have fuel for only about three hours. You'll have to go in from the west."

Flecker shows with his finger.

Gaspar doesn't like the approach from the west. "There are towns in there. Decazeville is a good-sized town. Then there's Aumont, Praysac—all those villages."

Flecker draws on the cigarillo and then sets it down on

the tin can. "You haven't got the fuel to go around to the north. It's another hundred kilometers. Those towns don't amount to much. They're not as big as they look on the chart. They're only hamlets. You can pass by Decazeville to the south. If you stay low the hills will hide you."

"You're the expert. But if someone sees us come in the whole thing will be foutu."

"Don't worry about people seeing you. You have to accept that. They're going to see you anyhow."

Flecker's French is fluent, but with a heavy American accent. Gaspar speaks with the rolled *r*'s and slightly audible final *e*'s of the region. Sara says nothing. She is tired of examining her nails and reaches over to the tin can where Flecker has left his cigarillo. She places it between her lips inexpertly and draws at it. She considers the taste, shrugs, and puts the cigarillo back. She exhales the smoke slowly.

Flecker shows the route on the chart with his thumbnail.

"You leave Montauban to the west, then turn northeast and pass by Decazeville through the hills. The final approach you make from the west, over this plateau. It's an hour from Toulouse, perhaps a little more."

Gaspar gets a ruler from a cardboard box to measure the distance. A little over fifty centimeters. The scale of the chart is $200,000:1$. A hundred kilometers.

"You say an hour. Is that all the thing will do?"

"It will do two hundred and fifty, probably. But the climb-out is slower. Then you have to make this dogleg around Decazeville. It's better to allow plenty of time."

Gaspar sets out to show that he is wrong. With a pencil and ruler he sketches out the route: Toulouse to a point east of Montauban, then northeast past Villefranche and Decazeville, then the short leg to the east. But Flecker takes the pencil away from him and throws it against the wall.

"Don't make marks on the chart. Anybody can look at it later and tell exactly where you've been."

He is right, of course. Gaspar says nothing. But his

56

dark Latin vanity is offended, especially since it happened in the presence of Sara.

"Did Patrick say he has found a place to set down?"

"He hadn't had a chance to look yet. He had just got there when I talked to him."

"I don't entirely trust him, ce bougre-là."

"Patrick's okay," says Flecker.

"He's an intellectual."

"What the hell are you?"

"Me? I'm me."

"Besides what's wrong with intellectuals?"

"They're always thinking, and while they're thinking someone comes up from behind and screws them in the ass."

This dialogue is unrewarding. Flecker glances at his watch. "It's a quarter after one. Are you ready to go?"

"Whenever you are."

Sara says, "Where are you going?"

"Out. You stay here."

"I like to go out once in a while too."

"We're just going to visit the local bordello," says Flecker. "We'll be back in an hour."

"What are you going to do? Maybe I can help."

"You stay here, Sara."

Down below in the boulevard the nearest street lamp is a hundred meters or so from the car and it is fairly dark. They load in the empty packing case. The car is Gaspar's rather battered Deux Chevaux camionette. It has only two cylinders and makes a noise like a motorcycle, but it has the advantage that it is the cheapest car in France and it always runs, more or less. It is painted gray, with a truck body on the back like a little hut made out of sheet metal. The lettering on the door is made with the same stencil used for the two packing cases: UNIVERSITE DE TOULOUSE-MIRAIL. INSTITUT DE GEOPHYSIQUE.

The thing starts with its usual clatter. Flecker looks around down the street, but there is nobody in sight at this time of night. They go down the boulevard to the river, then they cross over the bridge to the Saint-Cyprien district and leave the city by the avenue Muret. Gaspar drives fast, hurtling the small truck over the bumps and crossings in a way that makes Flecker's teeth jar. Once in the open country it is totally dark. The yellow headlights bob on the long strip of pavement ahead of them. They are on Départmentale 4, a back road that winds through the farm country toward Pamiers. After only about ten minutes Gaspar turns off on another road marked AUREVILLE 4 KM. The road is paved but it is barely wide enough for the Deux Chevaux. Gaspar drives aggressively, with his chin stuck forward a little, scratching his chest with one hand.

"How do you know where you're going?"

"I've been here before."

Aureville consists of a half-dozen or so houses at a crossroads. A kilometer or so beyond the village Gaspar turns off onto a rutty dirt road. The camionette climbs up over bumps and lurches into gullies.

He pulls up before a rather decrepit-looking farmhouse. The headlights illuminate spots of manure or mud on the whitewashed walls. In addition to the small house there is a barn made out of galvanized iron and a shed with an old car in it.

Before he has come to a stop Gaspar switches off the lights and the engine. The camionette stops with a wheeze, and it is so quiet that they can hear the countryside breathing around them. They get out and Gaspar knocks on the door.

Almost immediately it opens. There is a curtain or blanket hanging just behind the door, with a yellowish light trickling around the edges. Flecker can't make things out very clearly. The man who has opened the door disappears around the blanket, and Gaspar and Flecker follow him.

There is only one room in the house, with a kind of blackened alcove at the end where the cooking is evidently done. The light comes from an old-fashioned oil lamp, the kind with a glass chimney, on a table at the center of the room. There is only one chair at the table, so nobody sits down.

The man who has let them in is perhaps fifty. His face and hands are grimy, or else his complexion is dark and his skin disfigured with some disease; it is hard to tell which in the poor light. His yellowish eyes catch the gleams from the lamp. He seems to be wearing an extraordinary number of clothes. Starting from the outside, there is a brown army sweater with a rolled collar, then a sweater-vest, then a flannel shirt, and under everything a greasy turtleneck sweater coming up to his chin. Finally, a belt *and* suspenders, a sign of suspiciousness in Flecker's experience, and heavy farm shoes caked with mud.

There is a loaf of bread and a demijohn of cheap purple wine on the table, but he doesn't offer them anything. He doesn't have a hospitable air. He simply stands looking at them, his arms protruding slightly from his body because of the thick clothing.

Gaspar doesn't seem put off by these manners. He is quite cheerful. He looks around the room, and then back to the man buried in clothing.

"Alors Léon. On est toujours d'accord?"

"Oui."

"You have the fountain pens?"

"As I told you."

"Are they new or used?"

"Used, but rebuilt, in superior condition."

"MAT 49s?"

Léon seems to be unwilling to take his eyes off them. He backs across the room like a circus bear, still watching them, then reluctantly turns away and opens a battered leather trunk against the wall. He takes out several blankets and lays them on the floor, then removes an old ouija board, a cracked bedpan, a bayonet in a scabbard, a folding brass telescope dating perhaps from the Napoleonic period, and another blanket, which he lays down on top of everything. Finally, with another glance around, he takes out three curious objects. They look like pistols with odd mechanical attachments fastened to them on all sides: bars, pieces of tubing, lugs, and oblong metal boxes sticking out below the barrels. He sets two of these on the table, in the light of the lamp. The third he begins manipulating, a little clumsily, as though he is not very familiar with it. It unfolds like a trick jackknife. A telescoping steel stock slides out from under the gun, and the oblong box under the barrel, when folded down, turns into a vertical magazine housing with a magazine protruding from it. The handgrip locks with an oily click. Now it resembles an ordinary submachine gun, functional and light, of the kind that might be used by paratroops.

"Show me again how it folds up."

Léon does this too like a circus bear performing his trick. He doesn't really want to fold the gun up again, but he does it, slowly and reluctantly, looking at Gaspar and Flecker rather than at the gun.

"Let's see it."

He hands it to Gaspar, who pulls out the stock and unfolds the magazine housing more deftly than Léon himself has done. He also finds the magazine catch and ejects the magazine into his hand.

"Nine-millimeter Parabellum."

Léon nods.

Gaspar slips the empty magazine back into the housing with a click. "What's the firing rate?"

"Six hundred a minute."

"You have ammunition?"

Léon goes back to the trunk, swinging and sidling in his circus-bear manner and keeping Gaspar in sight. He comes out with four cardboard boxes of ammunition and a half-dozen magazines. These he sets on the table. He tries to arrange them neatly, with the magazines in two piles, but the piles fall over and he leaves them as they are.

"What do you want for them?"

"Twenty-five hundred."

"Each?"

Léon nods again. He seems to prefer to avoid talking whenever possible.

"You said they'd be a thousand francs."

Léon makes his only long speech. It seems difficult for him, his hardest trick so far.

"When I said that, I thought I would be able to get

surplus weapons licensed by the army. These are not licensed. Therefore," he says, "there's more risk in getting them, and more risk in selling them to you. So I have to charge twenty-five hundred."

To judge from Gaspar's expression he finds this explanation perfectly reasonable. He feels for the catch and ejects the magazine into his hand again. Then he begins loading it from the box on the table. The ammunition is slightly oily and he inserts each cartridge into the magazine carefully with his thumb and forefinger, pushing against the spring. The staggered-row magazine takes thirty-two rounds. When he is done he snaps the magazine back into the weapon.

Léon doesn't like this. He starts to make a move toward Gaspar, then thinks better of it. He makes a preliminary bearlike sound in his throat.

"What are you doing? Be careful."

Gaspar pulls back the cocking handle, then pushes it forward again. In the silent room the noise is surprisingly loud, an oily multiple click followed by a snap.

He says, "There are no licensed automatic weapons." He says, "That's too bad, Léon. You said a thousand francs each, but you cheat me and so I'm taking them for nothing."

Léon doesn't know what trick to do now. He looks from Gaspar to Flecker, and then to the things lying on the table. The other two guns are too far away, and besides they are folded up and the magazines are empty. He hesitates for a moment or two, his yellow eyes rolling to one side and then to the other. He says thickly, "Eh bien alors." He sidles forward, then abruptly throws himself at Gaspar and seizes the barrel of the gun.

There is a tussle. Léon is a good deal stronger than Gaspar, even if part of his weight seems to be sweaters. The two bodies bump against the table and bounce back. The barrel of the gun swings around like a conductor's baton. Both of them have their fingers inside the trigger guard, and it is only a question which way the thing will be pointing when it goes off. Flecker drops to the floor, hitting his head on the edge of the table as he goes down. This pain distracts him for a second or two during which he is unable to think of anything else. When the gun goes off he is lying on the floor under the table. Although the rounds are very close together, almost a single roar, Flecker distinctly counts eight detonations. He calculates in his mind: eight rounds, six hundred rounds a minute, eight-tenths of a second. It seemed longer. A cloud of dust and other small particles sifts down over him from the table above.

When he gets up he finds Gaspar with the gun in his hands, easing back the bolt to clear the chamber. Léon is lying on the floor with his arms stuck out at an angle to his body and his legs apart. The yellow eyes are still open. There is a ragged torn place in front of the sweater, but he is wearing so much clothing that no blood penetrates to the surface, at least not immediately. He still looks like a bear, an old stuffed toy that some child has dropped on the floor.

Gaspar shows something on the weapon to Flecker, a small tab on the back of the grip. "It has a grip safety. It's the bougre who has the palm of his hand on the grip that decides when it goes off. The other bougre, no matter what he has hold of, can't do much."

"We'd better get out of here."

"Find something to put the ammo and the magazines in."

Flecker looks around for a paper bag or a small cardboard box. There is nothing. He wraps the ammunition and the magazines up in the blanket and makes as neat a bundle of it as he can. Gaspar folds up the gun and takes the other two from the table. They go out into the night, which seems full of noises after the quiet of the room. Flecker can hear a cricket, the wind in the trees, and the distant muttering of a motor across the fields, perhaps a generator or a pump.

In the darkness they open the back of the camionette and put the three weapons and the ammunition into the packing case. Flecker shuts the small door at the rear.

"That thing made an ungodly racket."

"The nearest house is a kilometer away."

"Still."

"People around here don't want anything to do with him. No matter what they hear, they won't pay any attention."

"How do you know that?"

"You saw him yourself. You can see what he is."

"Where were you going to get the three thousand francs anyhow?"

"As it happened I didn't need it, did I?"

Gaspar starts up the Deux Chevaux and gets it going down the lane. The yellow headlights sway crazily along a stretch of white fence. Flecker starts to say something, then reflects that it is probably better to have the headlights on than to have someone notice them driving around in the dark with the lights off.

"I don't like to do things this way."

"What way?"

Flecker says, "I don't like to take risks. You may have to take risks, but you try to minimize them." He says, "I like to plan things in advance so that stupid things like this don't happen."

"It was an accident."

"You went there knowing you didn't have the money."

"It turned out all right, so stop worrying."

"What do you mean it turned out all right? We're still bumping along on this fucking dirt road. Anybody in one of these houses might take our license number."

Gaspar says, "You're a terrible old woman, do you know that?" He says, "You're worse than Patrick."

They carry the packing case up the stairs and into the bedroom, where they put it on the top shelf of the armoire with the blanket over it. Gaspar feels good. He scratches his chest through the opening of the unbuttoned shirt. Sara is in the bathroom, but the door is open. She is brushing her hair.

Gaspar says, "Viens."

"You first, or Martin?"

"Me first."

She turns from the mirror, sets the brush down, and follows Gaspar into the bedroom. The door shuts.

Flecker turns off the light in the bathroom, wanders around restlessly through the apartment, and drinks a glass of water in the kitchen. Then he goes back to the study and sits on the mattress with his back against the wall. It is a long time before Sara comes out. Gaspar takes almost forty minutes with her. Then he hears the door opening, and she appears in the doorway of the study. Her shirt is on, buttoned with a single button, but she is carrying the olive-green trousers in her hand.

He switches off the light, then opens the shutter. There is no moon, but a thin grayish starlight, faintly silver, comes into the room. Sara takes off her shirt and sits down on the mattress. She is out of sorts, he can tell. He is too, because of the business of Léon. They are both angry at Gaspar.

He says, "What's the matter with you?"

"Nothing."

Flecker sits down beside her and touches her arm, and she falls over onto her back like a mechanical doll. He removes his own clothing and lowers himself onto the mattress. His fingers move slowly over the familiar contours. She is better lying down than standing up, he thinks. Her breasts don't sag, and her rather short legs are not apparent. Everything about her is compact, firm, and businesslike, and at the same time soft.

He is finished with her in five minutes. He isn't a connoisseur like Gaspar, or perhaps his needs are more urgent. She says nothing, but from all signs she takes pleasure in the business, or pretends to. He lingers a little while longer, in fact, to let her finish.

He sits up and gropes for the towel that is kept tucked away under the mattress. Then, without bothering to put his clothing back on, he lies down again and pulls the blanket over him. He is sleepy. He hasn't noticed the time, but it is probably after three.

Sara attempts to arrange at least a small part of the blanket over herself. But the mattress is not very wide, and her knee slips over onto the floor. She sits up.

"Where am I supposed to sleep?"

"Wherever you want."

"I need a place for myself. I'm tired of this."

"Go sleep with Serge."

"He takes the whole mattress. He's worse than you."

"There's Patrick's bag over there. Sleep on the floor."

But he moves over a little toward the wall to make room for her. He feels the smooth rounded double shape of her bottom against his own back.

"Where did you go?"

"I told you. To the local cathouse."

"I heard you putting something in the armoire. You went out and got something."

"Go to sleep, Sara."

SIX

In the morning, to placate her, they tell her that she can go with them to the airport. They go down and get into the camionette, the two of them in the front and Sara in the back where she can sit fairly comfortably on a piece of foam rubber with a blanket wrapped around it. The airport is at Blagnac, a half hour out of town. There is quite a bit of traffic and most of it passes them. The small truck goes down the highway with a burring noise, something like a lawn mower. There is a small window between the front seat and the compartment in the back. Flecker slides it open.

Sara is more cheerful, as she always is after she has had some breakfast.

"Where are we going, Martin?"

"I told you. To the airport."

"Why? Are we going somewhere?"

"We're going to see the airplanes."

"The two of you are going somewhere, I imagine, and you expect me to drive the Deux Chevaux back to the apartment."

"Shut up, Sara."

"I'm talking to Martin. Not to you, Serge."

She is still quite blithe. There is no hostility. When

66

she is cross about something, which is quite often, it doesn't last very long. It isn't her nature to hold grudges. She is generous, clever in her way and quick to learn new things, and also she is good in bed. At one time, incredible as it may seem, she was Gaspar's student. Gaspar's field is political science, but he is on leave just now. Flecker tries to imagine Sara writing a thesis in political science. As an experiment in imagination this is not successful. He goes back to imagining her lying naked on the mattress in the starlight.

They find the office on the industrial side of the airport, near the freight terminal. It is a one-story concrete building with a sign : AEROSERVICE DU MIDI. There are several helicopters parked on the tarmac behind it.

Inside is a counter and a young woman working at a typewriter. There is only one other person in the large office. He seems too young to be the manager. He is perhaps twenty-five. He is coatless, in a shirt and tie with a company badge on the pocket. He wears glasses with light black frames.

"We would like to rent a helicopter."

The girl stops typing and looks up, and the young man at the rear of the office comes forward to the counter.

"For what purpose?"

Although Gaspar has spoken first, he says nothing now and lets Flecker explain it.

"Geological research. We're conducting a geomagnetism survey of the Rouergue, for the Institute of Geophysics of the University."

"The Rouergue?"

"On the plateau, about a hundred kilometers north of here."

"I know. You are attached to the University?"

"This gentleman is. I'm a consultant."

The young man looks out through the window. The Deux Chevaux is parked directly opposite, with INSTITUT DE GEOPHYSIQUE stenciled on the side in faded letters.

"How long will you require the aircraft?"

"A day, for the preliminary run. More perhaps later."

The young man's attitude, which was distant at first, now becomes somewhat more friendly.

"What type of helicopter do you require?"

"It has to carry three persons, and two cases of equipment weighing about fifty kilograms each. Magnetometers and other instruments. Good hover capability. Something that can land in rough terrain if necessary."

"You will be landing in rough terrain?"

"It may be necessary."

"We have an Aérospatiale Alouette II, in excellent condition, an almost new aircraft. There is also an Alouette III. It is perhaps larger than you need. It is essentially a military aircraft. It has five hundred and seventy horsepower."

Flecker says, "Poor visibility to the sides."

The young man studies Flecker for a moment or two.

"That is true. The Alouette II has better visibility. They are both Turbomeca powered. We also have a Bell 206B JetRanger."

He pronounces it as though it were a rather odd French word: j'étranger. It is clear that he knows no English.

"The Bell is not new, but it has been recently overhauled. It is an excellent aircraft. It rents for a little more than the Alouettes."

"I'd take the Bell," says Flecker in English.

"You've flown this machine?"

"Not the JetRanger. Other Bells. They're about the same."

The young man follows this conversation politely, without interrupting. For some reason he catches Sara's eye, perhaps because he senses from the expression on her face that she doesn't understand English either.

Flecker switches back to French.

"What is the working load of the JetRanger?"

"It is a lighter aircraft than either of the Alouettes. It will carry three passengers with baggage, in addition to the pilot."

"We want to rent the helicopter without pilot."

"Are you licensed?"

"No. I have military training."

68

"We can rent only with pilot. The rate will be fifteen hundred francs a day, plus five hundred per hour of operating time. We require a deposit of two thousand francs."

Flecker glances at Gaspar. "We can take it with the pilot."

Gaspar says nothing to this. He is leaving it to Flecker.

Flecker says, "We may need lateral access for our instruments. Does the canopy open on the sides?"

"The Bell has no canopy. It is a cabin aircraft. There are sliding windows that open on the sides."

"Of course. I was thinking of the Alouettes. Is the JetRanger here now?"

"I am sorry that it is out on a rental. It will be back tomorrow night."

"It doesn't matter. I know the aircraft. We're agreed then. Do you need the deposit now?"

"No. At the time of signing the rental contract."

"What documents will be required?"

"You have passports?"

"Of course."

"That is all that is necessary. You have an address here in Toulouse?"

"Yes."

The young man is becoming more and more accommodating. "If you take the aircraft for five days or more, I can discount ten percent. Suppose we make the contract for five days. Then, if you decide to use the aircraft for only one day, we can cancel the rest of the contract with no cost to you."

"Very good."

"Do you wish to reserve now?"

"We're not sure about the date. We'll phone you. What's your name?"

"My name is Lespinasse. But anyone can take the reservation."

Sara and the typist study each other. But evidently they decide that there is no rapport to be established on the basis of sex. Sara examines her nails, and the typist looks away.

"Alors au revoir, et merci."

The young man says, "By the way, the rate I quoted you is less fuel."

"Don't give it a thought."

They go out the door and get into the camionette, Sara clambering in the back. The typist and the young man watch the camionette swing around in a U-turn and head off down the road.

At nine o'clock Flecker goes out alone to make the phone call. Overhead swallows are flashing about in the dark, chasing insects. He crosses the boulevard and sets off. He dislikes walking, especially in the narrow streets of the old quarter where the sidewalks are crowded, but it is impossible to park in the center of town at this time of the evening. He passes the University and continues on down rue des Lois toward the center. People are just coming out to go to the cafés, and he frequently has to step off the sidewalk and into the street to get around them. Flecker dislikes crowds even more than he dislikes walking.

At the Capitole he turns left and crosses through the park to Place Wilson. The cafés are crowded. People in Toulouse go to the cafés at nine, then they have dinner at ten. He goes into Grignani's, turning his body sideways to work his way through the crowd, and finds a table at the rear. First he orders a Ricard, and when it comes he sips it for a few minutes. Then, leaving the Ricard on the table, he goes to the cashier and changes a ten-franc bill into coins. He goes back to the rear, in the passageway leading to the toilets. The phones are surrounded by a crowd of young pansies in tight jeans with their rears stuck out, as vain as girls. He pushes through them, producing a chorus of little murmurs. He ignores this. One of the phones is free.

He dials the region code and the number of the hotel in Conques: 69-84-03. The operator comes on and asks him for four francs, which he inserts into the slot. The hotel answers, and he asks for Room 9. After a short wait Patrick comes to the phone.

"Professor Proutey?"

"Yes."

"I hope I didn't interrupt anything."

"No. I developed some photos and I was—analyzing them."

"How is the research going?"

"Quite well. Some of the photos are very interesting."

"Is that all you've been doing? Taking pictures?"

"No." Patrick seems to hesitate at the other end of the line. "I made a detailed inspection of the site today. Also I think I've found an assistant to help me in the work."

"An assistant? What kind?"

"A . . ." Again the hesitation. "A person who knows the research materials thoroughly—and may be—sympathetic."

Flecker decides to argue about this later. "You've had a look at the surrounding countryside?"

"Yes."

"How about the place for birds to light?"

"I've found one."

"How far is it from the place where you're doing your research?"

"About three hundred meters."

"Excellent. Can the bird-watchers get there in a car?"

"Yes. It's a parking lot."

"Excellent. We'd like to see your photographs and sketches. Maybe we could make a short trip up there. Then we could go over the whole project and see if there are any problems."

"That's not a good idea."

"Why?"

"It's just that—circumstances are not quite right for you to come up just now. I'm establishing relations with some people here. It's a little delicate. In a week or two things will be different. Perhaps I can come down in a day or two, at least overnight."

Flecker glances around. Someone else is waiting to use the telephone. "We don't have that kind of time. We've got to get moving on this thing. The project has got to be completed in a few days. Why don't you come

71

down here right away, and bring your pictures and other materials."

"Right away?"

"Tonight."

There is a long pause while Patrick thinks about this. Flecker can hear him clearing his throat. Then he says, "I suppose I could do that."

"How soon can you get here?"

"In about three hours."

"We'll expect you then."

"All right." Patrick still seems dubious about the whole thing.

"Good-by, Professor."

Flecker hangs up and leaves the café without going back to his table. He often leaves a café in this way without paying for his drink. It is only five francs or so, but it gives him satisfaction. It is a game he likes to play. For some reason, even though he is a foreigner, there is something anonymous about him so that he is seldom recognized when he comes back after a few days to the same café. Sometimes he is recognized; then he can apologize and pay for the drink. But usually he isn't.

Place Wilson is jammed tight with traffic. Horns honk impatiently. Flecker sets off briskly through the crowds, stepping off the pavement now and then to get around the slower pedestrians. The thought occurs to him: Serge may be right about Patrick. He complicates everything too much.

When he gets back to the apartment he finds Sara sitting on the table eating cassoulet out of a pan. She makes it by opening a can of beans and putting canned goose into it. The table is littered with dirty pans and stacks of unwashed dishes. When they run out of dishes, sometimes they go out to a place near the Capitole for a steak and fries. Gaspar has opened the shutter a crack and is looking out the window. He turns as Flecker comes in.

"What did he have to say?"

"He's coming down. He'll be here in three hours."

"Has he checked everything out?"

"I don't know. It's hard to tell from what he says on the phone. He's bringing some pictures."

"What was he doing when you called?"

"He said he was analyzing some photos he had taken."

Gaspar says, "He probably took a picture of some girl and was jacking off with it."

"As a matter of fact he said he was trying to line up an assistant. To help in his research, was the way he put it."

"A woman?"

"He said a person."

Gaspar says, "Patrick has his own private dialect. When he says *une personne* he always means a woman."

"We were speaking English."

"It's all the same."

Sara says, "What would this assistant do?"

"She knows the research materials, he says, and she might be sympathetic."

"I don't see that she's necessary."

"Sara, lie down and spread your legs."

But Sara sulks. She is jealous. Flecker can see.

Patrick arrives a little after midnight. He comes in the door with his camera bag, looks for a place to put it, and finally sets it down on the floor.

"Why does this place have to be such a pigpen? Dirty dishes all over the table. Doesn't anybody ever wash them?"

"What the hell's the matter with you? You just got here and already you're complaining about the service."

"I want to show you some pictures, but there's no place to put them."

"Oh, for God's sake. Sara, take some of that junk off the table."

A place is cleared and Patrick gets the contact sheet out of his bag. The lamp is brought from the study. Gaspar glances briefly at the pictures and turns away, scratching the hair on his chest. Flecker says, "I don't see how you can tell anything from such tiny pictures."

"I have a magnifying glass but I left it in Conques. I'm going to enlarge them. I just wanted to show you what I've got in a preliminary way."

"What's this?"

"That's the parking. This is a general shot of the church. You see the road leading down. It goes right in alongside the church. Security in the whole place seems to be very loose. It's just a small town up in the mountains and no one seems to be concerned."

Sara says, "This is a picture of a girl. I told you it would be a girl."

"No you didn't, Sara. It was Serge that said that."

"These grilles in the chancel are very interesting. According to the legend—"

"I can't tell anything from these tiny pictures."

"I told you I'm going to enlarge them."

Patrick takes his enlarger, his trays, and several bottles and jugs of chemicals and goes away into the bathroom. He shuts the door. The light under the door disappears as he stuffs a towel in the crack.

Then there is a long wait. Gaspar smokes several cigarillos and Flecker goes off into the study to take a nap. After an hour or more Sara says, "I have to go to the bathroom."

"You should have gone before."

"I did go before. That was a long time ago. I have to go again."

Gaspar says, "Sara, you're the biggest God damn pain in the ass I have ever encountered." He says, "You're only good for one thing and you're not all that hot at that." He says, "Sometimes I think Patrick is right in sticking to his pictures." He says, "They don't cause so many problems and they're not such a pain in the ass."

Sara says. "I don't know why all this was brought on, just because I have to go to the bathroom."

Flecker comes out of the study. All this talking has woken him up. He says, "Use the kitchen sink, Sara."

Finally the door opens and Patrick comes out, bringing one damp enlargement after the other and laying them on the table. There isn't room enough for all of them and he has to set some of them on the floor. Gaspar takes a little more interest now. He sits down at the table and begins looking at the enlargements.

Patrick explains, "That's the church. The road leads down here from the main street of the town. You can drive right down. There's no chain or anything. This is the presbytery over on the side. You can't get the car right up to it, but it's only a few meters."

"What's this?"

"That's the Majesté d'Or of Sainte Foy. It's a gold statue over a wooden armature. You can see the dimensions from the meter stick. It's about eighty-five centimeters high."

"How thick is the gold?"

"I don't know. Pretty thick. There are gems all over the outside of it too as you can see."

"What's inside?"

"Some relics."

"Relics of what?"

"Some saint's bones. This," he says, "is called the A of Charlemagne. It's gold on a wooden base too. This is the Reliquary of Pepin." He looks around for another enlargement and finds it on the floor. "This is the Lantern of Begon. All these things are gold or silver, and most of them are encrusted with jewels."

Gaspar takes the Lantern of Begon and looks at it. "H'mm. Is that so?" He looks over the enlargement on the table and takes another one. It is the Majesté d'Or, viewed from the front. "She looks like a fat Gertrude Stein. What's this one here?"

"An arm."

"A what?"

"A saint's arm. Actually it's a reliquary in the form of an arm. There's supposed to be a bone inside."

Gaspar doesn't seem very interested in the bone. He picks up another enlargement. "What's this?"

"Careful, don't touch the emulsion. It's still wet."

"The hell with the emulsion. Is this your parking where you want us to set down?"

"Yes. You can see there are no trees or anything in the approaches. It's about three hundred meters from the church. There wouldn't be any cars parked there at this time of the year."

Gaspar moves the enlargement over by the lamp. "What's this up on the hill behind it?"

"I don't know. A building of some sort."

Gaspar looks more carefully. He puts on his Franklin glasses and examines the enlargement for some time. He says, "That's the gendarmerie." He points to a tiny spot on the front of the building, almost hidden by the edge of the hill. "That's a tricolor sign. It's too small to read but it says gendarmerie on it." He says, "Is that where you want us to land the thing? Right in front of the fucking gendarmerie?" He says, "That's a VHF antenna on the roof."

"It might be the post office."

"There's a brigadier standing in the window. You can even see his epaulets."

"All right. I'll look around for another place."

"How many gendarmes are there?"

"I don't know. I didn't know there were any."

"That's what you're supposed to find out."

Flecker says, "Let him alone, will you? He did his best. Some of these pictures are very interesting. Look at these four of the statue from all four sides. It's fantastic, from the point of view of art."

Gaspar says, "I'm not an art critic. I leave all that to you." He says, "Read Engels on the cash value of art. It just represents labor. Labor to dig the gold out of the ground. Labor to smelt it and refine it and pound it out into sheets and arrange them in representational form. The Sistine Ceiling is just a paint job. It took so many hundreds of hours. The rest of it is surplus value." He says, "In the name of the Front de la Jeunesse we are going to expropriate all this shit and return it to the people."

Patrick says, "The Sistine Ceiling isn't just a paint job. There's selection. Only Michelangelo," he explains as if to a child, "knew which paint to put where."

"He was a skilled worker. That means he got paid more. He was still a worker. Art," concludes Gaspar with an air of ending the discussion, "is surplus value."

76

Gaspar glances at his watch. It is a little after two. "Well, Martin?"

"Might as well."

Without explaining anything to the other two, they get up and go out the door, taking a canvas bag of tools with them. Patrick is left alone with Sara. For a while she sulks. She says, "They're always going out at night and not taking me along." She says, "They say they're going to a bordello, but that's not logical. They may be supermen, but not to that extent. Nothing else is open at this time of the night. The cafés are all closed and everything."

Patrick is still looking at the enlargements.

She says, "There's an after-hours club. If they're going there they might take me along."

"I don't think they're going to an after-hours club."

"You know what they've got in the armoire?"

"What?"

"Machine guns."

Patrick shrugs.

She looks over his shoulder at the enlargements. She says, "You're looking at the picture of the girl."

He sets it aside and pretends to look at another one.

She picks it up and begins looking at it.

"Don't—"

"I know, don't touch the emulsion. Who is she anyhow? She certainly is skinny. Is she French? She doesn't look French."

"She's a guide in Conques. Nobody in particular."

"Why did you take her picture then?"

"I had a film left in my camera."

"Patrick, are you really a professor?"

"I was."

"In America?"

"In California."

"Why aren't you anymore?"

"I didn't get tenure."

"What does that mean?"

"They fired me because I didn't publish."

"I thought," she says, "that when that happened the

students rose up and demonstrated. Then the university would have to hire the person anyhow, especially if he were a radical."

"That was true in sixty-eight. This was in seventy-four."

"I thought students were always radical."

Patrick pushes the photos aside. He turns around in the chair and looks at her. "Do you think Serge really has anything to do with the Front de la Jeunesse?"

"How would I know? I'm not into politics."

"You're into Serge and Martin. They're political."

"They're into me," she says, quite simply and without irony. She wishes to correct him for getting it the wrong way around. She says, "I tried being political once, when I was a student, but I couldn't understand it."

"Your clothes are a political statement."

"These clothes?" Her shirt says "U.S. Army" above the pocket and there are bullet loops in the belt. "They're not a political statement. I just got them at Clancy's in rue Saint-Rome. Everybody wears clothes like this."

"You look like a Palestinian commando."

"This shirt," she says, "cost two hundred francs."

He goes back to studying the photographs, and she disappears.

A few minutes later she comes back and stands in the doorway, totally naked. Her breasts are exactly the size of tennis balls, and rather pendulous. Still they are young and fresh.

She says, "Is this a political statement?"

"No, that's an idiotic statement."

"You don't want to?"

"No, I don't want to."

"Serge says you take pictures of girls and then jack off with them. Is that true?"

"Put your clothes back on, Sara."

SEVEN

The typewriter shop is in rue des Lois, one of the radial streets leading out from Place du Capitole in the center of the old city. It is a one-way street, for outward-bound traffic only. Gaspar has to drive in to the Capitole and then circle around through the Place to get into the street. He parks directly in front of the shop, blocking the view from the street. The narrow street is deserted. There are only a few cars parked along it here and there. The concrete wall across the street glows in the starlight. There is one of the usual student graffiti on it, painted in enormous letters with a spray can.

**FRONT DE LA JEUNESSE
B.P. 4004 31 TOULOUSE**

"They give their post office box," says Flecker, "in case you want to send contributions."

Gaspar says, "Can the chatter." They get out, closing the door softly, and Gaspar sets the canvas bag down next to the car. The sidewalk is narrow, only wide enough for one person, and there is a tunnel of darkness between the car and the shop only a meter away. From one point of view this is good, but they will have to use the flashlight. Flecker holds the light, and Gaspar gets out the battery-operated drill.

"The light down here."

The sliding steel shutter of the shop locks near the bottom. Gaspar touches the button of the drill and pushes. There is a humming sound, and an even metallic grating. Perhaps five seconds is required for the first hole. Flecker narrows the flashlight beam to a pencil with his enclosing fingers. Gaspar pulls out, wrenching the tool away with a twist, and drills again.

In less than a minute the lock drops out into his hand. He sets the drill down, and together they insert their fingers under the bottom of the shutter. It comes up with a slight screech of metal, a sound that is alarmingly loud in the quiet street.

"Easy, easy."

When the shutter is waist high they stop. Gaspar gets out the drill again, deftly inserts a diamond tip in the dark, and drills through the glass door. Into this small hole he inserts the circular glass-cutting tool. He rotates it eight or ten times, applying a steady pressure. Then he carefully levers the tool back and downward. The circle of glass comes away with a faint clink.

They open the door and duck inside. There is a night light on inside the shop. Everything is dimly illuminated. There is no burglar alarm. An electric clock circles slowly inside the illuminated ring of its frame. It is two thirty-seven.

"Okay, vite vite."

"Which one do you want?"

There are Olivetti portables, a Hermes, an American Coronet, an IBM office electric, and some Olympias.

"The Olympia portable."

Flecker takes the typewriter. He is still carrying the flashlight in his left hand, and he puts it in his pocket. Gaspar is carrying the canvas bag.

It is less than a minute since the circle of glass broke away. They are out in the street, in the inky pit of darkness between the car and the building.

"Close the shutter?"

"No. Leave it."

Flecker throws the typewriter in the back. The camionette starts with its usual racket, and they are away down the street: rue des Lois, Place du Peyrou, and then rue des Salenques. Gaspar knows these one-way streets in the old part of town by heart. This one leads directly out of the center to the University quarter. It is only two minutes to Boulevard Armand Duportal.

They go upstairs, Flecker carrying the typewriter and Gaspar the canvas bag. They usually use the stairs late at night, since the elevator makes a hum that can be heard through the building. Patrick is at the table looking at the photographs, and Sara is in the bathroom with the door shut.

Gaspar says, "Get all that stuff off the table."

Patrick removes the photographs, which are almost dry now anyhow, and Flecker puts the typewriter down on the table. Gaspar goes for the paper. It is a package of a hundred sheets, sealed in plastic, bought at Monoprix and absolutely anonymous. He slits the plastic with a penknife. Then, with a pair of tweezers, he slips out a single sheet, not touching it with his fingers. He inserts it into the top of the typewriter and rolls the platen. It goes in a little crooked but he doesn't adjust it.

"Okay, Patrick. Who owns this stuff anyhow?"

"The Monuments Historiques, I think."

"What's that?"

"It's a branch of the Beaux-Arts."

At the top of the sheet Gaspar types, *Service National de Monuments Historiques. Ministère des Beaux-Arts.*

"Or maybe the Church."

"Make up your mind. What diocese is it in?"

"Albi, I think."

Gaspar types, *Evêché d'Albi.*

"Anybody else?"

"It's a Dominican that lets you into the place."

"Dominican is just a nickname. What's the order really called?"

"Preaching Friars, I think."

Gaspar types, *Ordre de Frères Precheurs.*

He says, "Might as well get everybody in." He pushes over the space bar to make a new paragraph. Then he begins typing, slowly, with two fingers. He writes the note in French. It is two paragraphs long. This takes him five minutes or so, since he is careful not to make mistakes. Flecker and Patrick watch him, Flecker sitting in a chair and Patrick standing behind his back.

Gaspar reads what he has written. "Good, good."

"Let's see."

Flecker looks down into the typewriter. The light is poor and it is hard to read.

"Don't touch it."

"It's okay."

Sara comes out of the bathroom, fully clothed. She fastens up her hair at one side with a pin. This feminine gesture contrasts oddly with her clothes. From the neck down she is a Palestinian commando, from the neck up she is a girl in a flirtatious pose.

"I heard typing. What are you doing?"

"Writing a love letter for Patrick. It's to his girl in Conques."

"Where did you get the typewriter?"

"We are realists," Gaspar reads from the typewriter, "and for us these precious national treasures represent no more than their weight when melted down."

"I like your mention of the people."

Gaspar says, "Well, the stuff does belong to the people. Did the Church make it? Hell no, artists made it. Artists are workers. It belongs to us."

Patrick wonders where he has heard this before. Then he remembers that it is exactly what Marie-Ange said. The juxtaposition of the two personalities is slightly ludicrous. He thinks of them as belonging in different worlds.

Gaspar says, "Well, they can have it either way. If they want it back, they can pay for it. If they don't want it back, we'll put it in a pot and melt it." He says, "I know an outlet in Marseille that will pay eighty percent for the bullion, and no questions asked. I'd rather not do it that way, because it's a lot of trouble and you don't get as much. But we can do it either way."

82

Flecker looks at the note again. "You didn't say how much."

"That's for later. A hundred million."

"Are you crazy?"

"Don't forget, there are those bones that Patrick talked about. They ought to be worth something to the Church. How would you like it if you were a saint and somebody burned up your arm?"

"I'm not sure the Church has that kind of money."

"They could sell some of the stuff in the Vatican. All the priests and monks all over the world could go on a fast. What do you think, Patrick?"

"I think it's too much. I think you might get a million francs out of the Monuments Historiques."

Gaspar removes the sheet of paper from the machine and, still handling it with the tweezers, sets it down on the table. Then he finds a Pentel and, in lieu of signature, begins painstakingly drawing a design at the bottom of the page, a crossed O like a telescopic sight with its two cross-wires.

He says, "You don't think big enough, Patrick." He says, "If you ask for a million they'll think they're dealing with some small-time burglars from Toulouse." He says, "Some characters in South America got ten million dollars for an oil executive. That's fifty million francs. You've got to think big. If you think small, it's burglary. If you think big enough, it's politics."

Patrick says, "I don't like this talk about melting the stuff down. The value of the gold is not one-tenth of one percent of the value as art. The art is irreplaceable."

"That's what I'm telling them. 'For us these precious national treasures . . .' "

"A hundred million is ridiculous."

"They'll cough up the hundred million," says Gaspar. "They don't want us to melt the stuff down. Besides," he says, "I need enough to live comfortably in Algeria for the rest of my life. I can buy a villa on the coast at Mers-el-Kebir. There's no extradition for political fugitives from Algeria. Would you like to go to Algeria, Sara?"

"I don't know." She isn't sure whether he is serious or not. "Are you going to Algeria, Martin?"

"No, I'm going to Thailand. It's a beautiful country. I have an old girl there in Bangkok. I met her when I was on R-and-R from Vietnam."

She isn't sure whether he is serious either. "What about you, Patrick?"

Patrick doesn't explain that the whole thing is more a symbol for him than anything else. Probably Sara wouldn't grasp the point, and he doesn't care to discuss it either with Gaspar or Flecker.

Gaspar stares at the piece of paper on the table, his face underlit in the dim glow from the lamp. He still likes the note very much. He says, "Good, good."

"What about the envelope?"

The envelopes too come from Monoprix in a plastic package. Gaspar slips one out with the tweezers. It is a trick to fold the paper in thirds without touching it, and he doesn't get it quite straight, but at least it goes into the envelope. He bends down to lick it without touching it, a curious doglike gesture, and presses it with a rag to seal it. Then he puts the envelope into the plastic from the package of paper, and seals it with a bit of tape. He fits the cover back on the typewriter.

"Now let's get rid of all this stuff."

He and Flecker pack everything away into the canvas tool bag: the typewriter, the drill, the glass cutter, the paper and the envelopes. Flecker notices for the first time that Gaspar has carried away the cut-out circle of glass from the door, which he has perhaps touched with his fingers. He leaves this in the bag.

Sara says, "Where are you going?"

Gaspar says, "We're going to take the typewriter back to the shop."

"You two be good," says Flecker.

It is now almost four in the morning and the night has turned chill. In another hour or two it will be light. Gaspar throws the bag in the back of the camionette. They go off again, this time down the boulevard in the direction of the river. Gaspar turns to the left along the quay. In Place Daurade they pass a blue van going the other way with a figure in a képi dimly visible at the wheel and POLICE in white letters on the side. Gaspar watches the van in the rear-vision mirror; it continues slowly on down the quay in the opposite direction. Because of it, however, instead of turning onto the bridge immediately, Gaspar makes a circle up through rue de Metz and around the cathedral. It is five minutes before they come back to the river. There is no sign of the police van.

Gaspar drives out onto the Pont Neuf. In the middle of it he slows and motions to Flecker.

"Do it fast."

Flecker opens the door. The camionette is still moving at a walking pace. As it goes on past him he lifts the canvas bag out of the rear, takes it to the parapet, and turns it upside down. The heavy typewriter and drill slip out. The pieces of paper flutter down like large butterflies in the darkness. The piece of glass is last to come out; he shakes the bag.

The camionette has never stopped. It is still moving slowly along the bridge, the door waggling open. He catches up to it and slips in. Gaspar shifts to accelerate, goes on across the bridge, and turns off through the narrow streets of the Saint-Cyprien quarter. To the right they can see the Garonne, a black ribbon flowing on powerfully and silently in the darkness. They cross the river again on the Pont Saint-Pierre.

The typewriter is gone. It can never be traced. It was simply stolen from a shop in rue des Lois and then disappeared. Likewise the paper and the envelopes, the circle of glass, and the drill which might conceivably be matched with the holes in the steel shutter. Gaspar is pretty good at what he is good at, Flecker thinks. Still, he thinks, that business with Léon was an insanity. There was no need for it. All Gaspar had to do was stand farther back in the room where Léon couldn't get at him. Flecker has no use for these flamenco gestures. He has military training and he believes in planning everything carefully. That was the way he survived for four years in Vietnam as a helicopter pilot. Sometimes you have to take risks, he thinks, but they should be calculated risks and there should be a reason for taking them. Gaspar's training came from hanging around university cafés where they talk about the cult of violence. With him it is always a kind of macho game to see who will lose his nerve first. He does it because he gets a kick out of it. Gaspar, he thinks, is not really serious. Of course, Flecker thinks, he too plays the game of leaving cafés without paying for his drink. But that's only a small risk and it's an acceptable risk. It comes under the heading of training. You have to keep your hand in. If you don't take a few risks once in a while you get soft. This is how he, Flecker, justifies the game of leaving cafés without paying for his drink.

Patrick gets bored waiting for them to come back. He doesn't go to sleep because the sleeping arrangements in this pigpen are unsatisfactory. There is his sleeping bag, but it's filthy, and besides the floor is hard. There are only two mattresses. It has never been clear who they belong to and he could just lie down on one of them, but when Gaspar and Flecker come in they will turn on all the lights and have a big dispute about who is going to sleep where. Then there is the problem of where Sara is going to "sleep," as the saying goes; *coucher* is the French word. Patrick doesn't want to *coucher* with Sara and he doesn't want to *coucher* on the floor. So, when Gaspar and Flecker come back, he gets up (he has been sitting with his back against the wall, watching Sara who is buffing her nails) and announces that he is going to drive back to Conques.

"Now?"

"There's no traffic at this time of night."

"Tu peux bien coucher ici," says Sara.

"I know that, but I don't want to."

"It's because of his girl in Conques."

"Shut up, Sara."

Patrick gets his camera bag and slings it over his shoulder. "When are you coming up?"

"We'll be in contact. Stay in Room 9, by your phone."

"With your pictures," says Gaspar.

"Lay off him, Serge."

"A bientôt, alors."

"Your French is so idiomatic, Patrick," says Gaspar. "Don't use the elevator. It makes too much noise at night."

Patrick leaves the city by the Boulevard Lascrosses and the Avenue des Minimes. The night air is cool and pleasant. It is almost four-thirty but it is still dark. He is able to make better time than he did before, in the daytime, because there is no traffic on the highway. He lights a Silk-Cut from the lighter in the dash and smokes it as he drives along, feeling calmer now that he has left the apartment behind him with its three people who always seem to be quarreling about something. A little beyond Montauban the highway begins climbing up into the hills and a sheer stone cliff goes by on the right. The headlights pass across a legend crudely painted on the rock.

OCCITANIE

Half a kilometer farther on there is another one, this one in a more delicate, almost feminine hand.

Vòlem viure al país

This stretch of highway with cuts through the rocky hills is a good place for graffiti. There is one more before he comes out onto the tableland at the top. This one is a Front de la Jeunesse symbol a meter or more high, except that someone has taken a brush and added tails to the crossbars on the O, converting it to a swastika.

87

It makes very little difference anyhow. He remembers his old professor at Stanford explaining that the extremism of the right and the extremism of the left eventually converge. He now regrets discussing his academic career with Sara. She won't understand anyhow, and she will only tell it to Gaspar and Flecker, to whom he has never really explained why it was that he left California.

Although, as a matter of fact, there is nothing to his discredit in the whole business. He left because he failed to get tenure at Santa Barbara, and he failed to get tenure at Santa Barbara because he was cheated by his thesis director, who was one of the most eminent medievalists in the business. Patrick took his Ph.D. at Stanford in 1969. He did his dissertation on French illuminated manuscripts of the fourteenth and fifteenth centuries. His thesis director, Halbertson, had published a book on the Limbourg Brothers and their contemporaries, the artists to whom the *Très Riches Heures du Duc de Berry* is attributed. After Patrick got his job at the Santa Barbara campus, Halbertson wrote him calling his attention to Ms. Latin 9471 of the Bibliothèque Nationale in Paris, the so-called *Grandes Heures de Rohan*. With Halbertson's recommendation, Patrick got a grant to go to Paris to study these illuminations and spent a year there. He made several discoveries that seemed to him important. The most interesting of these came from an examination of Folio 45 of the manuscript, an Annunciation scene. This page, along with the whole manuscript, had previously been attributed to the unnamed artist known as the Rohan Master. But there seemed to him no doubt that, while the Master had painted certain figures in this folio, the Gabriel for example, he had left the Virgin to an assistant. The style was totally different; this could be seen clearly in the way the folds of drapery were handled. Only one other figure, that of the Deity hovering over the top of the page, seemed to him definitely attributable to the Master. A further examination showed the same evidence in a number of other folios; the Office of the Dead (Fl. 159), for example, and the Hours of the Cross (Fl. 135). For some reason this great artist had attempted to pass off the work of apprentices as his own, and for three hundred years he had succeeded. There was material here for a monograph that was sure to attract attention and controversy, and would also probably get him tenure at Santa Barbara. It directly contradicted the interpretation of the paintings offered by Canon Meissen, the author of the only authoritative book on the subject.

He spent the rest of the year making high-resolution Kodachrome slides of the manuscript, and when he got back to California he sent copies of them to Halbertson at Stanford. Then he sat down to study his materials carefully for a year or so. As he was working, however, Halbertson read a paper at Johns Hopkins which he planned to expand later into a monograph. In it he contended not only that the *Grandes Heures de Rohan* were the work of more than one hand, but that the illuminations had not even been planned and coordinated by a single artist. Somebody or other at a later time had assembled a number of different quires to make the book in its present form, and these quires had undoubtedly been painted in different workshops. About a third of them, he estimated, were probably done in Bourges by an artist commissioned by Yolande of Aragon, perhaps the same artist who did the *Hours* of René d'Anjou. The others were contemporary, but they were probably added to the book over a century later, when it came into the possession of the Rohan family. He arrived at this conclusion mainly through an examination of Patrick's slides.

This paper went far beyond Patrick's yet unpublished conclusions, not only in its findings but in the thoroughness and expertise of the argument. The fact was that Halbertson had stolen his material. Patrick told him as much the next time he happened to encounter him, which was at a meeting in Berkeley. He said, "You stole my material. In fact, you told me about the Rohan manuscript, and you suggested that I apply for a research grant, and you yourself recommended me for the grant, knowing that I would send you the slides as a courtesy, just to save yourself the trouble of going over to Paris and working in a drafty room in the Bibliothèque Nationale." He said, "You're worse than the Rohan Master. He passed his apprentice's work off as his own, but at least he did some work on the book. All you did was sit on your ass at Stanford and wait for me to send you the slides."

But Halbertson only said, "Ars longa, vita brevis. If I waited around for you to publish, I would be retired, or a dead man."

Patrick decided not to publish his own material. He was only two years from the tenure decision now. It was too late to find another research project, apply for a grant, do the research, and publish. He decided to be a "good teacher," which was a code word in those times for young faculty who didn't publish. He changed from tweeds to an old sweater and khaki pants without underwear, and spent a lot of time hanging around the student coffee houses in Isla Vista. As a matter of fact he made a good many friends among the students. They accepted him as one of their own, and he was even able to make out with several coeds, mostly art students who were not very attractive and confused sexuality with their interest in medieval manuscripts. When the department voted not to give him tenure, however, there was, as he explained to Sara, no great mass uprising of the ten thousand students on the Santa Barbara campus. It was not 1968 anymore and the students were into meditation rather than into politics. Anyhow he, Patrick, had no particular reputation as a radical.

This experience, however, thoroughly radicalized him if nothing else had. He threw his socks away as well as his underwear and became the Superfluous Man, Meursault the Stranger, l'Homme Aliéné. When he had referred to Halbertson's ass (thereby somewhat shocking himself), it was the first time in his life he had ever used a coarse expression. But now, as far as he was concerned the whole establishment could come crashing down and he wouldn't give a fuck. Especially the art establishment. To his mild surprise, when he was in the Louvre he felt an impulse to take out a knife and slash the Mona Lisa. But he didn't have a knife with him, and besides the Mona Lisa had glass over it. To the question, Are you a Marxist, he would have replied, No, because Marxism is an establishment too. This capability of violence in himself was the great discovery of his life. Just as other men discover that they believe in God, or that they are in love, he discovered he was not a coward. And yet with all this he was quite calm. He had never realized that radicals were calm in this way, that you could throw a bomb and at the same time think about the Gautama Buddha, or a meal you were going to eat that night.

For some time he has been driving in a trance, although skillfully. He is not quite sure where he is, but he seems to be on Départmentale 663 somewhere above Decazeville. The road turns ahead and dreamily, in the headlight beams, there comes up to him another legend on a vertical stone wall.

A toi le vote
A moi les armes

The vote for you, guns for me. It occurs to him that he has never voted in his life, either in America or in France.

EIGHT

It is nine o'clock. There is no wind, and the air is a little warmer today. Across the valley to the west there are some grayish clouds boiling up on the horizon, but overhead it is clear. The thin sun bakes through Patrick's shirt and feels pleasant on his back. With the camera bag on his shoulder he goes on down the street past the boulangerie, the tobacconist, and the dairy shop. After the houses are behind it is only a short distance to the parking lot with its stone balustrade overlooking the valley below. He walks slowly down along the balustrade to the end. At that point the parking lot dwindles away to a narrow asphalt road. A little farther on the road turns back to the left and ascends the hill to the building above.

The hill is rather steep. He is perspiring a little before he has reached the top. The road comes out onto a broad paved drive with the building on the right. It is the gendarmerie all right. The tricolor sign, which he hadn't noticed from the parking lot below, is clearly visible. In the end of the building facing him is a garage with a small blue car in it. There is no sign of life in the garage or anywhere else in the building.

Patrick takes the camera out of the bag, removes the

lens cap, and photographs the car in the garage from a range of about twenty meters. Then he backs away across the concrete and takes a shot of the whole building with the wide-angle lens. He switches back to the standard lens again and takes a third shot, almost vertical, of the antenna mast on the roof. Then he puts the camera away in the bag, zips it shut, and stands for a moment looking reflectively down at the town below.

There is a wall at the edge of the paved drive, similar to the one below in the parking lot except that there is no balustrade on top of it. The notion strikes him to sit down on this wall for a few minutes. He sits first facing the gendarmerie, then after a moment's thought he swings his legs around and sits in the sunshine looking down at the parking lot, the town, and the valley of the Ouche below it. Patrick is content. He doesn't feel like doing anything except sitting on the wall with the sunshine warming his back. After a while he gets out the camera, aims it at the town below clinging to the side of the hill, and looks through the viewfinder. The church is neatly lined up a little to the left of center. The three steeples with their slate hats are about on the level of the other roofs higher on the hill. He presses the button. There is the soft chunk of the shutter. He puts the camera away.

For some time Patrick has sensed that there is someone behind him. He has heard the footsteps on the pavement, stopping occasionally and then continuing on in a leisurely way. He has the impression that when this sound stops for the last time it is almost directly behind him. After another few moments there is a voice, casual but lucid, almost sharp-edged in the clear morning air.

"You have a light, monsieur?"

He turns.

The man before him is perhaps slightly less than normal height, although there is nothing unusual about this for a southerner. He is solidly built, with a broad chest and a thick bull-like neck. His face is tanned and there are pink splotches on his nose. He is wearing khaki pants, a short-sleeved khaki shirt with patch pockets, and a flat-topped képi with a narrow gold band around it. On the shoulders of the shirt are black epaulets with three narrow gold chevrons. He has a clear unlined face, an untroubled face. His expression is curious but not insistent; on the contrary it is thoughtful and contemplative, almost passive.

Patrick feels in his pocket and finds a folder of matches. He passes these over. Then he swings around, one leg at a time, to sit on the wall facing the gendarme.

"You smoke, monsieur?"

The gendarme offers a blue package of Gauloises. Patrick hesitates for a moment, then shakes his head. The Gauloises are too strong; they have a blackish biting taste that lingers afterwards. He reaches into his shirt pocket for the pack of Silk-Cuts and takes it out. It is empty. He puts it away again. The gendarme doesn't seem to notice this gesture. He lights his own cigarette, draws on it, then hands the matches back to Patrick.

"A fine morning."

"Very fine."

"However," says the gendarme, "it may rain later."

He has an odd manner. Except for his uniform there is nothing of the policeman about him. He is very calm, reflective. His movements are slow and measured, and he seems to think for a moment before saying anything, even something so conventional as remarking that it is a fine morning. He seems very interested in everything around him, and examines Patrick for long periods of time in silence, but in a totally objective way, as though these things are interesting to him for purely personal reasons. He gives the impression of a man who wants to know as much as possible about the world around him and the things in it, but only for purposes of philosophical reflection and not for any practical reason.

When he does speak his remarks are totally banal, but his measured way of speaking gives them a kind of weight.

"You are visiting Conques as a tourist?"

"More or less."

"I imagine you are interested in our church."

"It's a very fine church."

"Very fine," agrees the gendarme, in the same tone in which he commented on the weather. He sits down on the wall beside Patrick and crosses his legs. He draws at the cigarette, then presently remarks in a conversational tone, "A certain number of tourists come here to look at the church. But mostly in the summer. There are not very many at this season."

Patrick offers, not wishing to appear reticent, "I'm an art historian, as a matter of fact."

The gendarme doesn't seem surprised. He says, "Ah yes"—or perhaps "Ah yes?"—with the slightly rising inflection that in French may imply a question or simply an expression of agreement. Then he adds, "A professor" —or "A professor?"—again with the slightly ambiguous note at the end.

"How did you know that?"

"You registered at the hotel as a professor."

This isn't true, as a matter of fact. Although somebody at the hotel might have told him about the telephone calls. Patrick decides to be amused. He contemplates the gendarme with a small smile. "What other things do you know about me?"

"Very little. That you like to take photographs, and that you rented a car in Toulouse to come here."

"How did you know it was rented?"

"When a car is rented there is a small sticker at the back of the rear-vision mirror. It is not visible from the inside of the car, and most people don't notice it."

"I take photographs," explains Patrick, "as part of my research."

At this point the gendarme seems anxious, or concerned in a highly civilized way, that they do not know each other's names.

"Excuse me, Professor. You are called . . ."

"Proutey. And you?"

"Anstruc."

"You are a brigadier?"

He seems to consider this for a moment, which is curious, since he must know the answer. But this way of pausing before he says anything is simply a mannerism.

"Technically the rank of brigadier has not existed in

the Gendarmerie since 1918. My rank is called Maré-chal des Logis. But, in popular speech, any officer who is in charge of a detachment is called a brigadier."

"That is because the detachment is called a brigade."

"Exactly."

"How many men are there in your detachment?"

"Five, including myself." If he is curious about the particulars of Patrick's life he seems to have no reticence about his own. Again he gives the impression of a man who is interested in the banal details of life and finds them terribly important.

"Five isn't many."

"No. It's a small brigade. But until 1954, in fact, there was only one man here. There was no brigade. The gendarme in Conques was attached to the brigade in Decazeville."

"Why 1954?"

"Because it is only since 1954 that the Treasure has been displayed here in the church."

This, as Patrick knows, is not entirely accurate. He says, "The Treasure was not here before that?"

"Not exactly. Most of the relics were in the church, but they were not all on display. It was in 1954 that the collection was arranged where it is now, in the strong room of the presbytery. All the relics were cleaned and restored, and the present cabinets were built. At that time the Monuments Historiques requested that a brigade of gendarmerie be stationed here, because they were concerned about the security of the Treasure."

"The security?"

Anstruc seems to find this query perfectly reasonable. He is concerned to make everything perfectly clear to Patrick.

"Because of its great value, you see."

The two of them reflect silently, for a few moments, on the great value of the Treasure.

Then Patrick remarks, "Still, that can't take very much of your time."

"No," he agrees. "Actually there isn't much for us to do here. We are bored much of the time."

Patrick says, "In case of need, I imagine, you could call for reinforcements."

"Reinforcements?" Anstruc considers. "Yes, we could do that."

"Where would the reinforcements come from?"

"There is a brigade of twelve men in Decazeville."

"You would call them by radio, I suppose."

"Radio?"

Patrick point to the antenna on the roof.

"Ah. Of course. We have radio. But ordinarily, of course, we would use the telephone."

"Ah, the telephone."

Anstruc draws at the last of his Gauloise, examines it, drops it on the ground, and crushes it with his foot.

"Yes. Ordinarily we would telephone, to Decazeville, or to Villefranche, which is a subprefecture with a standard brigade of fifty men. But we have never had any occasion to call for reinforcements. There is very little crime in this part of France. You see, Professor, for a crime to take place there must be a passion. An unfulfilled passion."

"A passion?"

"A man must covet someone else's wife, for example. Or he must be jealous of his own wife. Jealousy too is a passion. Or another man perhaps doesn't want to work but wants to have money. So he becomes a thief. But, in order for men like these to carry out their crimes, they have to nourish their passion for a while in secret, until the passion is ripe. And this they can't do, here in Conques. Because everybody knows everybody else. We, the gendarmes, know everybody in the town, and we know what people are likely to do. We know if they have unfulfilled passions. And if they have, we watch them, or we talk to them."

"You talk to them?"

"Yes. We talk to them in a friendly way, about this and that, without mentioning unfulfilled passions, perhaps, but in a way that makes it clear we know what is going on in their minds. In this way a man who is thinking about a crime usually changes his mind. It's a very small town. I know everybody in this town, and I know what they're thinking, as though they were members of my own family."

Patrick might have remarked that it is possible to live for years in the same house with a person and not know what is going on in his mind, but he decides not to.

"That's why, you see, Professor, most crimes take place in the big cities and not in the towns like Conques. Because, in the cities, it's impossible for the police to know what everybody is thinking. There are too many people and it's impossible for the police to know them in the way that I might know my family. So most of the crime we encounter, here in Conques, comes to us from the city."

Patrick shifts his position on the wall, and stares back at him with aplomb. "For example?"

"For example, a man may steal a car in the city and attempt to hide it here in the hills. Or hunters come from the city, to shoot partridges or quail out of season. If someone here in the hills shoots partridges out of season, or hunts without a license, we don't call that a crime. Or sometimes people who commit a crime in the city may attempt to flee this way, through the hills. They let us know by telephone, and we set up a roadblock."

"You mean that no one here in Conques ever commits a crime?"

"Only occasionally. Out of insanity."

"Insanity?"

"You see, as long as people are in their right minds, it's possible to know what they are thinking and to anticipate their actions. But when a man is insane, no one can tell in advance what he is going to do. Last year, for example, a peasant in the hills near Aumont killed his wife with a mattock. He smashed in her skull. When we went to take him, he surrendered as meekly as a lamb. He was insane. He had no reason to kill his wife. That sort of thing, Professor, can never be anticipated. That, and the kind of crime that comes to us from the city. Except for that sort of thing, we have very little to do here."

"So you're bored?"

"I'm bored much of the time."

"How do you pass your time? Do you read?"

Anstruc considers.

"No," he concludes. "No, I don't read very much. There's not much to read here. I think, for the most part."

He gets up from the wall, feels in his shirt pocket for another Gauloise, and takes out a box of matches from his pocket and lights it. He shakes out the match, stands for a moment holding the burnt match as though he were examining it with interest, then for some reason puts the burnt match away in his pocket with the cigarettes. He does all this in a deliberate way as though he wishes to make it clear to Patrick that he has had matches all along.

Patrick gets up too, slinging his camera bag, and moves off across the paved drive toward the road. Anstruc accompanies him down the road to the parking lot, and a short distance farther, almost to the first houses on the outskirts of town.

At that point the brigadier stops on the road. Patrick invites him to the café for a cup of coffee, or a glass of wine, but he declines.

"Another time, Professor. Thank you very much. At the moment I am on duty. I have things to do."

"What sort of things?"

"I have to think, Professor."

This is perhaps a joke. Anstruc never smiles, but something appears at the corners of his mouth, a kind of flatness, that is perhaps his way of fixing his face when he tells a joke. "Il me faut penser." His tanned face is immobile in the sunlight.

An idea occurs to Patrick. He says, "Would you mind if I took your picture?"

After reflecting for a moment Anstruc says gravely, "Not at all."

Patrick gets out the camera. The ASA 400 film is almost too fast for the bright morning sunlight. He takes a shot at f.11 and a thousandth of a second. Anstruc, framed in the viewfinder, gazes with his usual abstract curiosity at the lens. The sun catches the gold on his epaulet. It flashes like a spark, very briefly, at the exact moment the shutter clicks.

After lunch Patrick decides to develop the roll of film in the camera, even though he hasn't taken all the twenty shots. He goes into the bathroom and shuts the door, but it isn't entirely dark. Even after he stuffs a towel into the bottom of the door a faint light still comes around the edges of the door, visible only after he has sat on the bidet for a long time waiting for his eyes to adjust. The fast film would be fogged. He will have to wait until after dark. He turns the light on and glances at his watch; it is almost two. He decides to go instead to the presbytery and have another look at the Treasure, which ought to be open at this time of day. The exposure counter on the camera reads fifteen. He still has five more shots to take anyhow.

Outside a light cloud cover has begun to drift over the valley from the west. It is not quite so warm now; there is a faint chill in the air. The street is almost deserted. Evidently everyone in Conques sleeps after lunch. He crosses the street and goes down the steep lane to the church.

When he enters the corridor of the presbytery he sees that the door of the strong room is open and the lights are on. There are voices, one a rumbling basso and the other feminine. Before he can reach this door, however, he has to pass another door, the one to the office. It is open too and there is someone inside, the priest who sells the tickets.

He is very old. He is not much larger than a child, although he gives the impression that he might have been larger at one time and simply shriveled as he reached his advanced old age. His face is a yellowish white and consists entirely of wrinkles, as though it were a piece of parchment that has been creased over and over again for several centuries. The wrinkles open up enough to allow the two eyes to appear, and the mouth is simply a convergence where a large number of wrinkles come together. He is totally bald except for a white tonsure, like an incomplete halo, running around

100

the back of his head. The top of his head is not wrinkled particularly, but it is scabby and covered with brown spots. His habit consists of a white cassock and scapular with a long black mantle, the cowl of which has fallen down on his shoulders.

"Hello," says Patrick. "I'm Professor Proutey. Probably you've heard of me."

"No, I haven't heard of you, my son, but there are many things I haven't heard of. Do you want a ticket? They are four francs."

His voice is faint and reedy, but it is extraordinarily complex. It seems to contain sounds of a number of frequencies, some of which are so high that they are not audible to humans but might be audible to a dog. It is the voice of a bat, Patrick thinks. It makes him feel a little strange.

"My name is Proutey," Patrick repeats.

"Yes. I'm Father Dion."

"That seems an odd name for a priest."

"It's not my real name," he says, staring at Patrick fixedly.

"Is that so?"

"Dion is the name that I took when I entered the Dominican order," he says in a voice that is hardly more than a whisper. "But there was a Saint Dion who lived at Aleppo in the fourth century, so you see it isn't an odd name for a priest at all."

"What did your parents christen you?"

"They didn't christen me at all. You see, they weren't Christians. They were very benighted people. But now, you see, I'm a Dominican and my name is Father Dion. But I'm not allowed to serve Mass any more, you see, because my hand shakes." He holds up the hand to show, and indeed it vibrates softly in the air in front of him. "A priest with a defect is not allowed to serve the Mass. However, I am still a priest."

"Is it true that Dominican means Domini Canes, the Hounds of the Lord?"

"Of course not, my son. The order takes its name from the Beloved Father and Brother Dominic, who came from Spain to preach the Doctrine in these parts."

101

"He came to preach against the heretics, as I've heard."

The old man stares straight at him, and the wrinkles around his eyes twitch.

"They were terrible heretics, my son."

"What did they believe?"

"Who?"

"The heretics."

"They believed that they were Perfect, you see, and that they could fornicate without sin, and that they had no need of the Blessed Sacraments."

"I thought they practiced total abstinence."

"Some of them did, my son, and that's a terrible heresy. If everybody practiced it, it would mean the end of the human race. It's called Arianism."

"I thought it was called Catharism."

"Don't confuse me, my son. I'm an old man, and I'm a Dominican and not a Jesuit. The heretics hereabouts, who believed they were Perfect, were called Cathars. The doctrine that the created world is evil is called Arianism. The Cathars believed that the created world was evil, therefore they were Arians. They also had a number of other mistaken ideas."

Patrick is rather enjoying this conversation. He looks for a place to sit down, but there is no other chair.

"I'm something of a historian myself, although my field isn't exactly the history of theology. The way I understand it, the Cathars denounced the corruption of the Church, and practiced abstinence, and Saint Dominic was sent from Spain to preach against them. A good many of them were burned, and finally the last of them were cornered at a place called Montségur, near Foix, and several hundred of them were slaughtered."

"Did you say you wanted a ticket, my son? They are four francs."

He tears one off the pad and rises, all tottering, to place it on the table in front of Patrick. Patrick takes it and sets down a five-franc coin. Father Dion opens the cash box, puts away the five francs, gets out a one-franc coin, and sets it on Patrick's side of the table. Patrick

102

pushes the franc back toward him. Father Dion pushes it back toward Patrick again, rather crossly.

Patrick puts the coin in his pocket.

Father Dion does not sit down again. He begins moving around the table, supporting himself with his hands. Since his legs are entirely hidden under the skirt of his habit, this gives the impression he is walking around the table on his hands, a difficult feat which he does rather shakily.

Patrick says, "Don't trouble yourself."

"I have to open the door of the strong room, my son. It's my duty."

"The door is already open."

But Father Dion has the bunch of keys in his hand and, shaking like a leaf in autumn, leads the way.

"Never mind"—his spidery voice comes from down the corridor—"it's my duty to open the door, to guard against thieves and other unworthy persons."

"You can't open a door that's already open."

"The door to Heaven stands eternally open, my son, and yet each Christian must open it for himself. There are many mysteries. The ways of God are not our ways."

"Ah," booms the deep voice from inside the strong room, "it's our venerable Brother in Christ and custodian of the Mysteries, Father Dion."

Marie-Ange is at the far end of the room in front of the glass cabinets, and with her is Johannes Brahms. Standing up, he proves to be a little less than normal height. He is lumpy and bison-shaped, and like all bisons has an air of weighty aggressiveness. If he lowers his head, however, it is not to charge Patrick but to look at him over his glasses. His goatee waggles; not because he has a tremor like Father Dion, but because he chews things when he is thinking about them.

Marie-Ange says smoothly, "I don't believe you've met the Professor."

She means not Patrick himself but Johannes Brahms. With an elegant Victorian gesture he reaches into his waistcoat and produces a card, which he hands to Patrick.

103

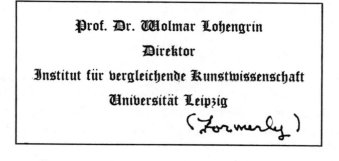

Prof. Dr. Wolmar Lohengrin

Direktor

Institut für vergleichende Kunstwissenschaft

Universität Leipzig

(Formerly)

"Formerly?"

"Upon the advent of the Bolshevik regime in Leipzig, I was invited not to participate further in academic activities."

He is very courtly. In saying this he might be paying Patrick a compliment.

"Proutey."

"I know. You are my colleague. You are affiliated with . . . ?"

"I am an independent scholar."

"You couldn't be an independent scholar, my boy, or I would have heard of you. I am thoroughly familiar with the bibliography." However he doesn't press the matter. He never seems to follow anything up. He immediately goes back to the discussion he was having with Marie-Ange. "I would contend that the Reliquary we are looking at is Byzantine in provenance. Look at the verflucht mosaics all over it. Or if they aren't mosaics, they are in mosaic style. I would say it's from Ravenna, fifth century."

"You should have heard of me," Patrick presses him. "I've written a monograph on the *Grandes Heures de Rohan*."

"Ah yes. It seems it's not by the Master of Rohan after all, but by several other people."

"That's what I demonstrate in my monograph."

"Are you Halbertson?"

"No, Proutey."

"Yes, so you say. I knew you weren't Halbertson. I met him once in Geneva. You can see that this so-called Reliquary, which is not from the Carolingian period at

104

all, is in the form of a house. It probably represents the House of God. There's a very similar one in the Church of San Vitale in Ravenna. Do you know Bloch's work on the Ravenna mosaics?"

"He contends they're based on pagan models. The house is a very common figure in antique Mystery art."

Professor Lohengrin waggles his goatee while he chews this. "Yes. Well, you seem to know what you're talking about. Of course, our Brother in Christ here would be scandalized by the notion that some Christian art is actually of pagan origin."

"I am scandalized by very little, my son," says Father Dion, who to Patrick's surprise is standing just behind his elbow. "The Church is erected on the ruins of the Temple. This is well known. In fact, this very church of Conques is said to have been built on the site of an ancient temple to Diana. Before the arrival here of the relics of the Most Holy Martyr Foy, this place was known as Fonromieu, which may be construed as Fount of the Romans."

"It may also be construed as the Fountain of the Pilgrims," says Professor Lohengrin. "There are many such place-names in the vicinity, such as Roumequiès, the Pilgrim's Repose.'

"That is the opinion of lay scholars."

"I bow to your piety, Father, if not to your erudition." He is still quite cheerful. He is a cheerful bison. He charges and overcomes his opponents with the greatest goodwill in the world. "Besides, the place was called Conques long before Sainte Foy was brought here. It takes its name from the fact that the valley is in the form of a scallop shell or *concha*, and also because the pilgrims from Compostela brought back scallop shells from the sea to show they had been there. Such double etymologies are common in philology. They are called Bruderstämme. Another example is the fruit we call orange, which derives from the Persian *nãrang*, but also from the Latin *aurum*, gold."

Father Dion is unable to stand up to this, if only because of his advanced age. "The Blessed Martyr Foy has always been here in spirit," he quavers. "However, you are right that the Reliquary is in the form of a house. More than twenty relics belonging to a number of different Saints are collected in it. Truly, in Our Father's House there are many mansions.''

"What is the material of construction?''

"I beg your pardon? It is gold, my son.''

"Gold over wood. Gold over wood,'' Professor Lohengrin rumbles, trampling over him. "Just gold leaf. Everything here is, except this lantern, which is no doubt the one that Diogenes used in his attempt to find an honest art historian. It is solid silver. The misconceptions about the objects in this room are infinite, and most of them are published. There is only one person who knows the provenance, material, and iconographic significance of these objects beyond the possibility of error, and that is Wolmar Lohengrin.''

"Excuse me,'' says Patrick, "but when you say it is only gold leaf, surely that is hyperbole.''

"Hyperbole?''

"It must be thicker than gold leaf. I believe the average gold leaf is only about a hundred-thousandth of an inch thick, or less than a micron.''

"It's less than that.''

"What's less than that? The average gold leaf, or the gold on these reliquaries?''

"You are full of questions, aren't you? Most of them have nothing to do with art. On the A of Charlemagne and the Reliquary of Pepin, probably, it's a half a centimeter or so. I've weighed the former and it comes to just short of a kilogram. This, combined with bathometric data, establishes the gold at about eight hundred and fifty grams.''

"Bathometric?''

"You compare the weight loss when suspended in water. The technique was devised by Archimedes.''

"You aren't taking account of the jewels.''

"Bah,'' says Professor Lohengrin, still quite cheerful. "They weigh almost nothing. If you expect to get very far in your profession, I advise you to be more scientific. The density of a ruby, for example, is about midway between that of wood and gold. When an object containing a ruby is suspended in water, therefore, the effect of the gem on the calculations is negligible."

"What about the Majesté?"

"I haven't suspended her in water. They wouldn't let me."

"I mean the provenance, the material, and the iconography."

Professor Lohengrin stares at him, the goatee moving back and forth. He launches into a lecture. "The Majesty-Reliquaries of the ninth century, of which the Sainte-Foy is the sole extant example, represent the first return to representative sculpture after the decline of antiquity. This accounts for a certain crudeness of representation. Most of the jewels were added in the Gothic period. The arms are modern, that is to say, they date from the sixteenth century, along with the flower vases. In the Middle Ages people were not very much interested in flowers. As for the shoes, which are ridiculous, they date from the nineteenth century."

For the first time Patrick notices the long narrow shoes, which indeed have a fake-medieval look about them, as though they were made in a Pre-Raphaelite workshop.

"The head is pagan. It derives from the late Imperial period, the fourth or fifth century, and is probably that of an emperor. Jean-Claude Fau, who is no fool, calls it a virile mask. You can see that it doesn't fit the body. It's too large and it's in a different style. That accounts for a good deal of the strangeness, which all critics have noted in the impression made by the thing. What looks like a crown is an imperial diadem."

"But the relics, my son. The relics," quavers Father Dion.

"What's this?"

"You've forgotten that the Most Holy Relics are inside the head."

"I've forgotten nothing. There is part of a human cranium, lined with silver, and confirmed as deriving from a young girl, lodged in a cavity in the head. The rest of the Saint, insofar as she still remains, is probably somewhere in the body."

107

"And the thickness of the gold?"

Professor Lohengrin examines him over the top of the glasses. "There is controversy about that. Some say it's very thin, some thicker. The roentgenological examination made in 1954 was inconclusive. Toward the end of the nineteenth century the Polish scholar Prybzyski developed a theory that the thing was solid twenty-two-carat gold. If this were true it would weigh over two hundred kilos."

"I hope not."

"What's that?"

"My son," interrupts Father Dion, "you make a mistake in saying that the Saint remains here. That is only the mortal envelope. The Blessed Saint herself is in Paradise, by the right hand of God."

"I'll concede you that," says Professor Lohengrin.

The four of them, including Marie-Ange, are standing around the glass cabinet, occupying its four sides in exactly the position of Patrick's four photographs. The impulse occurs to him to get his camera out, but he has very little use for a photograph of Professor Lohengrin.

Professor Lohengrin, however, still shows a considerable interest in Patrick's own person. He examines his feet, which obliges him to bend his head to its most bisonlike angle.

"Why don't you wear any socks?"

"It's a principle of economy. They aren't really necessary."

"I suppose everybody goes about like that in America."

Patrick says, "I beg your pardon. I'm English."

NINE

Patrick and Marie-Ange go together up the steep lane to the street. The weather has definitely changed while they were inside. The sky is filled with clouds, and the air has turned grayish, so that the houses in the town and even the church itself seem oddly gray instead of pink. When they reach the street at the top of the lane Patrick feels a single cool drop strike his cheek just beside the nose.

"What time is it?"

"Five o'clock. That's when I leave. I've told you several times that the Treasure is open from two to five."

"What do you want to do now?"

"You're so passive," she says. "You're always asking me what I want to do."

"Why are we quarreling?"

"We're not quarreling. At least I'm not." She suggests, "Shall we go to your room?"

"We've already done that."

"People sometimes do it more than once."

After reflecting why he doesn't want to go to the room, he says, "I don't like Mme Greffulhe."

"Mme *de* Greffulhe. Don't forget the noble particle."

"Yes, Mme de Greffulhe. I don't like her."

"You see, she represents the French aristocratic class, in our little drama. Just as Anstruc represents the police, Father Dion the clergy, and Professor Lohengrin the academic establishment. She represents the aristocracy, and that's why you don't like her."

"You know Anstruc?"

"In this town, everybody knows everybody."

"That's what Anstruc said. Why should I dislike aristocrats?"

"I don't know. That's your problem. I don't have all the answers."

"You have an awful lot of them. I suppose I resent countesses because they're on top of an unjust social system."

"Not any more."

"If she's on top, then it's unjust. If she's not on top, then she's not a countess."

"Now you're the one that's quarreling."

"No I'm not. Where do *you* want to go?"

"As I told you before," she says, "there is the place up by the campground."

A few more drops are falling now. They strike the pavement with a plop, sending up a pleasant smell of dampened dust.

"All right." It seems one of the less promising ideas that he has heard about lately, but except for the room it seems to be the only alternative. They go on down the street, past the Mairie and the Porte du Barry. Here the town ends and the steep road pitches down the brow of the hill. She seems blithe. She points out this and that in her mock-guide manner. To the left is the tiny chapel of Saint-Roch, perched like a bird on the very edge of the hill. He declines her invitation to walk out to it, even though there is a fine view of the town from there. The rain hasn't really made up its mind to start yet. The drops are falling at wide intervals, making a rustling sound when they strike among the leaves at the side of the road.

The road makes a sharp turn to the left, then comes out on the highway near the old medieval bridge. Patrick observes a line of telephone poles vaulting in over the hills from Decazeville. The last one is just by the edge of the highway, made of concrete as telephone poles are in France, holding up eight or ten wires and tilting slightly as though it were getting tired of its job.

"The bridge—"

"I know. Dates from the fourteenth century. I wasn't sure it would hold up my car. Is there a large open space anywhere around here, fairly level?"

"Open space?"

"Something like the parking in town."

"Well, there's another parking."

"Let's go have a look at it."

"That's where we're going."

"I'd like to get a picture. Do you think it will rain?"

"It already is."

"I mean hard."

"I'm not a meterologist. It's only water. You're a terrible old woman."

At that, playful but ferocious, he lunges at her and attempts to kiss her, pinning her arms to her sides. She averts her head and he is able to plant his lips only fleetingly on the corner of her jaw.

"Very well, I'll take it back. You're not an old woman. There are people in the Auberge."

Wrenching herself free, she points. Only a short distance down the highway, he now sees, is a kind of miniature inn with café tables on the porch. It is called the Auberge du Pont Romain. It is curious that he didn't notice it before when he drove in over the bridge. But he was coming the other way then and intent on finding his way into the town. There is even a small sign, CHAMBRES. But evidently Marie-Ange doesn't consider these rooms suitable for their purpose, or perhaps she wishes to punish him for not liking Mme de Greffulhe. In spite of her warning, the doors are shut and there doesn't seem to be anyone in sight in the place.

"It's not Roman," he says.

"What?"

"The inn is called the Auberge du Pont Romain. But the bridge isn't Roman."

"In this sense," she says, "the word means romanesque." She seems pleased at being able to correct him on a point of art history. She leads him on across the bridge, then down the steep bank and through a thicket of reeds to the river. The quality of the air, in the bottom of the green ravine, is remarkable. The elastic air seems to enlarge everything slightly, blurring the trees, daubing the greens so that they blend together in a faintly vibrating mass, fixing each twig in a glassy mass of particles. The raindrops, at wide intervals, fall into the leaves with a sound like the ticking of a clock.

"What about the large open space?"

"You are single-minded, aren't you?"

"I wanted to get a picture of it."

They are under the bridge now. He looks around. A short distance downstream is the confluence where the Ouche, hardly more than a creek, joins the larger Dourdou. She sets off upstream, along a path at the side of the river. The path skirts around a large pond dimpled with raindrops, then comes back to the river again. The path is exactly parallel to the highway above, and it isn't clear why they couldn't simply have walked up the highway instead of making their way tortuously along the river bottom with branches slapping them in the face. But she has dropped her guide manner now and pushes her way briskly up the path without explaining anything at all. He follows behind her, his eyes more or less mechanically fixed on her jeans at the place where the rebozo ends, a little below the waist.

They come to the campground, a grassy expanse with scattered trees. It is a very pleasant spot in the summer, no doubt; the river plashes along it on one side, and on the other side there are woods. Beyond the campground they mount up a slight rise, and all at once the parking comes into view, marked with the customary blue sign with a P on it. Cars are not allowed in the campground proper, she explains, and the campers (mostly Germans and such) have to carry everything down from the parking by hand.

"They bring their own food," she says, "and they don't stay at the hotel. There is a saying about them,"

she says. "An egg in hand, they look at the church."
After a moment she adds, "It's better in Occitan."

"It's not bad in French."

"But now," she says, "there are no Germans, and so
we cross the parking, and go up into this grove of
larches, where we find a grassy sward to sit down. As
I explained, this is a local custom."

The parking is smaller than the one in town, but it
is still a good-sized one and almost level. There is the
larch grove on one side, but the approach from the south
is clear. A graveled road in good condition leads up to
the highway. The parking is only five minutes from the
town by car. While she watches him, with a crease on
her mouth that may be impatience but may be only
amusement, he gets out the camera, switches to the wide-
angle lens, and takes several shots of the deserted asphalt
expanse which is gradually darkening as the rain dampens it.

"Are you finished?"

"No." He puts the standard lens back in, looks
through the viewfinder, then moves up closer, closer to
her until her face fills the rectangular glassy frame and
spills out over the edges, rotates the camera ninety de-
grees for a vertical, turns the focus ring, and *chunk*.
He puts the camera away.

It is still not clear why she has led him upstream along
the river, when the highway parallels it just above.
Perhaps because it would be too conspicuous for them to
leave the highway and cross the open space into the
larches, or perhaps simply because it is the local custom.
There is a steep embankment leading up into the larch
grove, almost a miniature cliff, and she passes her hand
down to help him. Together they scramble up, grasp the
roots at the top of the embankment, and pull themselves
up into a kind of green aquarium under the branches.
They have to push their way through; twigs snap and
slap against Patrick's face, and he has to fend his way
with an outstretched arm. In here under the trees the
sound of the rain is more constant, a steady rustling
patter. There are not really any grassy swards to sit

down in. Still pulling him by the hand, she finds a shallow bowl in the floor of the grove, the size of a large bed perhaps, and covered with a blanket of pungent-smelling larch needles. Stumbling a little, she half lowers herself and half falls into this depression, pulling him down after her. They are both panting a little from the exertion.

Now there is a curious moment of—not of embarrassment exactly, or of awkwardness—but of stasis. Nothing happens. She sits with her hands around her knees, and he falls over onto his back with his knees stuck into the air, looking up into the branches overhead. It's not very comfortable, to tell the truth. A twig is sticking him in the back. There is the smell of larch needles, slightly medicinal, and the soft and steady rustle of the rain falling. Marie-Ange seems pensive. She is watching him, he knows, but he is looking up into the trees and not at her.

He says, "This is what is called a Bower of Bliss."

"Yes."

"Such a reference," he says, "is known in literature as a *topos*. A recurring motif, that is a cliché."

"Yes. The plural is *topoi*. I told you I studied letters at Toulouse."

"Do you know any more *topoi?*"

"Worm eats man, bird eats worm, man eats bird."

"That's not a very cheerful one."

"Do you know any better ones? Give us," she says, "a lecture on the subject, Professor."

"Carpe diem."

"Seize the day. Ah, let us. And we are seizing it, are we not? More."

"The Eternal Return. For example, you are Virginia Woolf."

"Are you a *topos* too?"

"The Fox in the Henhouse."

"You have already," she says, "made a wide swath among the pullets." Removing her hands from her knees, she lunges over abruptly to kiss him. The Cross of Twelve Pearls dangles before his eyes, the tiny round points gleaming. Distracted by this glittering bangle swaying before him, he attempts to grasp her, but she eludes him and sits up again.

"So this is the way you spend your afternoons."

"Don't be silly."

"You said it was the local custom."

"I only heard about it," she says, "from the lycéens. Besides," she says, "I work every afternoon in the strong room, except Tuesday. This is getting on toward evening, and furthermore it's going to rain too."

"Is Professor Lohengrin there every afternoon?"

"Not every afternoon."

"But Father Dion is."

"Yes."

He peers out at her from his half-closed eyes. She is lying on one elbow now and the rebozo has fallen apart. The Cross moves slowly in the gray light, and emits a tiny silver spark. Like a signal to mariners, it exactly delineates the location of the neat breast under her shirt. The rain is making a sound as though someone were softly scattering rice in the leaves overhead.

"You said you knew Anstruc. He doesn't seem very bright."

She says nothing.

He persists. "Does he?"

"Patrick, you want to steal the Treasure, don't you?"

"Why do you say that?"

"All your questions are thieves' questions."

After a pause he says, "How would you feel about it?"

"I suppose," she says, "it would depend on what you're going to do with it."

"Return it to the people."

"And who are they?"

"I don't know. Perhaps the Occitan movement, or the Front de la Jeunesse."

"That's the wrong answer, Patrick. You should have said, 'You and I.'"

"We're the people?"

"If there is any people," she says, "it's us, because we're all there is."

"I don't quite follow that."

"We're all there is. There's nothing else. Nothing nothing nothing." This *rien rien rien* is an odd noise, one that might be made by a wildcat; it accords strangely with her grave and slightly ironic composure. He is still lying on his back. She stares at him for a long moment, her gray eyes thoughtful. Then she falls over onto him, as though she were springing onto an animal that might try to escape. Their arms and legs tangle together, then straighten out except for occasional slithers. They roll over several times on the rustling larch needles. He is aware of her long bony face pressing against his, of her lean body, which seems extraordinarily muscular; he can hardly resist its pressings with his own strength. When the rolling ends he is on his back, as he was in the bed in the hotel. From somewhere he hears a voice in a rather inarticulate murmur. "Comme je t'aime je t'aime je t'aime."

"What are you saying?"

"That I love you."

She doesn't ask him to say the same in return, even though in his experience women almost always do. Her hair falls over his face, blocking everything from sight. There is a kind of hushed rustle like the flurry of angel wings in the trees overhead. It begins to rain in earnest.

When he wakes up it is because he is cold. He is stark naked and lying on his back. The rain is dripping through the branches and falling in thin but steady threads onto the blanket of larch needles under him. One of these miniature rivulets is aimed exactly at his groin. He sits up.

"You're a very good sleeper, Patrick."

She is sitting there cross-legged watching him, naked except for the cross around her neck. He wonders whether she has put the necklace back on after she got up from their embrace, or whether she has had it on all along. He tries to recall whether she had it on when they were slithering around like two wet snakes on the larch needles, but in fact he can't even remember her taking her clothes off. For a time they only contemplate each other in silence. It is the first time either of them has had a good look at the other's body in the daylight. Her tiny triangle of pubic hair, resting on the rather bony mons veneris, is a tuft something like a mustache, except that it is not ridiculous, only neat. This detail is not like Cranach, but like Modigliani. All his perceptions of the external world, he reflects, are drawn not from life but from the history of art.

"I didn't sleep last night."

"Do you always," she asks, "do it upside down?"

"It was you who grabbed me."

She has no response to this. It is self-evident. They sit there examining each other for a moment longer. The water falls onto her skin in tiny pearls, which cling glistening for a second and then slide off into the larch needles. The Occitanian Cross rests exactly between her water-dotted breasts. It has so many points on it that its cruciform shape is no longer apparent and it is only a kind of round badge in complicated fretwork, with sprouts and pearls projecting from it on all sides. No one, he thinks, could possibly be crucified on it.

Everything is soaking wet. His clothes are strewn around like abandoned rags. Hers are by her side in a neat pile which, probably, she arranged only after the débâcle, while waiting for him to wake up. The camera! But the bag is closed and the zipper is probably water-proof; he decides not to open it to check. He reaches for his khaki pants. She stands up, raises both hands to her neck, and shakes her head. Her hair whirls around with a snap. A few drops fall onto Patrick. In contrast to that other water, dripping in rivulets from the leaves, they are curiously warm.

The town is deserted and it is getting dark. The rain is still coming down and there is no one in sight. They separate in the street; Patrick goes into the tabac and Marie-Ange goes on up the hill toward her rented room. He buys a pack of Silk-Cuts and some matches, and then looks around to see what else there is. The tabac is also a kind of souvenir shop, in the summer at least. There are sew-on badges that say "Languedoc" and "Conques," some plastic dolls of the Majesté d'Or, and the usual sort of junk. Under a glass counter is a collection of silver pins and jewelry. He catches sight of a Cross of Occitania.

"May I see that?"

The girl takes it out. It is not as large as Marie-Ange's cross, only about half the size, and it is not of the same quality; it appears to have been stamped out by a machine. The twelve pearls are uneven and there are little burrs of metal on it where the finishing is imperfect. He decides to buy it for his car keys.

"Twenty francs," she says.

"Then it's not silver?"

"No. It's *étain*."

This may mean either tin or pewter. It doesn't seem shiny enough for tin. "That is, *potin*," he says. This *really* means pewter.

"That's it, *potin*," she agrees.

He pays her and puts it in his pocket. He would like to put it on the key ring right away, but he remembers now that the hotel boy took the keys away from him again when he came back from Toulouse. Because, of course, the Citroën with the Paris plates is still there in front of the Renault, and might have to be moved. But whom does this other car belong to? he wonders for the first time. The Belgians are gone, and Professor Lohengrin would hardly drive a Citroën CX Pallas, which is an expensive luxury car. Perhaps it belongs to Madame herself. But with Paris plates? He distinctly remembers the 75 at the end of the number. Patrick becomes, all at once, very curious about this Phantom Guest who comes from Paris and drives a Citroën CX.

Because of his wet clothing he attempts to sneak into the hotel something like a a truant schoolboy. But Madame is standing by the desk in her tailored suit.

"Ah. Professor Proutey. Someone has left this for you."

She hands him a folded slip of paper.

"Also, there have been several telephones from Toulouse."

"Am I to call back?"

118

"No, the party said he would continue to call every so often."

"Very good."

She stares at his wet clothing. "You've been having a look at our countryside."

"Yes."

"Have you visited the chapel of Saint-Roch?"

"No."

"Perhaps the viewpoint of the Bancarel? It's across the valley."

"No."

"What have you seen then?"

"The campground."

"There's not much to see there this time of the year."

"There's a nice parking." He feels slightly feverish and is perhaps not entirely aware of what he is saying. But she makes no comment on this. She only says, in her arch and significant manner, "Dinner is at seven thirty."

"Isn't it always?"

"Yes," she says smoothly. "That's what I meant to say."

God knows what she meant to say. He goes up to his room, locks the door, and opens the slip of paper. There are only five words on it, in a careful and slightly old-fashioned hand.

Emil, asleep, peels a lime

In his state of mind this doesn't seem at all an extraordinary message, even though it is meaningless. After a moment of reflection it occurs to him that it is in English. He knows no one in the town who speaks English, unless it is Madame herself. Another moment, and he notices that the sentence reads the same backwards as forwards. Perhaps it is from Professor Lohengrin, who certainly knows all languages including English, and whose handwriting quite possibly resembles that of an unmarried female schoolteacher. He looks at the slip again. It may be fraught with some terrible significance,

119

for him or for someone else, but if it is he can't figure it out. He drops it into the wastebasket.

Checking once more to see that the door is locked, he kicks his shoes into the corner, takes off his wet clothing, and drops it on the floor. Then he gets into the tub and takes a hot bath. It is amazing the difference this makes to his clarity of mind. He remembers everything that happened in the afternoon with a keen exactitude, as though it were a cinema running through his mind. And, oddly enough, he finds himself satisfied with this little movie. He had accomplished two things for this day that he set out to do. He found the parking and photographed it, and he has . . . he was with Marie-Ange in the larch grove. Perhaps it is only the warm bath. He pulls the plug, gets out of the tub, and is drying his hair when there is a knock on the door.

"Who is it?"

"C'est moi, monsieur. Hyacinthe."

He opens the door. It is the boy who helped him park the car. Patrick is stark naked, but he nevertheless stands holding the door open.

"It is, monsieur, that I have come to take your wet clothes away and press them dry."

"It isn't necessary. I have others."

"I'll just give them a touch of the iron."

"You yourself?"

"Oui, monsieur."

"Why not the chambermaid?"

"There is no chambermaid, monsieur. Or rather, I am the chambermaid, such as it is. You see, Madame does not like women working in the hotel. She says they get notions. So all the employees are men. The cook, the waiters, and I myself make the beds and do things like pressing out damp clothes for the guests."

"She's the only female in the place?"

"Oui, monsieur. So if you'll give me the clothes, I'll just touch them with the iron."

Patrick takes some soggy franc notes and a few coins out of the pants and hands them to him with the shirt. The sweater is beyond touching with the iron; it resem-

120

bles a drowned cat. The boy goes away and the door
shuts. Almost immediately the phone in the room rings.

"Hello, Professor Proutey?"

"Yes."

"This is Gabriel. Where the hell have you been? I've
been trying to get you all afternoon."

"I've been out doing some research."

"Is that so?"

"Yes. I've found a place for birds—"

"Is this a green phone?" Flecker interrupts.

"What? I don't know. It's an extension in the hotel.
Anyone else can listen in on it."

"Go out and call me on a pay phone. I'll wait here."

"I'm not sure where there is one. It's a very small
town."

"Go out and look."

"It's raining here."

"It's raining here too. Get a move on, Professor."

Patrick is still naked and he hasn't even dried himself
properly. He doesn't feel like going out. "What's the
number where you are?"

Flecker gives it to him. "It's a café. I'll wait here."

"I'll call you in five minutes."

"Very good, Professor Proutey."

Patrick dresses in a dry shirt and khaki pants, the
only two remaining garments he possesses. He puts his
money in his pocket. There is no point in putting on the
soaked sweater over the dry clothing. It is still raining
outside; a kind of steady hushed roar is falling over the
rooftops. He finds some coins, puts them in his pocket,
and goes out. Madame is not at her desk and he manages
not to encounter anyone else on his way out. As soon as
he steps out from the doorway he is immediately
drenched. It is a little after seven and pitch dark outside.
A black layer of water is slithering down the slope of
the pavement. It sloshes over into the tops of his shoes,
which begin to squish as though he were walking
underwater with them. To his surprise he finds a pay
phone almost immediately, in the Café de la Terrasse.

121

The girl shows him where it is, then disappears again into the kitchen. He puts in the coins and direct-dials the number in Toulouse.

Flecker answers almost before it starts ringing. Patrick can hear the sound of glasses clinking, and conversation in the background. A laugh. Over these sounds Flecker's voice is succinct and military, a kind of subdued bark.

"Professor Proutey?"

"Who else would it be?"

"Is this phone green?"

"Well, it's about as green a phone as you're going to get in Conques. The town is so small that you can't get more than ten feet from anybody."

"Don't be a smart-ass, Professor. This is an important call so pay attention, will you?"

"All right."

"Get this straight, but don't write anything down. This is Wednesday the sixth. Tomorrow, the seventh, your wife will be driving the Deux Chevaux up to Conques. I want the two of you to put it somewhere. Now listen carefully. The place I want you to put it is in the churchyard of a village, up in the mountains. The village is called Aumont. It's—"

"I know where it is."

"You do?"

"I know the churchyard. I got a look at it the other day."

Flecker sounds dubious. "Okay, if you say so. Now listen. Are you sure this phone is green?"

"There's a girl called Sylvie in the back room. I think she's making frites, to judge from the smell of it."

"Fine, fine. Now listen. Did you say you'd found a bird sanctuary?"

"Yes. It's fine. It's another parking, near the campground. It's on Départementale 601, about five hundred meters up the highway from the road that turns off to the town."

"Six oh one?"

"Yes. That's the main road that comes up from Rodez. The parking is paved and level and there's a good approach from the south."

122

"South." Flecker seems to be writing things down, even though he told Patrick not to. "How far from the place where you do your research?"

"A kilometer. Five or ten minutes at the most."

"All right." He is still writing. "Listen, Professor. The bird will light on the eighth, that's Friday. At exactly 1650 hours, that's ten minutes to five."

"The place closes at five."

"I know that. You said five or ten minutes, didn't you? We want to get there just as it closes. Get this straight now. You be at the sanctuary with the car, at exactly 1650 hours. What about this assistant of yours?"

"She's all right."

"I thought it was a she."

"What's wrong with that?"

"Nothing. We'll leave it to you to be sure that all the lights are green up there. Is there anything else you need?"

"Have Sara bring up two firecrackers and some Silly Putty. And some friction tape."

"Firecrackers. Silly Putty." It is as though he were making a grocery list. "All right. Got you. Good, good. Until Friday, then. What's the time at the bird sanctuary, once more?"

"1650 hours."

"Very good, Professor." Flecker hangs up without saying good-by.

No one notices Patrick coming back in either. His clothes are soaked again but the warm and pressed pants and shirt are lying on his bed. He changes once more and goes down to dinner. Since the Belgians are gone now he and Professor Lohengrin have the dining room to themselves. The prix-fixe is Truite Bleue, then Cassoulet with Confit d'Oie, salad, fruit, and cheese. A rustic menu. Specialties of the region. This time, on Madame's advice, he takes a white Quatourze with the fish and a strong, slightly resinous Gaillac with the cassoulet. Il faut toujours boire le vin du pays, says Madame as a general piece of wisdom. The Gaillac, he decides, has a very faint flavor of armpit. It is not un-

123

pleasant, especially with the cassoulet, which is a gamy dish tasting slightly of corruption.

Professor Lohengrin is not so far along. He is reading a newspaper and he seems to have been provided with some pickled mushrooms, which are not on the prix-fixe. When his fish comes he ignores it. He looks in Patrick's direction, ineffectually and myopically because through his glasses. He lowers his head to look over the glasses. Identifies that there is a person sitting at the other table. Shows no sign of recognition whatsoever. Instead he turns back to the plate before him. He shoots both cuffs. He extends his arms straight out before him, a fish knife in one hand, a fork in the other. And he charges at his trout.

TEN

When Patrick wakes up the next morning he has, it seems to him, a slight sore throat. Perhaps, he thinks, he has caught a fever from not coming in out of the rain (the classic definition of a fool), and from engaging in activities under these conditions that made him perspire. He gets up and goes down to breakfast. Madame is not there, only the waiter, who may or may not be the same waiter who has always served him. He has not paid very much attention to the waiters. Things seem a little better after he has had his coffee. He leaves the croissants untouched in the basket on the table. They look scratchy, and he isn't hungry anyhow. Has he a sore throat? It is difficult to say. There is a slight hoarseness, but he talked a great deal the day before, much more than he is accustomed to. He remembers this same hoarseness from the time when he was a university instructor. It is probably only functional laryngitis.

Back in his room, he takes everything out of his camera bag and begins feeling around in it for the vitamin C. He finds a five-hundred-milligram tablet hidden in the seam at the bottom, brushes some grains of tobacco and a little dust off it, and takes it with a glass of water from the bathroom. He knows that, in all probability, there are several more tablets hidden in the seams and corners of the bag, and under a kind of flap that covers the bottom. These tablets are like the coins that can always be found by taking apart an overstuffed sofa. Patrick does not take vitamin C all the time, only when he thinks he may be catching something. And he does not carry it around in a small neat bottle with the pharmacological description, dosage, and warnings for misuse on the label. This he would consider bourgeois and overorganized. Yet he does not want to be caught without vitamin C. So he arranges that there are always a few tablets lost in the seams of the bag. The fact is that he has never caught a cold from the time he began taking vitamin C at the earliest onset of symptoms. I am really quite anxious to stay alive, he thinks. This surprises him a little. He puts everything back in the bag, including his passport and money, and zips it shut.

Sara arrives a little before eleven. She is better organized than he thought. Instead of having him called from the desk below she comes right up to his room and knocks on the door. She is in her usual paramilitary garb, and since it is cool in the mountains she has added a leather jacket with LT HAYMAN on a label over the pocket. The leather is cracked and worn and perhaps it is an authentic surplus Air Force jacket. Her boots, which are Russian leather, must have cost at least five hundred francs in rue Saint-Rome.
"Patrick. Comment ça va?"
"Where's the car?"
"Down the street, by the café."
"Is it blocking the street?"
"No. There's a little hole I stuck it in." She demonstrates with her middle finger.
She has nothing with her but the cheap imitation-leather suitcase. "Did you bring the stuff?"
"I brought *my* stuff."
"Martin was going to send something."
"Oh yeah, there's some other stuff."
"Let's go see the car."

126

Just as she said, it's parked down the street by the café. She has managed to find a little spot to jam it in, just wide enough for the Deux Chevaux, between the café and the fountain. There is a note under the windshield wiper which says, "Please do not leave cars in this position. There is a parking just at the outside of town, by the gendarmerie. Anstruc."

"Who is Anstruc?"

"A policeman."

"He's very polite. In Toulouse they just give you a ticket."

"Yes. Where's the stuff?"

In the back of the camionette is a gray cardboard box, a rather flimsy one of the kind used for envelopes and stationery. There is something heavy in it. He has to carry it carefully, with his hand under it, so that the contents don't spill out or break the fragile box.

They go back up to the room. Sara goes into the bathroom, to make pipi as she says, which she does with the door half open. Patrick opens the stationery box. There is a block of plastic in it the size and shape of a book, and two American M3 hand grenades. Also, a roll of black friction tape, partly used, but there are still several meters left on it. Flecker is reliable. There is that to be said for him. He has some obnoxious qualities, but he is reliable. He puts the box away in the bottom drawer of the bureau.

Sara comes out of the bathroom, wiping her hands on her pants, and they go out again, Patrick with his camera bag. Patrick looks around at the desk for Madame. There is nobody in sight. He opens the door to the kitchen, and investigates another door which proves to lead down a corridor to the employees' toilet. He comes back out into the foyer.

"Hello!"

In only a few moments Hyacinthe appears, wearing a white apron and wiping his hands on it.

"I need the keys to my car."

"Very good, monsieur."

Taking a key from his own pocket, he unlocks the drawer of the desk and finds the keys to the Renault.

127

"I'll go down with you, monsieur, just to be sure there isn't some other car behind yours, blocking it."

This doesn't seem very likely to Patrick, since there are only two cars in the garage. He explains, "This is my wife."

"Ah," says Hyacinthe. "You are going away together?"

"We have to take my wife's car to be repaired."

"Ah. It doesn't march?"

"It marches, but with pain."

"Ah. So you are taking it to Rodez to be repaired?"

"Perhaps."

"But," says Hyacinthe, "the camionette has something about the university on the side of it."

"What camionette?"

"Your wife's car down by the café."

"That's really my car. We've traded cars. Her car is the Renault."

"The Renault is rented."

"Yes," says Patrick. "Does everything get around in this town? Do you have meetings all night in which you discuss the affairs of strangers?"

"I beg your pardon, monsieur. We sleep just like everybody else. I was just making conversation."

They have reached the garage. "Now you tell me something. Who does that Citroën belong to?"

"Ah. That's the car of Madame."

"It has Paris plates."

"Yes. Madame has a town house in Paris, on the Île Saint-Louis, and also a château in the Touraine."

"Then why does she stay in this place?"

"She has to be here to run the hotel. And also," says Hyacinthe very simply, "I believe she has a great affection for the church."

Patrick takes time to pry open his key ring and put the small Cross of Twelve Pearls onto it, as a kind of handle or bangle. Then he starts up the Renault, backs it out of the garage, and drives down the street to collect Sara. She follows along behind him in the Deux Chevaux. As they leave town he can hear the muffled popping behind him, like a motorcycle running inside a garbage can. They come to the highway, go down it to the medieval bridge, and cross it onto the narrow country road. For about an hour they go up, down, and around the endless hills of the Rouergue without meeting a soul, although they pass an occasional farmhouse. He is careful not to climb the hills too rapidly, because the Deux Chevaux is even more underpowered than the Renault. He has the map clipped to the dashboard but he hardly needs to glance at it, since he has been over this route before in the other direction. On the outskirts of Aumont he glances into the mirror to be sure Sara is still following. He slows down.

There is only one crossroad in the village and you could throw a stone from the highway to the end of it. He turns into the road, then pulls over to one side and motions for Sara to go on ahead of him.

She stops abreast and slides the window open with her hand. It doesn't roll down.

"What?"

"Pull into the churchyard," he shouts over the clanging and popping of the camionette, "and leave it there."

"Why?"

"Just do it, Sara."

The camionette goes on down a rocky lane into the churchyard, pitching like a boat in a seaway. She parks it next to a crude stone cross with a snake wrapped around it; perhaps it is the grave of the local physician. The camionette dies with a final shudder. She gets out and comes back to the Renault.

"What are we doing this for?"

"Did you lock it?"

"Yes."

"Give me the keys."

He has some difficulty turning the car around on the narrow road. There are stone walls on either side. From the path that runs by the church a woman stands watching them, the same one who stared at Patrick when he passed through the village before. She is even carrying the same pail in her hand. She raises the other hand to protect her eyes from the sun, and gazes at them with a kind of brooding intensity. She doesn't seem to have noticed the camionette in the churchyard.

"Most people in the country," says Sara, "are morons."

They drive back through the hills without very much discussion. When they get back to Conques it is after two, and too late for lunch at the hotel. They have to eat at the café. Sara prefers this anyhow; she is a passionate devotee of junk food. She has a jelly pastry, a little bag of potato chips, another of chocolate wafers, and a Coca-Cola. Patrick has a ham sandwich and a glass of milk.

She says, "Serge will never let me order Coca-Cola. He says it's conspicuous."

"Is that so?"

"Yes. He says it's a capitalistic drink. It's conspicuous consumption."

"Oh I see. Sara," he explains, "he didn't mean it was conspicuous. He meant it was conspicuous consumption. This is a term used by Veblen in his *Theory of the Leisure Class*. According to Veblen, the leisure class spends money in a way that is intended almost exclusively to demonstrate its wealth. The spending must be publicly visible and it must be useless. For example, women of the leisure class wear high heels, in order to show that they have cars to take them everywhere and don't have to walk, and they have long fingernails to show that they don't have to do anything with their hands. Women of the leisure class are useless luxury objects. In the same way, Chinese women of the aristocratic class used to bind their feet."

"But I don't wear high heels."

"I didn't say you did. Do you have to refer everything to yourself?"

"I don't understand what you're talking about. I have long fingernails and I can do lots of things."

There is nobody around in the hotel, so Patrick simply leaves the keys to the Renault, with the Croix de Languedoc now attached to them, on the desk. Sara follows languidly after him, trailing her hand along the banister of the stairs. Her relation to things is largely tactile. After the door is shut behind them she *feels* the room, running her fingers with their silver nails over the door handle, the armoire, the foot of the bed.

"There's not much to do in this place."

"You could go and look at the church."

"Patrick, do you want to—"

"No I don't."

"Okay," she says complacently, "then I'll take a bath."

"That's a good idea."

"In Toulouse," she says, "somebody always wants in the bathroom, and you've got all your developing junk in there." She says, "Sometimes a girl likes to take a long bath." She unbuttons the shirt, dexterously in spite of her Veblen fingernails, and slips it off. Incongruously enough, under the military shirt she wears a see-through bra of black net and lace. When she gets the trousers off, the rest of her underwear is in the same style. Now, instead of a Palestinian commando, she resembles one of those girls in a fin-de-siècle whorehouse by Toulouse-Lautrec. He has got to get rid of this habit, he tells himself. The whole world is not an anthology of art reproductions. He picks up his camera bag and goes out, locking the door and taking the key with him.

It is not quite four o'clock. There is a concert in the church at five thirty, and he has promised to go to it with Marie-Ange, but she won't get off from her work until five. Patrick goes up the street, past the boulangerie-pâtisserie, the tabac, and the milk bar. In the parking he sits down on the balustrade, facing outward with his feet dangling, and looks out over the valley. Sure enough, after a few minutes Anstruc appears. He can sense his presence behind him. He turns around on the balustrade and sets his feet on the pavement.

Anstruc reaches into his shirt pocket. "A smoke?" He holds out the pack of Gauloises. "Ah, you prefer Silk-Cuts." He withdraws the pack, takes one out for himself, and puts the rest away in his shirt again. Patrick gets out a Silk-Cut. This time Anstruc provides the match.

They smoke at each other in silence for some time. Anstruc is built like a wrestler, Patrick thinks. In fact, he is a little muscle-bound. His neck is so thick that it doesn't allow very much movement to his head. He has to turn his whole upper body from side to side, like a figure in a Swiss clock, when he wants to look at something. He has the motions of a man wearing a neck brace. But the neck brace is simply the cylinder of muscles around his neck.

He says, "So your wife has arrived."

Patrick nods.

Anstruc says, "It's better not to park a car by the café. It blocks the way for people coming down the hill on the lane. The car can be left here in the parking."

"It's in Rodez now, being repaired in a garage."

Anstruc has nothing to say to this.

Patrick says, "Have there been very many crimes in Conques, since I talked to you last?"

Anstruc considers. "No," he says. "No, there haven't been very many crimes, serious ones at least. Somebody ran off the road and hit a tree, on the Départmentale. He had been drinking white wine. And then, of course, there was your car parked between the café and the fountain." He says, "It's a slow period, this time of the year. Not many crimes. The crimes all come from the city, and there's nobody here from the city at this time." He says, "In fact, I'm able to release two of my four men to go on leave. They've gone to visit their relatives for a week. Lomiers has gone to Albi, and Barthes has gone to Kremlin-Bicêtre. That's a suburb of Paris. Barthes," he explains, "is a Parisian. Kremlin-Bicêtre is in what they call the banlieue de Paris."

"So there are only three of you here."

Anstruc considers this. "No," he says, "I have a man sick. Casteljaloux has an infected finger. He cut it with a paring knife working in the kitchen, you see, and then he picked his nose with it. At least he said he picked his nose. I think he was probably picking something else.

So he's in the hospital in Rodez. And tomorrow," he says, "Hutrac has a dental appointment in the city."

"So you'll be all alone."

Anstruc has to think about this too. "That's true," he says after a moment. "Tomorrow I'll be all alone. But the next day Hutrac will be back, and perhaps Casteljaloux too. So it's just tomorrow that I'll be all alone." It is not, Patrick feels, that Anstruc hasn't realized this himself. He is explaining the matter systematically because he wants it to be clear to him, Patrick. "However," Anstruc says, "there's not much for us to do this time of the year. Not much crime. Although," he adds, "it was just this time last year, in April, that the peasant in Aumont killed his wife with a mattock. They buried her up there," he says, "in the churchyard."

Patrick says nothing to this. There is a silence.

"However," Anstruc concludes, "that type of crime can't be anticipated. He was insane. It can happen any time of the year."

"Did he do it with one blow?"

Anstruc does not seem to find this question at all peculiar. After his usual pause, he says, "Yes. With one blow. He was a peasant, you see, and he was skilled with the mattock."

"What a terrible crime."

"So tomorrow," says Anstruc, "I'll be all by myself."

Five twenty. Patrick and Marie-Ange sit on a hard narrow bench in the vast nave of the church. Tapers are lighted in huge candlesticks distributed around the ambulatory. Complicated shadows come through the iron grilles, wavering slightly. The light of the tapers hardly reaches into the soaring vault overhead, which is gloomy and indistinct. A shadow from the grille wanders back and forth on Marie-Ange's face.

"Guides, I imagine," says Patrick, "have to know foreign languages."

"It helps."

"Do you know English?"

She looks at him and smiles faintly.

"Ah lee-tell. Ah—ee—"

"I know. You studied letters at Toulouse. Are you interested in palindromes?"

"Able was I, ere I saw Elba."

"A man, a plan, a canal, Panama. What about Emil?"

"It's because, I suppose, you sleep a lot. And if you can make love in your sleep, you could peel a lime."

Patrick lets this pass, and decides to keep the conversation on linguistics. "Do you know any palindromes in French?"

"No. I don't believe there are any palindromes in French. It has something to do with the endings of words. In French, words begin one way and end another way, so you can't turn them around. I don't understand it very well."

"How about Occitan?"

"No. Palindromes are a joke, and no one jokes in Occitan."

This seems unlikely, but he doesn't pursue it. "Sometimes I wonder," he tells her, "if you have a sense of humor. But you must, if you like palindromes."

"I find many things funny," she says, "but not in Occitan."

Perhaps it is only the echo in the church, but her voice sounds hoarse. There is a slight pinkness too around the edges of her nostrils.

"You have a cold?"

"No. It's just from talking all afternoon in the Treasure. There were some visitors." But, as if reminded of it by Patrick's question, she takes out a handkerchief and blows her nose.

"You do too have a cold. We shouldn't have—"

Marie-Ange doesn't care for references of this sort to her body. She says, "Quiet, the music's starting."

The chorus consists of boys from a home for the mentally retarded in the hills nearby, at Saint-Cyprien. They file into the choir, slowly and gravely and not looking around very much. Some have jerky motions, others the slack chin and vacant eye of the mongoloid, but in general they seem in control of themselves and thoroughly confident about what they are doing. They are arranged in three rows by a young man who himself seems normal except for a slightly haunted stare like a figure in Edvard Munch. (Another artistic allusion.) They sing medieval chants, very sweetly and movingly. Some are sopranos, or countertenors, but since they are mentally retarded it has not occurred to them that there is anything unmanly about this. The voices are exact; not once is there a wrong note or a hesitation. They seem to enjoy what they are doing; there is a beatific look about their faces. When they finish with the chants they sing some Renaissance songs, some of which are rounds and quite complicated. Then, as a finale, they sing some modern songs in Occitan. These are religious in nature and based, Marie-Ange explains, on Cathar hymns. Yet the boys are Catholics.

The four or five parts of the song touch one another, then come together in a single prolonged and seraphic note: "Amen."

Marie-Ange says, half-wonderingly, or pityingly, "They believe."

"Yes. But they don't know *what* they believe."

"There is absolutely no way," says Marie-Ange, "of distinguishing between the piety of an idiot and the piety of St. Thomas Aquinas. Piety is not of the intellect. In the Middle Ages, it was possible to be an intellectual and believe. Now, in order to believe, it is necessary to be an idiot."

"You sound as though you envy them."

She says nothing to this. The concert is over. They get up and walk out of the church with the rest of the audience, only a dozen or so people. Mme Greffulhe is there, he notices, but she sits in the back and slips out first so that he catches only a glimpse of her. Patrick and Marie-Ange, going down the aisle, are forced to stop for the others, who loiter and block the way as even a small crowd will.

Patrick says, "She doesn't like me."

"Who?"

"Mme Greffulhe."

135

Marie-Ange says, "First you say you don't like her, then you say she doesn't like you. She doesn't like you or dislike you. She just runs a hotel." After a moment she says, "You know, that woman in your room isn't your wife at all."

"She isn't?"

"Everybody can see that."

"How?"

"She's not your type. And besides you don't—you know—with her."

"Perhaps there's a peephole in the wall of my room."

She says, without any expression on her face at all, "We line up. They charge a franc. The money goes into the box for the restoration of the church."

"Did they watch you and me too?"

Still gravely, she says, "Don't joke, Patrick."

Outside on the parvis, in front of the darkening façade, they meet the boys, who have been led around the side of the church by the Edvard Munch young man and are walking to their bus at the top of the lane. Now that they are not singing the boys look less confident and their defects are more obvious; some of them can walk only in a shuffle and the procession goes very slowly. Marie-Ange's glance meets that of the young man. He smiles.

"Adiou, Gustou. Bas pla?"

He smiles again and says, "Oc."

It is the first time Patrick has heard the word spoken. It seems to him an odd object, a kind of verbal fossil, like something one expects to see in a museum and is surprised to find in the real world.

The young man adds, "Quand parlam occitan dins lo païs, tot ba plan."

When he is gone Marie-Ange asks Patrick, "Did you understand that?"

"Yes. He said, 'When we speak Occitan in our land, all goes well.' "

She blows her nose. "You're almost one of us, Patrick."

She smiles at him and he realizes he wants to be one with them—with her, actually.

136

The great bell of the church booms out the half hour.
Seven thirty. The shutters are tightly closed and only the
small light by the bedside is on. Sara has washed out her
various pieces of black lingerie and hung them about in
the room. She is very clean; he concedes that to her.

He says, "You're not my wife, Sara."

"I never said I was. You're acting very queer, Patrick."

"I just wanted to make it perfectly clear, so that you
wouldn't be under any misconceptions."

"I *could* be your wife. But all you want to do is jack
off with those pictures."

"Let's go to dinner."

They have the dining room to themselves, except for
Professor Lohengrin. Madame, who takes the order,
shows no sign of interest in the fact that Patrick seems
to bring different women to meals in the hotel one after
the other. The menu is Cold Veal in Aspic, then Rôti de
Boeuf, Pommes Parmentiers, and Haricot Beans. Sara
speaks only once, to ask if there are frites. Yes, says
Madame, the potatoes with the dinner are pommes parmentiers, but she can substitute frites. Sara is easily
pleased; she eats the fried potatoes with her fingers. The
wine: a red Gaillac, which Patrick is developing a taste
for. Perhaps in time, if subjected to the influence of
Madame, he might become a gourmet. A Chevalier du
Tastevin; one of those fat florid old gentlemen who taste
wine out of little silver cups. To arrive at that age, however, he will have to live not quite so dangerously. He
reminds himself to take his vitamin C.

Professor Lohengrin does not even deign to turn his
head in their direction. At the end of the meal he orders
a Cabriou. Patrick tells the waiter, "Two Cabrious."

When the cheese comes it consists of two round white
pellets the size and shape of hockey pucks. It has a gamy
odor. Sara looks at it suspiciously.

"Ugh! It's from goats."

"Well, ordinary cheese is from cows."

"Ugh!" she says. "Don't talk about it."

Ten o'clock. In Room 9, with its quaint dormered ceiling, they get ready for bed like an old married pair. First Patrick probes in the bottom of the camera bag for another vitamin C tablet, and finds one in the seams. Then he takes off his clothes. Sara sleeps in her black lace underwear, but Patrick, possessing no underwear, has the choice of sleeping in his clothes or naked as he usually does. He is damned if he is going to rearrange his habits for Sara. He climbs into bed with her, hurrying to get under the covers before he shows some visible sign of her influence. He turns out the light.

"Now be good, will you?"

"Why should I?" she complains. "It's not what I'm accustomed to."

However, she turns her back and scrunches up into a fetal position, the shape of a cashew, a natural one for her firm and compact body. He can feel her lace-covered bottom touching his own. Patrick recalls the early Christian saints who, according to Gibbon, slept chastely in bed with naked women, to chastise the flesh. It probably took a lot of faith. And it wouldn't help much even if you were mentally retarded. He remembers now what Gibbon said about it. "Sometimes," he said, "outraged Nature revenged herself."

He gets out of bed and, in the darkness, gropes around the room for his box of photo equipment. When he finds the box he carries it into the bathroom.

"I may have to go in there," says a muffled voice from the bed.

He ignores her. Getting out the developing tank and setting up his trays, he develops the roll of film from the camera and makes a contact sheet from it. Stark naked, chilled in the damp bathroom, he rocks the tray with his hand. Some gray ghosts appear on the white piece of paper; they spread and darken, the edges acquire solidity, and finally the twenty tiny images leap out and freeze in their four rows of five. He fixes the sheet and washes it.

At the beginning of the roll are several shots of the gendarmerie and the small blue car in the garage. Then the panorama of the town taken from the parking. A nice composition; the three steeples of the church dominate, a little to the right of center. There is Anstruc—his bull neck, his blank stare, the spark of gold gleaming on his epaulet. In the other parking, the one down by the campground, there is not much to see. Some trees, and an expanse of asphalt. Wasted film. At the end, however, is the closeup of Marie-Ange. Her face fills the frame, white and somehow tremulous in spite of its icy clarity, long and brooding, calm. There is a blurry spot just over her throat—a raindrop on the lens, no doubt. The expression is vaguely reproachful. It is an expression she often has. Perhaps it is only irony. Patrick becomes aware of a curious thing : he was aroused when he was in bed with Sara, whom he does not love, but he is not aroused by looking at the photo of Marie-Ange, whom he does love. Sara is totally wrong about what he does with the pictures. Probably she got it from Gaspar, who is a simple-minded animal and totally unable to understand anyone more complicated than himself. Patrick puts the developing equipment back in the box and sets the print on the bidet to dry.

Going back into the dark bedroom, he looks in the direction of the bed. A hump is dimly visible, and a sound of breathing is coming from it. He puts on his pants and shirt and slips into his shoes. Then, taking the key, he leaves the room.

It is a little after midnight. There is no moon and a few clouds are creeping across a steely gray sky. The peach-colored stones of the town seem to glow faintly, especially the church. He goes up the street, which curves slightly to the left and then to the right before it arrives at the parking at the edge of town. Patrick stops before he reaches the parking and sits on a wall. In the dark, he thinks, photography is impossible and so he is obliged to sit quietly and look at things with his own eyes. The town is absolutely silent except for the faint soughing of breeze in the trees across the street. Not a light is showing. The town might be deserted, or everyone in it might be dead. Everyone except himself is asleep. He meditates over the strangeness of this swoon that everyone falls into more or less at the same time each night, as though some invisible plague has stolen into the town, unnoticed by anyone. Everyone, as though by mutual agreement, loses consciousness for eight hours, during which God also turns out the lights. Only policemen stay awake. And monks, praying in their cells, or chanting mass at midnight in their cold chapels. Patrick glances down the street behind him into the town. There is nothing; only the blacker irregular shadows of the houses on the black asphalt.

ELEVEN

Patrick has set his mind to wake up at six o'clock, and as a matter of fact he wakes up a little before this. This is the big day, he thinks banally. It isn't as though it were a football game. It is barely light. There is no sound from the other parts of the hotel. Sara is still asleep, with her bottom in exactly the same position against his.

He gets out of bed and puts on his shirt, pants, and shoes, after some thought adding the old gray sweater, which is still a little damp but will probably keep him warm anyhow to some extent. He leaves the room, taking the key and his camera bag. He has formed the habit of locking the room when he leaves Sara in it, although she has never shown any signs of wanting to go out alone. He steals down the stairs. His shoes are damp too, which has the advantage that it keeps them soft and prevents them from squeaking. In the foyer the night light is still on over the desk. All the other downstairs rooms are dark and the shutters are closed. In the dining room the tables are bare and the chairs set upside down on them. He goes to the sideboard and finds what he is looking for: a sugar bowl. He puts it in the camera bag, wedging it carefully so it won't fall over.

The room key also opens the street door, so he will be

able to get back in. Although probably, by the time he gets back, the door will be unlocked. He goes up the street in the morning twilight, past the shops, which are still shuttered and dark. The ground is still wet from the rain the night before. The air is crisp with a slight chill to it; it feels good. Even the damp sweater feels good. Patrick thrusts his hand into the bag hanging from his shoulder, gropes in the seam along the bottom, and finds a vitamin C tablet. There is no water to take it with so he chews it. It is quite sour, but, like the chill air and the damp sweater, this is also somehow pleasant.

The houses are behind. He crosses the empty expanse of the parking, turns into the road beyond it, and climbs up the hill. He notices now for the first time that the small red-white-and-blue sign of the gendarmerie is illuminated at night. No one has turned the light out yet, so probably it is still officially night in the gendarmerie. The small blue car with the emergency light on top is sitting snugly in the garage, which has no door and is really only a kind of open cave in the end of the building.

The gas cap is on the right rear fender. He takes off the cap and pours in the sugar from the bowl. This has to be done carefully, because the bowl isn't designed to have sugar poured out of it and the filler tube in the car is rather small. He holds his hand under it and spills only a little. These few grains in his hand he scrapes carefully into the tube. Then he puts the cap back on. He has spilled nothing on the ground.

He looks around; the gendarmerie is apparently deserted and everything is silent. He meets no one in the walk back to town, except for the usual old woman with the milk-can on her way to the crémerie. She is early this morning, he thinks. It is only six thirty. No one is up yet in the hotel, and he has to unlock the street door with his key. He goes up the stairs and into the dining room, and replaces the sugar bowl on the table. It is empty, but sugar bowls often become empty in hotels. Probably no one will notice. He still feels good. It is a fine morning, and he always feels good in cold weather.

*   *   *

142

Now he has to get through the day somehow until 1650 hours. Patrick's watch is an inexpensive American one, a Timex, but it is sturdy and reliable. It gains two or three minutes a day; the rate can be counted on. The trouble is that he can't remember when the last time was he set it. Probably it was in Toulouse, a week or more ago. There is a synchronized electric clock in Toulouse in front of the post office, and he sets his watch whenever he passes it. In Conques there don't seem to be very many clocks, and the ones in the hotel are mainly antiques. He could get accurate time signals from Radio Paris, except that he has no radio. The only thing to do, he decides, is to set his watch by the bell of the church. It seems to clang out in a reliable way, every quarter of an hour.

At breakfast, which he takes with Sara and which is served in the small enclosed garden or patio of the hotel, he waits for the bell to ring. But at seven forty-five he is distracted by Sara who is talking about something or other, and he misses it. He and Sara have long since finished their coffee and the waiter—who this morning is Hyacinthe, the chambermaid—can't understand why they go on lingering at the table.

"May we have more coffee, please."

"Tout de suite, monsieur."

He brings the carafe and fills their cups.

"And sugar."

"Ah, you take sugar?" He goes away to the dining room and comes back with the bowl. "Ah, this one is empty. Excuse me. I'll get another one." He brings another bowl with some sugar in it, and Patrick puts a spoonful in his coffee. According to his watch it is slightly after eight, but the watch is fast.

He waits. The watch says seven minutes after eight. Madame comes out into the patio, looks around for something, and stops and fixes her glance at the table where Patrick and Sara are sitting. She probably wants them to get up and leave so Hyacinthe can clear away. The small brassy bell in the church begins intoning slowly. BONG. BONG. BONG. BONG. BONG. BONG. BONG. BONG.

143

He sets the watch. Madame observes it all from her post at the corner of the patio.

After breakfast he gets rid of Sara, which is not very difficult because she seems perfectly content to stay in the room polishing her nails with a little buffer, and goes for a walk with Marie-Ange. "Let's go up to the parking," he tells her.

"Why?"

"I want to look around." He has his camera bag with him but he hasn't loaded the camera. In fact, the thought occurs to him, he has used up his last roll of film. Perhaps they would have some at the tabac. However, they pass the tabac and he doesn't stop. The film doesn't seem very important.

The sun is out now and the wet street is steaming. However it still isn't very warm. Marie-Ange clasps the rebozo around her and holds it together in the front. She sniffs, and takes out a handkerchief and applies it to her nose once in a while. Not only are her nostrils pink but there is a little rim of pink around her eyes as well. She doesn't refer to her cold, and her manner is exactly as always, calm, self-assured, and faintly ironic.

"It's a lovely morning."

"Yes," she says. "It's Good Friday, you know."

"What's so good about it?"

"It's the day they killed God."

He hardly knows how to take her when she is like this. She may be serious, but it is probably only a joke. However she doesn't smile.

He tells her, "I'm sorry about the larch woods."

"What?"

"Getting wet."

"It's all right."

"Do you really love me?"

"I've already told you that once before. I advise you to make a note of the fact and put it in a place, somewhere, where you won't lose it."

"Don't be cross."

"I'm not."

If she says she isn't, he decides, she isn't. They have arrived at the parking. She says, "Now where?"

"Come on."

He leads her a little farther, across the parking and halfway up the road to a point where they can see the paved driveway in front of the gendarmerie. The blue car has been pushed out of the garage into the open. The hood is lifted up and Anstruc is bending over into the machinery. A part of his shirt, his khaki pants, and his polished shoes are visible. The rest of him has disappeared into the engine compartment.

Now Patrick does wish he had film in the camera. It would take a telephoto lens though. The car is a hundred meters or more away. Anstruc may come up out of the engine compartment at any moment. He leads Marie-Ange away down the road again. Halfway down the hill, at a place where some trees obscure the view from the town, he finds what seems to be a good place to kiss her. For some time he has had a strong desire to do this. They stop, and he turns her around with her back against a tree.

Her lips are strong, firm, and slightly tremulous. But she won't open her mouth. Perhaps she is afraid he will catch her cold. They go on down the road. Patrick reaches for the camera bag, which is on his right side, the side away from Marie-Ange, unzips it, and feels down into the seam for a vitamin C tablet.

"That was a nice kiss," he says.

"Really?"

"No, not really. But perhaps we can have another one later."

"Don't you have something else to do today?"

"It's a long day. I'm free until evening."

"I have to work in the afternoon."

"We still have this morning. What else is there to see in this town?"

"What do you mean?"

"You're a guide. What else is there to see?"

"Well. There's the Site de Bancarel, across the valley. It has a view of the town."

"Yes. Madame told me about that. It doesn't sound very interesting."

"There's the cemetery."

"That seems sufficiently lugubrious, for the holiday." They wind their way down past the rear of the church and around the apse. Here they come out onto a lane that leads down a gentle slope to the cemetery, which is built on filled land at the very edge of the valley, held up by a retaining wall. This wall, in contrast to the one above the church, doesn't seem very substantial. It appears to have been made of cast-aside chunks of building stone, perhaps fom Roman times. The whole cemetery is a ramshackle affair. There is a tomb here, a gravestone there, but everything tilts and the weeds spring up like fountains among the stones. The weeds are the only vigorous thing in sight. Patrick walks to the edge and looks over the wall. Beyond the wall the slope is *really* steep. It drops off almost vertically. The gorge below is a void, an abyss, so deep it looks almost black. There is the sound of water talking to itself far below.

They sit down on the wall a few feet apart. Patrick looks at her in silence. It is a composition : at short range is Marie-Ange with her long pale face and dark hair, in the middle distance a medieval tower at the corner of the cemetery which has been converted into a chapel, and in the background the hillside beyond the Ouche, still shadowy but with a bit of sun beginning to creep across it. Her hair is in the sun, back-lighted as though there were a ring of fire around it, standing out clearly against the dark hill. He reaches for the bag but remembers once more that he has no film.

"The little chapel," she says in her guide manner, "may date from as early as the tenth century. As you can see it is fortress style, a tourelle. In those days, sometimes they were not sure whether they were building forts or churches."

"Perhaps the tower was part of the ramparts of the city."

"Perhaps. At any rate it's a chapel now. All the abbots are buried in it."

"All of them?"

146

"Why not?"

"The chapel seems very small."

"Well, they weren't very large men. Oh, merde. Here comes Father Time."

He turns around. In fact Father Dion has appeared at the corner of the church and is making his way down toward them. He is wearing his black cloak over the white cassock, with the cowl thrown back over his shoulders. He has a heavy gnarled stick to hold him up, and with this he advances in tripod fashion, moving no more than one of his three supports—the leg, the other leg, and the stick—at a time. It takes him some time to arrive at the edge of the cemetery, where he perceives them, and another length of time to make his way through the tilting gravestones to the wall.

"Good morning, my children," he says. "My children, this is a blessed day. This is the day of the Most Holy Passion of Our Lord Jesus Christ, for the Atonement of Mankind."

"Yes, Mademoiselle was just remarking as much."

"The bells have been ringing from the church. Perhaps you have noticed. That is why."

"But they ring every day."

"They ring every day. But today they are ringing because it is the Most Holy Passion of Our Lord and Savior."

"Is it true that all the abbots of Sainte-Foy are buried there in the chapel?"

"Which chapel is that, my son?"

"The little tower there, at the corner of the cemetery."

"Ah. That I can't say, my son. You should ask Mademoiselle. She is a certified guide to the church and environs. I only know that it is a holy place, and I come here to pray on mornings when it is fine. When it rains I don't. I expect to be buried in the chapel."

"Which chapel?"

"This little chapel that you speak of. It doesn't have a name."

"Father," says Patrick, "do the dead have names?"

Father Dion seems to understand this rather odd question perfectly. "In my opinion," he says, "they

don't. It is a point on which the Church has not pronounced a doctrine. Certainly souls before they are born
do not have names. This is the way I reason the matter.
Names are an invention of man, even though they are
conferred by the priest in the Holy Sacrament of Bap-
tism. The souls when they are in the Bosom of the
Creator do not have names, but they are given names
when they are born. It follows that, after death when
they are once more in the Bosom of the Creator, they
no longer have names, which are an invention of man
and therefore a part of their ephemeral earthly attachments. The dead are nameless," he concludes.

"Perhaps," says Patrick, "the damned in Hell have
names."

"How is that, my son?"

"Since they are not in the Bosom of the Creator. Perhaps they can have names."

"That," considers Father Dion, "is possible. Certainly
they do have names in Dante."

It surprises Patrick a little that Father Dion has read
Dante.

"And you," says Patrick, "are called Father Dion."

"I am at present."

"And after you die," persists Patrick, "you won't be
called anything at all."

"I hope not."

"What," says Patrick, "do you think, Marie-Ange?"

"I am not very interested in the subject. Let the dead
bury the dead," she says. "Quickly if possible."

Later in the day, after lunch, when Marie-Ange is
working, Patrick takes another walk up to the gendarmerie. Anstruc is still working on the car. Parts of the
carburetor are sitting on the fender.

TWELVE

The taxi stops in front of the office of the Aéroservice du Midi. Gaspar and Flecker get out, then the two packing cases are taken out and set on the pavement. Flecker pays the driver. The packing cases are not heavy, but they are large and an awkward shape. The two of them carry one into the office, then they come back out and get the other.

The same young man is behind the counter. His name, Flecker remembers, is Lespinasse. The girl behind him is typing and doesn't even look up. Lespinasse gazes with some curiosity at their costumes. Gaspar is wearing coveralls and a camouflaged military fatigue hat; Flecker is in Levi pants and jacket, and a high-crowned red cap with a visor and the word "Caterpillar" embroidered on it. Lespinasse has also noticed the taxi pulling away.

"Ah, you don't have your little camionette anymore?"

"It's gone on up to the Rouergue with the advance party."

"Ah, I see. Well, your aircraft is ready on the tarmac. Do you have the document you told me about on the phone?"

Flecker looks at Gaspar. Gaspar reaches into his cover-

149

alls and takes out the requisition. Lespinasse studies it for some time.

"But this document is from the Institute of Political Science."

"The research is actually being funded by the Institute of Political Science. They're doing an entire demographic survey of the Rouergue. We're only doing the geophysical part of it, as a background."

Lespinasse is clearly impressed by the words demographic and geophysical. Also, the packing cases are stenciled INSTITUT DE GEOPHYSIQUE.

"I see. Well, do you want to bring your—equipment —out to the tarmac and I'll introduce you to the pilot."

The JetRanger is sitting on the concrete behind the building, baking in the afternoon sun. It seems to waver slightly because of the warm air rising from it. It is painted white and blue, with a darker blue stripe around the fuselage and the tail. Flecker and Gaspar load the packing cases into it. The pilot is introduced, although Lespinasse doesn't mention his name. He just says, "This is the pilot." He is evidently a southerner; he looks like a young Italian movie star. He has curly hair and a friendly tanned face. He is wearing a flight suit and is bare-headed. However he has aviation-type sunglasses that give him a ready-for-anything look, cheerful but tough.

"That's all?"

"That's all."

"Okay. Allons donc."

They get in. Gaspar takes the rear seat, next to the packing cases, which are piled one on top of the other. The pilot slips in behind the controls, and Flecker takes the right-hand seat. He was hoping it would have dual controls, but only trainers have dual controls, and this isn't a trainer. He looks over the instrument panel, to be sure he knows what everything is. It is a beautiful machine.

"This is a 206A?"

"A 206B. It has the larger Allison engine. It will hover up to eighteen hundred meters. The 206A was only good for sixteen hundred."

150

He sets the throttle and pushes the starter with his thumb. The turbine rises to a whine, coughs, and takes hold with a roar. It starts easily, Flecker observes. It is in excellent condition.

They are north of Montauban, with the escarpment of the Rouergue already visible over to the right. There is a gap in the hills where the highway goes up through Caylus. The pilot glances at his map, then looks out the window to identify this gap where in a few minutes he will make his turn.

Flecker says, "Have you flown up here before?"

The pilot pushes the phones up a little above his ears so he can talk to Flecker. "Once or twice. I came up on a medical once, to take somebody out of a village."

"Did you learn to fly in the military?"

"Yes."

"In Indochina?"

"No. I was only fifteen then. I was in the lycée."

"In Algeria?"

"No. It was all peacetime service. I stayed right here in France."

'What did you fly?"

"Alouettes. The Alouette II, and also the Alouette III. The three is a beautiful aircraft. It has the Turbomeca Artouste, which gives six hundred horsepower. It goes to almost twenty-five hundred meters."

"Yes."

"However it is rough, and it makes a lot of noise. It hurts your ears unless you wear phones. I like the Jet-Ranger. It's quieter and it handles beautifully."

"Yes."

It is a very friendly conversation. They recognize each other as fellow pilots. A camaraderie is established, even though Flecker doesn't explain anything about his own military service. While they are talking the pilot has taken them up through the gap in the Rouergue, with the altimeter needle fixed on about five hundred meters. The monotonous hills roll by underneath them, with the highway winding its way through them. Caylus

151

is behind, and Villefranche visible ahead and a little to the right.

"From here we want to go up to the left." Flecker points on the map to the deserted high country north of Decazeville, between Decazeville and Aumont.

"Okay."

He swings the JetRanger around in a long curve to the left, and pulls up on the collective lever at the side of his seat. The JetRanger begins to climb: to five fifty, to six hundred, to six fifty. It also climbs beautifully.

Flecker glances around behind him. Gaspar is unscrewing the wing nuts on the first case. He removes the plywood cover, and takes out a Walther P-38 automatic on a web belt which he snaps around his waist. Next he takes out one of the MAT 49s, pulls out the telescoping steel stock and locks it, unfolds the magazine housing, and slips a magazine into it. He pulls back the cocking handle.

Flecker says, "There are some five-hundred-meter hills around here. The altitude at Aumont is around three fifty."

"No problem."

The pilot glances around to see what all the activity is that is going on behind him. Gaspar has stood up and is moving forward in a crouch with the MAT 49 in his right hand. Flecker pulls out the phone jack.

The pilot says, "Oh no."

"Get out of there and let my friend take over."

"I can't. This thing will plunge."

"No it won't. Set the frictions on the controls," Flecker tells him. "It'll be okay for a few seconds if you tighten the frictions."

He seems reassured by the fact that Flecker is a pilot. If Flecker is a pilot, then perhaps everything will be all right. Reluctantly he gets up, with slow motions as though it were a film running at half speed, and squeezes his way out through the narrow space between the seats. Gaspar motions him to the rear with the barrel of the gun. Flecker slips in behind the controls. He backs off the frictions, and waggles the aircraft a little by touching first the right pedal and then the left. He swings the cyclic back and forth. The JetRanger rolls to follow it, then settles back to level. The throttle is on the end of the collective, which is down to the left of the seat. Since it is a turbine aircraft, once you are in the air the throttle is set at a hundred percent and left there. The RPM is controlled automatically. To change the pitch, you move the collective.

Gaspar says, "Is it okay?"

"Beautiful," Flecker says.

Flecker looks out through the windscreen in front of him, and down out the window to the left. He banks the aircraft a little to get a better view out the window. Far over to the left he can see the highway going up though the hills to Figeac, and ahead through the windscreen is the tiny village of Aumont perched on top of its mountain. It is eight or ten kilometers to the north, and directly below there is nothing but broken hill country and an occasional farmhouse. He swings over the cyclic and touches the pedal to begin a turn to the left. He pushes down a little on the collective. The JetRanger turns in a wide coil, sinking down through the clear air toward the hills below. This coming down in a spiral is an old military trick, so you can get a look at the terrain out the window and pick your place to set down. He watches the altimeter: four fifty, four hundred. The terrain here is probably about three hundred. He checks it on the map, but he doesn't want to turn his attention away for too long from this aircraft which is still new to him. The JetRanger goes on down in its wide spiral. He glances out the window; the ground is about a hundred meters below. It is high pasture country. The ground is uneven and covered with a short tough grass, and there are occasional clumps of trees. At fifty meters he begins to feel the ground effect. The descent slows; it is as though the aircraft were sinking into a gradually thickening molasses. He picks out a flat spot without any rocks on it.

"Don't touch the throttle until you are on the ground," says the pilot.

Gaspar rumbles, "Shut up."

Flecker puts it down, with only a slight bump. He locks the collective and sets the cyclic at neutral, then he backs off on the throttle. The whining note of the engine descends.

"Get out," says Gaspar to the pilot. The door flops open.

"Go over there," says Gaspar, "by the trees. Keep moving."

The pilot is white under his tan. He begins moving slowly away from the helicopter toward the trees, with Gaspar following him.

"Serge," says Flecker in English, "for God's sake don't lose your head again."

Gaspar's English is not very good. "Loose my ed?"

"You know what I mean."

"Don't worry," says Gaspar. "You either," he tells the pilot reassuringly. "Ne t'inquiètes pas."

The pilot doesn't seem very reassured. He would feel better if Flecker told him this, since Flecker is a pilot. Gaspar still has the gun in his hand, carrying it lightly at the balance point. They reach the trees. The pilot's mouth seems dry. He licks his lips, and doesn't take his eyes off the gun in Gaspar's hand.

Gaspar says, "Sit down. There by the tree."

"No. Listen——"

"Sit down."

The pilot sits down. Gaspar hands the gun to Flecker. "Don't *you* lose your head. That thing is cocked." He takes a length of chain out of his coveralls, and two padlocks. The chain is the kind used for locking bicycles. He wraps the end tightly around the pilot's ankle and locks it. The other end he puts around the low branch of a tree and locks it with the other padlock. The branch is about waist high, and the pilot's leg is suspended a little off the ground. The pilot looks at the chain, and at his leg in the air. Gaspar reaches into the other pocket of his coveralls and takes out a small rat-tail file.

"With this," he says, "you ought to be able to saw yourself loose in about three hours."

154

The pilot says nothing. He is still pale and looks at the file.

"Notice that it is triangular. It has three cutting edges. When one edge gets dull, rotate it and go on to the next one. Otherwise it'll take you three days and not three hours."

He gives the pilot the file, and takes the gun back from Flecker. They walk away, leaving the pilot sitting under his tree like Jonah under the bush, hoping that God won't wither it. He feels in his flying suit for a pack of cigarettes, and pulls it out. He pats his pocket for a match but can't find one. He almost calls after them to ask if they have a match, then thinks better of it. He hasn't started filing yet.

Gaspar and Flecker reach the helicopter and climb into it, and Flecker pulls the door shut after him.

"That was better. I'm glad you didn't lose your head this time."

"Of course," says Gaspar, "if he had tried to grab the gun like that other bougre, it would have been the same thing."

They are flying at five hundred meters over a high shallow valley, like a huge pie pan dotted with pines and oaks. Flecker has the JetRanger almost in a hover. They are a little early anyhow and he barely pushes forward on the cyclic between his knees. They are making only about seventy kilometers over the ground. The pie pan underneath slips by quite slowly, the individual branches and even the leaves visible on the trees below. Ahead, on the rim of the pie pan, is a ridge with a line of trees at the top. Beyond that is the valley of the Dourdou, with Conques on the other side of it.

Gaspar gropes around in the packing case and finds a flat white jar. This is the last thing he needs out of the packing case. The three MAT 49s are laid out on the floor of the cabin, each fitted with a magazine. He puts the plywood top back on the packing case and tightens the wing nuts. The other packing case has never been opened.

155

Gaspar unscrews the top of the white jar. "You first or me?"

"Give it to me."

"Can you do it with one hand?"

"I think so."

"If not I could do it for you."

"Let me try."

Flecker takes the jar and balances it on his thigh. He digs his fingers into the black greasepaint and begins smearing it onto his face. By looking forward and slightly upward he can see a dim reflection of himself in the plastic windscreen. In this way he is able to do a fairly decent job. When he is done his face is black up to the Caterpillar cap, and his eyes show whitely in the shadow under the visor. He gets a certain amount of the stuff on his Levi jacket. Gaspar passes him a rag, and he wipes his hands.

He glances at his watch. It is 4:35. They are still a little early. He tilts the cyclic over and begins a long circle around the pie-shaped valley. From old habit he likes to turn to the left, since in a left bank he can see the terrain below out of the window. Behind him Gaspar is applying the greasepaint to his own face. Gaspar takes off his camouflage hat to do a good job of it, watching his reflection in the side window.

"Do you think the times are going to work out?"

"We've got a little over ten minutes. It's only five minutes from here to Conques."

"I mean afterwards."

"Just about as we figured. We ought to put down at Aumont some time between five thirty and six. It'll just be getting dark. We can transfer everything to the car, and before anyone figures out where the copter's gone it'll be dark, and they won't find it till morning. By then we'll be clear over the mountains in the Vaucluse."

"What about the people in Aumont?"

"I've checked it out. Nobody lives there except an old woman and a priest. There's no phone."

"An old woman and a priest," Gaspar says. He says, "They probably make out every night in the church." He says, "There's probably not much else to do there."

Flecker has nothing to say to this. He has finished his circle and begins going around again. He glances over his instruments, then looks out to the left again through the tilting window.

Gaspar says, "What did you do in these things in Vietnam?"

"We shot at people on the ground."

"Did they shoot back?"

"Not very often. It wasn't smart of them if they did."

"Were they civilians or military?"

"You couldn't tell the difference. And if you can't tell the difference, there is no difference."

Gaspar looks out at the concave valley with its scattering of trees rotating slowly under them, only about a hundred meters below.

"I wouldn't want to be in this thing and have somebody shooting at me."

Flecker says, "I'll try to keep your preferences in mind." It seems to him odd that Gaspar becomes so fearful when he is only a little out of his element.

THIRTEEN

Patrick glances at his watch which has been accurately synchronized with the bell of Sainte-Foy. It is 4:03. He takes his camera bag and checks to see that everything is in it. Then, with Sara following, he goes down the stairs to the foyer. There is no one in sight. He knocks on the desk, and then after a moment calls out, "Hello."

Hyacinthe appears from the kitchen, wiping his hands on a white apron.

"I need my car."

"Bien, monsieur."

"You'll have to give me the keys."

"Ah, the keys." He takes the keys out of the desk, then he remembers something. "Ah, we moved the cars last night, monsieur. Madame went out to visit a friend. So now your car is at the bottom of the garage, and it's blocked by Madame's car. Monsieur, just at the moment I'm occupied in the kitchen. Perhaps you could take both keys, and move Madame's car so that you could get out your own car." He takes another set of keys out of the desk.

"Fine."

"You know how to drive the CX, monsieur?"

"Yes."

"It has air suspension and power steering, so it won't move until the engine is running."

"I know."

"If you'll excuse me, monsieur. I'm occupied with something in the kitchen."

"It's quite all right."

He takes the keys and goes off, with Sara still trailing him. She says, "That boy is sneaky. He knows about us."

"He's not a boy. He's as old as you are."

"No he's not. He's just a boy. I'll bet he's never been laid."

"Oh, come on, Sara."

"He's just like you," she says in a low tone as though to herself. "You've probably never been laid either."

He looks at his watch again. It is 4:07. "Just keep quiet, will you, Sara. And do exactly as I tell you."

"What is it that I have to do?"

"Mainly keep your mouth shut. I may think of something else for you to do."

"In some ways," she says, "you're as bad as Serge."

"I wish I were."

"You know, Patrick," she says, "sometimes you say really goofy things." She says, "Sometimes I don't understand you." She says, "Sometimes I think you're a little crazy."

"More than a little."

He goes on down the corridor and out the door briskly, and she almost has to hop to keep up with him on her short legs. "What's the rush?"

He looks at his watch: 4:08.

They arrive at the garage. Just as Hyacinthe has said, the big Citroën is parked behind the Renault, blocking it.

"Stay right here," he tells Sara.

He starts to give her the camera bag, then changes his mind and leaves it over his shoulder. He gets into the CX and looks around for the place to put the key. The car is really luxurious. It is instrumented like an airplane and the velour seats are exactly contoured to the human body. He puts in the key and starts it up. With a faint hiss the car rises up on its haunches. This is the air suspension that Hyacinthe spoke of. He backs it out of the garage.

Once he is out in the sunshine, with Sara standing there by the right-hand door, there seems to be no compelling reason to park it in the street, go in and back out the Renault, and then laboriously regarage the CX.

"Get in," he tells Sara.

She climbs in and shuts the door, and Patrick drives smoothly off up the street. The car is a dream. It makes almost no noise and seems to move by magic; when he pushes the accelerator even slightly it goes forward with a rush. He is impressed by the idea that he is driving the car of a countess, even as one wonders what it would be like going to bed with a countess, knowing at the same time that it would be only a human body like the others. It is what we think about things (he tells himself) that is important, and not what they really are. The phenomenal world is a drawing by Escher. If we think the stairs are going up, they go up; if we think they are going down, they go down. He drives on up the street past the shops, but instead of continuing to the parking he turns left up a steep and narrow lane through the houses.

Sara says, "Why can't I drive?"

"Because I'm driving."

"I've never driven one of these things. It looks like fun. Look at all those instruments."

"You have to know what they all are," he tells her, "before you can drive the car."

The lane gets narrower and narrower, but it is wide enough for him to follow along under the brow of the hill to the rear of the gendarmerie. Here he stops. The problem is in turning around. There is a little space where the gendarmes put their garbage cans, and by backing and filling several times he manages to turn the car around so that it is facing back the way it came.

"You stay here," he tells Sara, "and keep your mouth shut. If there is any kind of trouble, you beat it in the car."

160

"What kind of trouble?"

He sees this is not going to work. The rules would be far too complicated. "You stay here no matter what," he tells her.

At a point a little farther down, the lane ends and the steep hill actually becomes a cliff which almost touches the roof of the gendarmerie. He scrambles up this cliff, the camera bag dangling, and goes along the top to a place where he is able to step off onto the roof of the gendarmerie. It is only about a meter, an easy jump. He goes on up the roof, which is steeper than it looks from the ground. The slates are slippery. The antenna pole is mounted almost at the peak of the roof. There is a complicated pyramidal system of guy wires holding it up, a Christmas tree of wires. These he ignores. He goes straight to the metal pole, takes out the friction tape, and winds a few turns onto it. Then he takes out the hand grenade and fits it against the pole, winding several more turns of tape around it. He glances around him. He can't see anything from his position on the roof, except the town with the three steeples of the church sticking up out of it. The driveway in front of the gendarmerie is invisible, and so is the Citroën in the lane behind with Sara waiting in it. He applies a little pressure to the handle of the grenade, pulls out the pin, and releases the handle.

Now he has seven seconds to get down off the roof and into the car. He slithers down the slates, falls onto his bottom, and slides the rest of the way. At the edge of the roof he gets up and jumps over to the cliff. He is halfway down the cliff, again sliding on his bottom, when there is a deafening bang that makes the dust jump up on the cliff. Several windows shatter in the gendarmerie; he hears the tinkle over the ringing in his ears.

He dusts off his pants and gets in the car. It is moving off down the lane in only a second or two.

Sara says, "What was that?"

"What?"

"Something exploded."

"Yes. It was the antenna. Don't talk so much, Sara."

161

* * *

In some ways the telephone pole is easier, in some
ways harder. It is easier because it is right beside the
road and he doesn't have to climb up a roof to get to it.
It is harder because of the plastic. He has never used
the stuff before (although he had never used a grenade
either, so it's a tossup) and he is not quite sure how it
will work. One thing he is sure of, he will have to get
away from the thing with celerity and not hang around
to watch the spectacle. There is a choice he has to make.
It would be safer to park the car a little distance away,
so that neither Sara nor the car will be damaged if the
thing goes off early. But if it goes off early, where is
he? He wouldn't need a car. Of course there is Sara.
But gallantry, he decides, is a secondary consideration.
Sara will just have to take her chances. The alternative is
to park the car directly against the pole, so that it is
only a step from the pole to the open car door. The time:
4:29.

He props the door carefully open. It will stop in two
different places—a beautiful design. Then he takes the
things out of the camera bag. He hopes he is going to
have enough tape. The pole is bigger than he realized
when he only looked at it from across the road. It is
rectangular in section, perhaps ten centimeters by twenty
at a point shoulder high from the ground where he wants
to work on it. However it is not solid, luckily. It consists
of two flat columns, connected by crosspieces every meter
or so. In between it is hollow. This is done to save weight.
He sticks the chunk of plastic into the hollow between
the two columns, and reaches back onto the car seat for
the grenade.

Sara says, "Is that little thing enough to blow up that
great big pole?"

"No."

"Oh I see. It's that other stuff you're putting up
there."

"If you keep chattering, Sara, I'm going to make some
mistake."

"I don't think you will, Patrick. You're very intelligent. You're the most intelligent person I know."

162

"More than Serge?"

"Serge," she says, "is a piece of merde."

"Then why do you go to bed with him?"

"Patrick, sometimes I think you know nothing about life."

Patrick jams the grenade in next to the plastic, then he begins wrapping tape around the plastic, the grenade, and the pole. After he has used up most of the tape he takes a look at what he is doing and realizes that he has the grenade jammed in against the pole in such a way that, even if the pin is pulled out, the handle won't release. He takes off the tape and starts doing it all over again.

The time: 4:33.

This time he fits the grenade into the hollow in the pole with the handle facing outward. It is a little more difficult to remove the pin, but once the pin is pulled the handle will snap right out. The grenade is flat against the concrete pole on one side, and on the other side it is jammed flat against the plastic, which fills up the rest of the space between the two columns of the pole. He thinks it will work.

All this has taken two minutes. 4:35.

"Don't," he tells Sara, "touch any of the controls of the car. I don't want it to stall at the wrong moment."

"What kind of a fool do you think I am?"

He could deliver quite a discourse on this, but it will have to be for another time. He looks up the highway, and down it the other way. There is nobody in sight. At the Auberge du Pont Romain the shutters are closed and the chairs on the porch are upside down. It is not the tourist season. Patrick pulls the pin and jumps into the car.

He tears off like a race driver in a Le Mans start. The tires screech on the pavement. But the car has gone only a stone's throw or so when the highway seems to lift up and bang against the tires. The car is slammed down the road so that his head whips back and bumps against the headrest. He is not aware of any noise, until a second later when he realizes he can't hear anything. There seems to be a great deal of smoke, above the car and out in front of it. Perhaps it is dust. He looks into the rear-vision mirror, but the rear window of the car has turned into a thousand tiny diamonds that sparkle in the late afternoon sunshine. Both the windows on the left are broken too. The windshield seems to be intact.

Sara says, "I think that probably broke off the pole, all right."

To his surprise he is able to hear her, in spite of the ringing in his ears. As soon as his head clears a little he realizes he has made a blunder. The car is facing the wrong way down the highway, toward Rodez, instead of up the highway toward the campground. He will have to turn it around on the narrow mountain road, somehow, and drive back past the telephone pole. But still, it was necessary to have the car facing this way if he was to park on the left-hand side of the road, next to the pole, and still have the driver's door of the car beside the pole. He certainly wouldn't have wanted to take the extra time to run around to the other side of the car. He thinks all this out by picking his way, so to speak, through the wreckage left in his mind by the violent shock of the explosion.

The solution to all this is fairly obvious, he realizes as his mind clarifies a little. Only a short distance down the highway is the inn where the road turns off across the medieval bridge. He turns the car into the side road, backs it up, and gets it facing the other way. Then he tears off again, not because he is in a hurry this time but because he has forgotten how much more powerful the CX is than the Renault. He finds he is going at a dizzying pace and lifts his foot from the accelerator. After a short distance he drives past the former telephone pole. There is only a hole in the dirt where the pole itself used to be. The pavement is covered with shards of concrete, and there is also a great deal of dirt and vegetation thrown across the highway. The eight or ten telephone wires have been flung up into the air, the broken ends landing in the meadow on one side and down in the river bottom on the other. One wire, however, still droops across the highway, ending in a gleam of bare copper just at the edge of the pavement. He drives across it gingerly, even though he knows that it probably carries only a few volts. The car teeters and scrunches on the broken concrete.

"You see," says Sara, "it broke it off just fine."

The highway curves on around to the left, following the river. It is only a short distance now to the graveled road that turns off to the parking. Patrick has been squinting to see where he was going for some time, and now he realizes that the reason it is so hard to see out the windshield is that it is covered with dust. He rolls down the window on his left; to his surprise the broken glass goes down smoothly. His ears are starting to work again, along with his mind.

For some time now there has been a sort of growling in the air, coming and going and sometimes subdued, along with a kind of pot-pot-pot that seems to be connected with it. These sounds, Patrick realizes, he has attributed to the shock in his head when it was flung violently back against the headrest. Now they suddenly increase in volume, and the helicopter bursts out over the top of the hill. The blue-and-white shape comes down toward the parking in a blur. The sound is quite loud: POT-POT-POT-POT-POT-POT.

FOURTEEN

The two of them, Patrick thinks, look like stage minstrels. Their faces are black, their eyes white, and their mouths red. He waits for them to say Yassuh and break into a buck-and-wing. They climb down out of the helicopter.

Flecker says, "What's this car, Patrick? This isn't the car you rented."

"This is a better car. How did you expect to get all of us in that little Renault?" This doesn't really make sense, and Patrick realizes he is mentally including Marie-Ange, his "research assistant." The Renault might hold four of them, and the two packing cases, but not five.

"Patrick," says Gaspar, "is probably including his research assistant."

Flecker examines the car. "How'd you break all the windows?"

"It was the Silly Putty."

"You should have kept the car a little farther away."

"Thanks, I will the next time."

"Cut the chatter," says Gaspar, "and get this stuff out of the copter."

The two packing cases are transferred to the trunk of

166

the Citroën. It would be a lot easier to get them in and out, Patrick realizes, if they had the Renault with its hatchback. Still, this is the car of a countess. Gaspar reaches in for the three MAT 49s. He fits a magazine onto one of them and hands it to Sara, who is sitting in the open door of the helicopter with her feet hanging out.

"Here," he tells her, "see if you can figure out how to work this thing."

"You just pull the trigger."

"First you ought to have it pointed at something. Don't pull the trigger now. You see this little bump on the back of the grip, Sara? That's the safety. Keep the palm of your hand off that until you're ready to fire."

"That little button there?"

"That's it."

"What do I do?"

"Don't let anyone," Gaspar tells her, "come anywhere near the helicopter." He says, "If anyone comes near, tell them to go away." He says, "If they don't get the idea, give them a burst with the gun." He says, "But don't give them too many bursts, because there are only thirty-two rounds in the magazine, and the gun will empty itself in about four seconds."

"Don't I get any more bullets?"

"When you use these," he tells her, "you can have more."

"Okay."

Gaspar hands one of the MAT 49s to Flecker and keeps the other for himself. He looks around at the parking and at the town across the valley, sucking his upper lip reflectively. "Okay," he says. "It looks like we can go." He opens the right-hand door of the car and slides in sideways, holding the gun by the middle. Flecker takes the back seat, and Patrick gets in behind the wheel. He glances at his watch: 4:52. It is only two minutes since the helicopter landed. It seems like longer.

Patrick still feels as though he were floating. It is perhaps the air suspension of the Citroën, or perhaps the pieces of his head have not quite finished arranging themselves after the bump on the headrest. He drives up the road into the town and past the Mairie in an odd leisurely mood, as though he were a tourist looking over the place. The sun has gone down behind the hill now and the town is shadowed. Only the three pointed hats on top of the church still catch a little light. Arriving at the wide place in the street by the café, he turns the car down into the lane to the church. It is a fairly busy hour of the day, at least for Conques where there is almost never anybody on the street, and a few people gaze curiously at Madame's car with its broken windows. The Citroën will barely fit into the narrow lane with the wall on either side. In fact Patrick is not sure whether he can negotiate the turn at the bottom. There are a number of disadvantages, he can see, to driving such a big car. But perhaps Madame feels she owes it to herself as a countess.

In the parvis in front of the church he swings the thing around, jams it into reverse, and swivels his head around to back into the space between the presbytery and the church, at least as far as the car will go. There is a little boy standing on the pavement, apparently smoking a cigarette. He is only about eight. He steps aside, reluctantly, as the Citroën grinds backward toward him. It is only a candy cigarette. He takes it out insouciantly, like a French movie star, and blows some imaginary smoke. "Get out of the way," Patrick tells him. The little boy flattens himself against the church.

"This is as far as I can go," says Patrick.

"Okay. Where's the presbytery?"

"Just over there on your left."

"Fine," says Gaspar. "We can leave the car here and cover it from that corridor."

"If you say so."

They all get out, Gaspar and Flecker carrying the MAT 49s and Patrick empty-handed. It occurs to him for the first time that he no longer has the camera bag. It isn't in the car either. He remembers now where he left it: at the base of the telephone pole, in his haste to get back in the car. He thinks: a Pentax 35 SLR, a standard lens, and a 28-millimeter wide-angle. Also his passport and travelers checks. So long, Adrian Proutey. It's a shame, he thinks, that Madame never saw the passport.

They get the packing cases out of the trunk. Since Patrick is carrying nothing, he takes one of them himself, and Gaspar and Flecker share the other one, each supporting the packing case with one hand and holding the gun in the other. The empty packing case is light and Patrick has no difficulty carrying it. It's a slightly awkward shape, that's all.

The little boy, with the cigarette in the corner of his mouth, is watching everything with a studied blasé air. Perhaps it is a show. Two of them are Black Men. It's like the movies. They are Americans.

"If you touch that car," Gaspar tells him, "you'll be electrocuted."

The little boy's tongue comes out. The end of the cigarette flips up, describes an arc, and disappears into his mouth. He swallows it.

They go off down the corridor toward the strong room, Patrick leading. He glances back once behind him. The little boy stretches out his finger, carefully, and touches the fender of the car. Nothing happens.

Father Dion is not in his office and the door is closed. The door to the strong room, however, is open, and Patrick can see lights inside. Just as he crosses the threshold into the room the bell of Sainte-Foy begins booming. It is five o'clock.

There are three persons in the strong room: Father Dion, Professor Lohengrin, and Marie-Ange. Oddly enough they seem to have noticed nothing odd going on outside in the town. However the strong room has thick walls and perhaps the pot-pot-pot of the helicopter was not audible. Still the door is open. The three of them are studiously examining the allegedly Byzantine reliquary in its glass cabinet. They look up as the little procession enters: Patrick staggering a little with his awkward box, then Gaspar and Flecker carrying the packing case between them, each with a MAT 49 in the other hand.

"Set it down here," says Gaspar.

They put their packing case down. Patrick, uncertain, still holds his.

169

"Martin," says Gaspar, "you stand out there in the corridor and cover the car. Stay by the door where we can see you. That's fine. Right there. Can you see the car from there?"

"Yes."

"Fine. Patrick, what are you standing there holding that thing for? Put it down. You three over there, get down to the end of the room." He waves the barrel of the weapon at them. "Who are you anyhow?"

"That's my research assistant," says Patrick.

Marie-Ange is wearing her usual jeans, shirt, and rebozo, and the necklace with its cross is around her neck. Her nostrils and the pink rim around her eyes are slightly redder than they were in the morning. She presses a handkerchief to the bottom of her nose, then puts it away in her pocket.

Gaspar says, "She looks like a rotten lay." He says, "If she doesn't get over there with the others I'm going to blast her." He says, "What's this priest doing here?"

"He's in charge of the place."

"Not now. We are. He doesn't look very robust. I could knock him over from here, by blowing a puff of air at him."

"When you get done with all the macho rhetoric," says Patrick, "what are we here for anyhow?"

"The macho rhetoric?"

"Let's get on with it," says Patrick, surprised himself that he is the one who wants to engage in action instead of talk.

Flecker is still visible in the doorway. He spends part of his time looking into the strong room and the other part looking out in the corridor toward the car. Professor Lohengrin, lowering his glasses in order to focus on the middle distance, is examining the word Caterpillar on the cap one of the black men is wearing, as though the most important thing for him at the moment is to comprehend what this means. He finally identifies it as an English word for the larva of one of the Lepidoptera. He turns his attention to Patrick.

"You know," he rumbles, his goatee moving back and forth, "I've finally recalled who it is you are. You aren't

Proutey. There's no Proutey. I've never encountered the name in the bibliographies. You're Halbertson's student. I can't recall your name, but you're Halbertson's student. I used to see you in the Bibliothèque Nationale, taking slides of the *Grandes Heures de Rohan*."

"Is that so?"

"You know," says Professor Lohengrin, "I think probably Halbertson was right about the attribution of the *Heures de Rohan*." He says, "It's just a hodge-podge." He says, "Somebody pasted it together. Some handyman around the castle."

"Yes," says Patrick.

"You were lucky to be his student," says Professor Lohengrin. "A fine scholar."

"Yes," says Patrick. "Get over there against the wall, or my friend will shoot you with his gun."

Professor Lohengrin waggles his goatee at this. It is a new idea. His small eyes blink in the swollen face. He pats his stomach. Before he can do anything about it, Flecker without warning lets off a blast of the MAT 49 at something outside. Since he is standing directly by the doorway, the strong room with its stone walls acts like the sounding box of a violin, or the inside of a drum. Two pneumatic hammers, one on either side, pound at Patrick's eardrums. Sharp stabs run through his brain. When it is over the ringing in his ears begins again.

"Don't destroy the car," says Gaspar. "We need it for later. What are you doing?"

"There's some guy out here. Patrick, come here. Who is this?"

Patrick goes to see. Anstruc is standing behind the car, his head visible from the flat-topped képi down to his eyes, calm but watchful, as if he too like the little boy wants to see the show. He is carrying some kind of service carbine, but he shows no signs of using it and perhaps he has forgotten he has it. There are several bullet marks in the wall of the church just over his head.

Gaspar comes out to look at him too.

"Ah, there are the MAT 49s," says Anstruc.

"Who is this bougre?"

"He's the local brigadier. His name is Anstruc."

"If he's a brigadier where's his brigade?"

"They're all sick, or on leave, except one that's gone to see his dentist."

"That's fine. He must be a prize idiot."

"He's a rather interesting person."

Gaspar studies Anstruc for a moment. Then he shouts at him, "We've got the girl in here."

"What girl?"

"What's her name, Patrick?"

"Mlle Duplexis."

"Mlle Duplexis!"

"Who?"

"The guide."

"Oh, that one. You're going to hurt her?"

"We may."

"All right," says Anstruc. "I'll think about it."

Gaspar turns his back, leaving Flecker to watch Anstruc and the car. He reaches into his coveralls and takes out a short piece of cotton rope. There are many pockets in the coveralls and he has room for a lot of different things. "Here," he tells Patrick. "Tie up the girl."

He throws the rope to him. Patrick goes to Marie-Ange, pulls her arms around behind her, and ties her wrists together. Immediately he gets an erection. With his face flushed, he looks around to see if anybody has noticed. He is standing directly in front of the Majesté, and the saint is staring straight at him. Marie-Ange passively allows this to be done to her.

She says, "I need to blow my nose."

"Where's your handkerchief?"

"In my shirt pocket."

Patrick helps her blow it, then he puts the handkerchief away in the pocket for her.

"As you were saying," Gaspar says, "let's get on with it. What do we take?"

Wordlessly Patrick points to the cabinets along the wall.

Gaspar's eye is caught by the A of Charlemagne, which is the most striking object in the cabinets. He smashes the glass with the butt of his gun. Then he kneels down, holding the gun in his left hand, and unscrews the wing nuts on one of the packing cases. He takes out the A of Charlemagne and puts it in the case.

"Ah, mon Dieu," says Father Dion. "The Most Holy Relics."

"You're a most holy relic," says Gaspar. "You keep quiet or I'll break your teeth."

"Take the Reliquary of Pepin," says Marie-Ange with her hands bound. "It's the most valuable."

"Try to play your role," Patrick grits at her between his teeth.

Gaspar smashes some more glass. "Are you going to help me or are you just going to stand there?"

Patrick clears away the pieces of glass and starts taking things out and packing them in the packing case. Working together, they stow in it the Reliquary of Pepin, the Lantern of Begon, the silver-and-porphyry portable altar, and the jeweled processional cross. Along with the A of Charlemagne this just about fills up the box. Gaspar looks at the humerus of Saint George and rejects it. It's somebody's arm in a tin container, the one in Patrick's photograph.

"Ah, mon Dieu mon Dieu mon Dieu," says Father Dion.

"What is he, some kind of phonograph? His needle is stuck. Where is the famous statue?"

If Gaspar hasn't noticed it yet, Patrick thinks, he has a real blind spot. It is at the end of the room, dominating everything with its brilliant and indifferent gaze. Again he points without speaking.

Gaspar slams the gun butt against the cabinet. Nothing happens. The metal stock of the gun is bent slightly, but the glass is intact.

"It's not going to be easy to break that glass," says Marie-Ange. "It's a special kind."

"What kind?"

"I don't know. A kind that won't break."

Gaspar tries again. This time he hurts his hand, which is clasped around the barrel just by the sharp clip that holds the magazine housing. Four or five blows; to no avail. The Saint totters a little but continues to gaze at him imperturbably.

"How is the fucking thing held together?"

They look. The glass comes down on all four sides and joins smoothly to the wooden pedestal. There are no screws or other fittings. It is as though the glass and the wood were one substance, joined like the bone and flesh of a living body. Gaspar raises the gun and bangs it again. The metal stock is bent a little more. A slight scratch is visible on the glass.

"If you will pardon me," rumbles Professor Lohengrin.

"No I won't. Instead I'll ram this thing up your sitter. What do you want?"

He sucks a little blood off his hand and stares at Professor Lohengrin.

Professor Lohengrin comes forward, waggling his goatee. He thrusts his stomach out in his most bisonlike fashion. And he embraces the glass cabinet, as though it were a fat lady. The glass slips off the wooden pedestal and he lefts it up. Carefully he maneuvers the cabinet around the head of the saint and sets it on the floor.

"All right. Get over by the wall again. What are you, some wise guy? Who is he anyhow, Patrick?"

"He's a very eminent scholar."

"He's a very eminent pain in the ass. Move, Patrick. Vite, vite. Is that thing heavy?"

"I think so. There's a lot of gold in it."

"Let's get it in the box."

"Ah, mon Dieu mon Dieu mon Dieu," says Father Dion.

Patrick embraces the Majesté exactly as Professor Lohengrin has embraced the glass cabinet, except that, since the statue is smaller, one does not need to be a bison to do it. He pulls up. Nothing happens. Perhaps it is attached in some way to the pedestal. He jerks again. This time it comes away and he is holding it in his arms. It isn't attached to anything; it is just very heavy.

In order to lift the Saint he has approached her from the front. Her Roman emperor's visage, still quite calm, is gazing at him from a hand's-breadth away. It is too close for him to see clearly. It is only a golden blur. At this distance she has only one eye; it is like the game that children play, staring at each other at close range so that the two eyes merge into one. Alabaster and ebony fill the center of Patrick's vision, with gold shimmering around it. He feels a little dizzy.

He backs away from the pedestal. The thing weighs more that fifty kilograms, probably. A part of Patrick thinks: there's more gold in it than we thought. Another part of him thinks: this thing is too heavy, I'm going to fall down with it, it will break and all the relics will fall out.

Patrick is like a man who has lifted a heavy flagpole out of the ground and is now staggering around with it, first in one direction and then in another, in an effort to stay under its center of gravity so it won't fall. He lurches toward Father Dion and then away again. Father Dion comes forward with his hands raised in a gesture as though of benediction, except that they are trembling like leaves in a storm. It is for this that he is not allowed to serve Mass. Patrick whirls around with his back to him, as though he were waltzing.

His back bumps against something. There is a sound as though someone has dropped a soft object, like a laundry bag. When Patrick is able to turn around again he sees that Father Dion has fallen down and is lying quite calmly on his back with his eyes open, looking at the ceiling. He is not breathing.

"Father!"

"Come on, Patrick."

Patrick feels very odd. He fights at a kind of blackness around his eyes. "Wake up, Father!"

"I think the old fellow has fainted," says Professor Lohengrin. "He's getting on in years."

Gaspar takes the Majesté out of his hands. It doesn't seem heavy for him. "You're nothing but a fucking intellectual," he tells Patrick. "Everything is such a big deal for you." He carries the Majesté off toward the packing case as though it were a bag full of groceries.

Feeling numb, Patrick kneels down beside Father

Dion. He is quite dead. His eyes give the impression that he is looking up through the ceiling, past the clouds and the stratosphere, to something that is quite a bit higher. Except for that he has his usual expression on his face, benign but rather tired. Now, Patrick thinks, he has no name.

He gets up slowly to see what Gaspar is doing. He has just finished setting the Majesté into the second packing case.

"It fits fine."

"It's eighty-five centimeters," says Patrick dully.

"Fine. The box is a meter." He replaces the plywood top on the packing case and screws down the wing nuts. "Now, shall we get out of here, or do you want to look around at some other things and make notes for a monograph?"

"What about these people?"

"The girl we'll take with us. The priest we don't need. We'll leave him here. And you"—he waves the gun toward Professor Lohengrin—"go out first. Explain to them that we've got the girl so we don't want anybody to bother us as we leave."

Professor Lohengrin waggles at him, breathes, and heads for the door.

"Wait a minute."

Professor Lohengrin stops.

"Take this to that flic out there."

He produces the Front de la Jeunesse letter out of a pocket of the coveralls. It is still in its plastic envelope, and he slips it out, holding it by the corner with his fingernails.

Professor Lohengrin takes the letter. Since Gaspar has handled it only by the corner, with his fingernails, Professor Lohengrin holds it by the corner with his fingernails too. Perhaps it is a letter bomb and will explode if grasped firmly. Who knows. There certainly have been enough loud explosions in Conques this afternoon. The young mademoiselle, the guide, said they were sonic booms, but he, Professor Lohengrin, doesn't know.

Gaspar stands in the doorway, watching Professor Lohengrin go off down the corridor. The late afternoon

176

shadows have fallen now and his bulky shape is dim once he is outside. He gives the letter to Anstruc, who frowns and opens it. Everybody waits.

"H'mm," says Anstruc. "This looks like it was typed on the Olympia that was stolen in rue des Lois."

"What about it?" shouts Gaspar.

"All right. Come on out."

"Do something or other with your weapon."

"All right," says Anstruc. "What?"

"Put it on top of the car, where we can see it."

A khaki arm appears and puts the carbine on top of the car.

"Have you got any other weapons?"

"No."

"Well, we have to believe him," says Gaspar.

They come out in a little procession, laden with Treasures, like the Magi coming to visit the Child. Gaspar goes first, pushing Marie-Ange ahead of him, the stock of the MAT 49 resting on his hip and his finger on the trigger. Patrick and Flecker come after with the two packing cases. Patrick isn't sure any more which is which, but he believes he must have the one with the smaller relics in it, since it doesn't seem to weigh as much. Flecker has slung his MAT 49 in order to be able to carry the packing case with both hands. He is staggering a little. He has the one with the Majesté all right.

They arrive at the car. Anstruc is standing motionless behind it with his képi showing over the top. Professor Lohengrin has disappeared entirely. Perhaps he has another engagement. A few people are standing up above the church by the retaining wall, looking down. Not very many; perhaps eight or ten. Patrick and Flecker go to the rear of the car and set the packing cases on the ground. Patrick opens the trunk of the car.

Anstruc says, "Professor, you put sugar in my gas tank. It took me quite a while to figure out what was wrong. You have to clean out the fuel line with a mixture of alcohol and water."

"Is that so?"

"Also the carburetor. I hope you aren't going to hurt that girl."

"You," Gaspar tells Anstruc, "get out from behind there."

"All right. Where shall I go?"

"Go out in front of the car, where we can watch you."

"All right."

Anstruc comes out from behind the car and walks a few meters into the parvis in front of the church. There he stands, the gold on his epaulets glinting. He swivels the upper part of his body to look at the people watching from the street above. Then he swivels it back toward the Citroën. He has a neck, Patrick thinks, like Henry VIII in the well-known portrait by Holbein. Holbein probably couldn't make Henry turn his head either. He would have had to turn the whole king.

"Allez, allez," says Gaspar. "Let's go. Vite, vite, vite."

The two packing cases are stowed away in the trunk. Patrick slams the lid and they all get in the car, rather self-consciously since Anstruc is still watching them with his interested expression. Gaspar gets in the rear with Marie-Ange, holding the gun upright between his knees, and Patrick and Flecker get in the front.

"If that bougre tries any acrobatic tricks," says Gaspar, "let him have it."

Patrick says, "He's not very acrobatic."

All four doors slam and they start off. As the car crosses the parvis Anstruc reaches out quite matter-of-factly and takes the carbine off the top. Perhaps this is what Gaspar meant by acrobatic tricks. He doesn't attempt to fire it though. Probably this is on account of Marie-Ange, who is sitting in the back seat with her hands tied and Gaspar watching her. In any case Anstruc wouldn't be able to see anything through the rear window to fire at, since the rear window has turned into an opaque lacework of diamonds. Anstruc swivels to watch them as the car climbs up the steep cobbled lane and turns into the street.

Patrick looks out carefully, through the broken window which he has left rolled down, to be sure there is no traffic before he pulls out onto the highway. He realizes that he has been carefully observing all the traffic rules with the idea that it would be a bad time to be stopped by the police. He covers the half kilometer to the campground a little more briskly, and wheels up into the parking by the helicopter with a certain élan. Everybody gets out except Marie-Ange, who can't reach the door because her hands are tied. A little gleam of mucus has appeared on her upper lip below her nose.

Gaspar tells her, "You stay in the car."

"What's this?" says Patrick. "I don't get it."

"You don't have to get it. I'm getting everything."

"What are you going to do with her?"

"Let's go, let's go," says Gaspar. "Get the stuff out of the car. Quick, quick, quick."

He keeps saying this, Patrick thinks, *vite vite vite*, the way Father Dion said *mon Dieu mon Dieu mon Dieu*. He's the one that's the phonograph.

Patrick and Gaspar lug the packing cases over to the open door of the helicopter. Sara is still sitting in the opening with her feet hanging out, holding her MAT 49.

"Get out of the way, you dumb broad," Gaspar tells her.

Sara scrambles back into the rear seat. Flecker is already behind the controls, pushing various buttons. There is a low whine that gradually builds and rises. Flecker pushes something else. The rotor overhead stirs and begins turning slowly, like an old-fashioned ceiling fan.

The two packing cases are in the back, one under Sara's feet and the other in the empty rear seat. Gaspar climbs in beside Flecker and pulls the door shut.

"Fine, fine," says Gaspar. "Let's go, Martin. We'll meet you in Aumont," he shouts to Patrick over the quickening whine of the engine.

"What the hell are you talking about? The helicopter will be there in ten minutes and it'll make me an hour in the car. Do you mean you're going to wait around up there for us?"

It occurs to Patrick now that there wouldn't be room

for all of them anyhow in the Deux Chevaux which he left in the churchyard at Aumont. The rotor whirls around so fast that it becomes invisible. The whine of the turbine now hurts the ears. Flecker pulls up on the collective. The dust flies all around Patrick, there are leaves whirling in the air and something tiny hits him on the side of the head. Futher conversation is impossible because of the noise. The helicopter heaves up, tilts, and climbs away into the sky.

FIFTEEN

Patrick unties Marie-Ange's hands.

"You might as well sit in the front seat."

When she hesitates he tells her, "Hurry up. We have to get out of here."

The first thing she does, when she is installed in the front seat, is blow her nose. Then she looks around, examines Patrick, looks at the departing helicopter through the windshield, and fastens her seat belt, all without a word. It is only perhaps fifteen seconds since the helicopter left. It is still mounting up toward the ridge, making its loud grumble and its pot-pot-pot. The car is still running. Patrick whips it around on the gravel drive and spins off toward the highway. He is not so much concerned about the traffic laws now.

When he gets to the highway the first thing he sees is Anstruc. He comes trotting down the road above with the confident assurance of a fox, holding his carbine by the balance point. He stops and rests the carbine in the crook of a tree. Patrick can see everything: Anstruc through the open window on his left, the helicopter through the windshield, and Marie-Ange next to him who is blowing her nose and seems not to notice what is going on. Anstruc fires. Nothing happens. He pulls back the bolt, sights, and fires again. This time some chips of black fly off the end of one of the rotors. The helicopter begins to wobble. The pot-pot-pot develops a fuzzy quality at the edges; it becomes a kind of pfot-pfot-pfot. The whole helicopter seems to shake like a dog that has just come out of the water. It is high up over the ridge now and still climbing.

The rotor blade flaps up and down for a second or two, then it breaks off and tumbles away like a leaf, turning end over end in the air. The helicopter plummets down behind the ridge, thrashing futilely.

Patrick stares at this without being able to pronounce a word.

"Anstruc," says Marie-Ange with an odd detachment, "won some kind of medal as a marksman. He wears it on feast days."

Patrick clamps his teeth together, jams the shift into second, and hits the accelerator. The tires squeal against the asphalt and the car shoots forward. They fly by under Anstruc, who looks down, turning to follow them like a sunflower. In only a few seconds they pass the site of the ex-telephone pole. A truck has stopped by the side of the road, and an employee of the Ponts et Chaussées is sweeping the pieces of concrete off the pavement. He turns to look at them as they flash by. The car is almost at the inn. Patrick twists the wheel to break the rear end loose and puts the car in a slide. Going partly sideways with a trill of rubber, it shoots into the side road and over the narrow bridge. There is a bang of sheet metal as a fender hits the stone parapet, but the car keeps going and is ejected out the other side of the bridge like a squeezed lemon pip.

Marie-Ange says, "I don't want to die quite yet, Patrick."

"Neither do I."

"I don't think Anstruc's car will work yet. He can't follow us." After a moment she says, "What's happened to your friends, do you think?"

"They're all dead."

Patrick slows down a little. She is probably right; there isn't all that much hurry. In fact, thinking what they will find when they get there, he slows down even more. The road climbs up over the top of the ridge, runs level for a while, and then starts down into the saucer-shaped valley below. The helicopter is just a little off the road, in a clearing where people have evidently been camping. There are papers scattered around and the remains of a campfire. The helicopter has nosed down at a steep angle and struck the ground almost vertically, like someone who has fallen down and hit his chin. The front end of it is smashed up but the rear, sticking up in the air, is relatively intact. In the thin gray of the twilight everything is lucid but colorless, like a black-and-white photograph.

"Stay where you are," he tells Marie-Ange.

He gets out and walks to a place about thirty meters or so in front of the impact point. When the helicopter struck the ground in chin-first position, Gaspar was evidently hurled forward and up, and the single remaining rotor blade caught him squarely in the middle. The body is cut almost in two; it is held together only by the spine, like a rack of lamb that has been cut apart for easy serving. A good deal of blood has gushed out, along with the viscera and some pieces of lung. The circle of offal and blood around Gaspar is two meters wide.

Flecker evidently flew out in the same way, but somehow passed by the blade unscathed and landed on the hard ground only a short distance away. He lifts his head off the ground as Patrick approaches. His white eyes are visible in the black face.

"I've got both legs broken. I don't feel like moving to the car. You'd better just leave me here."

"That's what I intended to do."

Patrick walks back to the helicopter. Sara is still sitting in the rear seat. She has to bend over sharply because the roof of the helicopter has folded in on her. The rear end of the cabin has contracted to only a third of its previous height. One of her Russian-leather boots is jammed in at an angle between two aluminum beams, and she has a nosebleed.

She says, "I don't like this. I want to get out of here."

"Somebody will be along in a while, Sara. We don't have room for you."

"You've got that big Citroën."

"Yes, but after a while we're going to change to the Deux Chevaux."

Patrick pulls out one of the packing cases. He can't get to the other one because it is jammed in under Sara. It is impossible to tell the packing cases apart and he can't tell whether he has got the one with the Majesté or the one with the smaller relics. It doesn't really matter. He puts it in the trunk of the car and goes back to the helicopter. One of the MAT 49s is lying on the aluminum floor. He takes this, and also fills his pockets with as many magazines as he can carry. There doesn't seem to be anything else in the helicopter that might be useful. He puts the gun and the magazines in the back seat of the car and gets in the front. He takes time to adjust his glasses, and also the rear-vision mirror. He fastens his seat belt.

"See if there's a map in the glove compartment or somewhere," he tells Marie-Ange. "I think I know the country, but it's better to have a map. It's Michelin number eighty, folds one and two."

She finds the map and spreads it out on the dashboard.

It is almost dark now. Patrick switches on the headlights. Only one of them works. Probably the taillights don't either, and it now occurs to him that there wasn't much point in adjusting the mirror, since the rear window is opaque. All he saw when he looked into it was a granular white surface. Well, the Citroën still runs. The engine seems undamaged by all the rough treatment, and it corners beautifully when you break the rear end loose. Patrick jams on the brakes, comes to a stop with the tires protesting, and flings the door open. He vomits onto the road.

After he breathes heavily, perspires, and spits for thirty seconds or so he feels better. He shuts the door and goes back to driving on down the road, a little slower now.

"You didn't get a good look at it," he says. "That's why I didn't want you to get out of the car."

"Thanks."

It is too dark now to see the map, and besides he remembers the country perfectly. There is only one side road and it is impossible to make a mistake. All he has to do is stay on Départmentale 606. A sign at the side of the road is illuminated in the single wobbling headlight; it's D606 all right. He has been driving in second, because of the hills and turns, and now he shifts into third.

The road now is a little straighter. They are almost to Aumont, although he is a bit vague about how far they have come. He accelerates down a straight stretch a kilometer or so long, and the car shoots across a ditch that has been left by workmen and filled with loose dirt. There is only a slight bump and the air suspension takes it nicely. A few seconds later there is a sharp brittle tinkling: *spring!* like the sound that the fairy's wand makes in a movie. In an instant the windshield has turned into an intricate lacework of crystal, very beautiful, almost opaque. Only here and there can a scrap of road be seen through it.

"Well, look at that," says Marie-Ange.

"It's tempered glass," says Patrick. "It's not as good as the laminated they have in America. It was fatigued from the explosion, and when we ran over the bump that was enough to finish it off."

"What explosion?"

"When I blew up the telephone pole."

"I thought it was a sonic boom," says Marie-Ange.

The last of the light has disappeared from the sky when they arrive at Aumont. It is completely dark. Perhaps this is because it is always darker in the country than it is near even a small town. Aumont is not a town at all; it is only two houses and a church. There are no lights showing in the houses, and from the open door of the church there is only a faint bluish glow, flickering slightly. Is someone watching television in the church?

185

No, it is probably only some kind of votive lamp or other liturgical illumination inside the church, although Patrick has never heard of such lights being blue. He turns off the highway and drives carefully up the rocky lane into the churchyard.

He shuts off the Citroën and it expires with a sound of escaping air, settling down on its wheels. The Deux Chevaux is exactly where Sara left it. The keys! He told Sara to give them to him, and probably he left them in the camera bag. He gets out of the car and gropes madly through his pockets. No, by some miracle they are in his pants pocket. This is contrary to his habit; usually he carries everything in the camera bag. His heart pounds. He has been more terrified by these missing keys, he realizes, than he was by the helicopter going down.

He gets the packing case out of the trunk and puts it in the rear of the camionette. It doesn't seem very heavy; probably it is the one with the smaller relics and not the one with the Majesté. Then he gets the gun and the collection of magazines out of the back seat and puts them in the camionette too. Marie-Ange stands in the churchyard blowing her nose. The usual Woman of Aumont has come out to watch them. This time she isn't carrying her pail, but she is standing where she always stands, just by the wall not far from the door of the church. It isn't easy to see her in the dark, even though a little of the blue light from the church touches her face. Patrick gets only an indistinct look at her. The two of them stare at each other across the gloomy churchyard. She isn't as old as he thought; fifty perhaps. A peasant woman ages like a cathedral. A cathedral is supposed to be old. If it were young, we wouldn't like it. She is wearing the usual peasant black, but her face is unlined and there are only a few touches of gray in her hair. Her eyes are in the shadow and he can't see them, but her face is pointed directly toward the two cars in the churchyard. Still it isn't as though she were watching him in any hostile or even curious way. She is just a spectator. What else? The map—he gets it out of the car and puts it in the front seat of the camionette.

186

A priest has come out of the church and is standing behind the woman. He is a good distance from her, and behind her back, but Patrick has the impression that she knows the priest is there. She has lived a long time in this hamlet, and she knows where the priest is at all times. He can't make out very much of the priest, because he is silhouetted in the blue light from the door. He is white-haired but hale, perhaps sixty.

Marie-Ange says, "What are we waiting here for?"

"Nothing. Let's go."

The two of them get in the camionette. Patrick turns on the key and presses the starter, which in the Deux Chevaux is a funny little lever. The engine groans for a while, and finally it blatts once or twice and begins running, after its fashion. It has only two cylinders and is really more like an outboard motor than an automobile engine. One cylinder isn't as strong as the other, and this gives it a kind of permanent lurch. It might be better to take the Citroën CX, except that you can't see through the windshield, and after a while the broken glass will fall out entirely. Also it is a luxury car and rather conspicuous.

"Conspicuous consumption," he says.

"What?"

"Veblen. *The Theory of the Leisure Class.*" He is still feeling floaty and odd and hardly knows what he is saying.

He gets the camionette going: backwards first, bumping into a gravestone, then forward to turn around. He leaves the headlights off for the moment. Through the windshield he can see the woman and the priest still standing in front of the church. As he watches, the priest comes forward until the two figures merge, then his arm slips around her waist. She remains motionless. The camionette bumps its way past them. When he reaches the point where the lane comes out onto the road Patrick glances around. They have turned and are going arm-in-arm into the church, framed in the blue light.

It's too dark to see the map anyhow. The camionette has no dash lights and the headlights are two yellow orbs, like jackal's eyes, that glow a little in the dark but don't illuminate the road perceptibly. Patrick drives cautiously on down D606 in the general direction of Decazeville. The narrow road winds its way through an endless succession of hills. It is such an unimportant road that it doesn't even have a center stripe. There are no towns.

Marie-Ange gazes out through the windshield. It is perfectly flat, like a piece of window glass, and rather dusty. It too will probably shatter if anyone makes a loud noise near it. She keeps the handkerchief pressed more or less permanently to the bottom of her nose.

"Where are we going?"

"Gaspar has a farm in the Vaucluse, near Gordes. That's where we were all going. Afterwards," he adds awkwardly at the end.

"In the Vaucluse?"

"Over beyond Avignon."

"That's a long way from here."

"I know the way. I've been there before."

She thinks about this for a while.

"Won't they be looking for the car?"

"There are a lot of Deux Chevaux camionettes."

"Yes, but this one says Institute of Geophysics on the side."

"Well, it's all we've got."

She says nothing. She is curiously withdrawn. After a while he asks her, "How do you feel?"

"All right."

"Do you have a fever?"

Half keeping his eyes on the road and half looking at her, he reaches over to feel her forehead. He has never been able to tell very much by feeling people's foreheads. It simply feels like a forehead, that's all. If she has a fever, he isn't going to be able to tell it without a thermometer.

"We'll stop after a while."

"It doesn't matter."

But a little farther on, when they are passing through a stretch of woods, he finds a good place to stop. There is a rough trail leading off through a thicket of oaks,

188

just wide enough for the little truck. He goes down it a hundred meters or so and then stops and shuts off the engine. He has forgotten to turn the headlights off, and as the engine stops the yellow glow dies away until it is hardly visible.

They get out and lie down in a little round clearing or dell near the car. The trees are some kind of mountain oak, like the scrub oak in America, and they are hardly higher than a man. Under them there are lots of these small fairy-bowers, and on the dry leaves it hardly seems cold. Perhaps the foliage overhead protects from the night chill. Patrick is lying on his back, and Marie-Ange is propped on her elbow looking at him, as well as she can see him in the darkness which is almost total. She seems more cheerful now. She is even a little chatty. Perhaps she is slightly febrile.

"Now," she says, "we are like the Cathars. We're hiding in the mountains. The Inquisition will never find us. Now," she says, "we are Perfects."

"Do we have to give up fornication?"

"Oh no. We can be Perfect in our own way."

"I'm glad of that at least." He tells her, "I've given up smoking. I hadn't noticed, but I just don't want to any more."

"Bravo. Now you can start in on your other vices. Still," she says, "smoking does pass the time. What are we going to do all night?"

"I don't know. Are you sleepy?"

"No."

"Neither am I."

She says, "I could tell you stories."

"All right."

She begins in a prim schoolteacherish voice, lightly ironic. "Sainte Foy," she says, "was originally a girl called Conagund, who came from the town of Agen not far from Toulouse. In those days there were Roman soldiers in the Land of Oc, who commanded everybody and said the place was their province. They were pagans and they put to death anyone who believed in Our Lord Jesus Christ. Conagund was an orphan. Her parents had

189

been put to death on account of their faith, and she was raised by a young priest who was called Father Caprus. He took care of her and fed her and clothed her."

"What's all this?"

"It's about Sainte Foy."

"Are you making it up?"

"No, it's from the Legend of the Saint."

"You mean you know it all by heart?"

"Just about. When she was old enough, Father Caprus taught her her catechism. He also told her that her name was now Foy. He called her Saincte Foy, which in the language of that time means Holy Faith. Then he told her that if you are a saint you must not eat anchovies, you must not go barefoot, you must not sing after dark, and you must not speak any language except your own. Also, you must not put kohl around your eyes, or shoot a bow and arrow. She asked if there were any special advantages to being a Saint. He told her that there were no special advantages, except that none of the herbs of the forest will harm you, and they can't make shackles and irons lock on your body."

"It's a pre-iron-age legend," says Patrick with his eyes closed. "Older than Christianity."

"Yes. At this, Conagund decided that she didn't want to be a saint. Also, Father Caprus told her, Saints couldn't ride stallions, eat asparagus, or sing songs in two or more parts. They were not allowed to commit sexual intercourse, and they were forbidden to kill anything including insects on Friday, because that was the day on which Our Lord was put to death. Shortly after that, a kind of cold fire appeared around her head, which was visible at twilight or after dark, and in church. Father Caprus told her to cover her head in church, on account of this Fire which was distracting to other people and might lead her to vanity. Conagund tried to run away, but she found that she only ran around in a circle through the woods and came back to the church. So she put a cloth onto her head, went into the church, and prayed."

Patrick, lying on his back, has almost fallen asleep. There is a kind of wavering buzz in the air, a high zzzzz sound. Marie-Ange slaps rather fretfully at the mosquito, then, remembering that it is still Friday, she tries to set it to rights again, feeling in the dark to bend the legs back into place and straightening out a wing. It makes a feeble buzz; perhaps it will recover.

"Are you still awake?"

"Yes."

"Once," she says, "a painter came from Guccio in Italy to take her portrait. He did it in miniature, on a board which he prepared first with a gesso ground. She said, 'It's a rather small board.' He told her, 'We do the more important ones on a triptych, or sometimes a ceiling.' However, in order to please her, he added a dove carrying a sprig of oregano in its mouth, and a ribbon reading 'Fer non serre.' "

"Iron won't hold."

"This same painting," she says, "is in the church in Agen."

"There's no such painting. I've been in the church in Agen."

"It's from the Legend of the Saint," she tells him.

They pass the night in the woods, sleeping in each other's arms. At some point in the middle of the night they wake up and, taking off their clothes, they have a try at being Perfect in their own way. At the very last moment she sneezes. This is a curious sensation for Patrick. It has never happened to him before. It is as though she has had an orgasm, but it lasts only an instant, not long enough to enjoy it.

SIXTEEN

The sunlight is shining through the leaves into the bower. She touches his nose with a twig.

"Wake up, Emil."

He sits up. It is cold, and he is stiff from lying on the ground all night. The bed of dry leaves and twigs is not nearly as soft as it seemed the evening before and during the night.

She is fully dressed, with the rebozo around her shoulders and the Cross of Twelve Pearls exactly in the middle of the opening. "I've already been for a walk to look around," she says, "and I found a spring to take a drink of water, and I washed out my handkerchief, and also I defecated. Not of course in the same place."

"Good girl," he says rather numbly.

She spreads the handkerchief over a bush to dry. She doesn't need to blow her nose so much this morning anyhow. However, she has developed a cough.

"Are you all right?"

"What?"

"How do you feel?"

He tries feeling her forehead again. He can't tell very much from this. Everything is cold: his hand, her forehead, and the air, which makes her breath hang from her lips like a pale wisp of fog.

"You can't," she says, "tell anything by feeling a person's forehead with your hand. The palm can't feel the warmth. Anyone who's taken care of children knows that. You have to lay your forearm on the head."

He rolls up his sleeve and tries it with his forearm. Her face feels warm this way all right.

"You've got a touch of flu, that's all."

"I suppose so."

"You should take better care of yourself. You should take vitamin C."

"I don't believe in drugs. I don't believe in anything that violates the body."

"Don't I violate the body?"

"No, that's the worshiper coming into the Temple."

Is this another sample of her irony? It's too early in the morning for him to engage in these deep thoughts.

"We didn't," he tells her, "have any dinner."

"No."

"Are you hungry?"

"No."

"Neither am I. I would like some coffee though."

"Yes. There's a farm," she says, "right down through there." She points. "I saw it on my walk."

He sets off through the oaks in the direction she indicated. After a quarter of an hour or so he comes out into a small clearing. The farmhouse is just below, in a miniature valley with a small stream running through it. There is a house built out of grayish-black chunks of rock, some outbuildings, and a curious structure like a large masonry lantern on stilts. This last is perhaps a pigeon cote.

There is nobody in sight. Patrick crosses the farmyard, which is full of manure, toward the kitchen door on the other side of it. At this point a man comes around the house. He is a typical peasant, in a white shirt with no collar to it, baggy pants, and a flat cap which he wears pulled down over his eyes.

"What do you want?"

"I'd like to buy some coffee. I don't mean coffee that's made, you understand, but ground coffee so we can make our own."

Although, it occurs to him, they haven't anything to make it in. Perhaps they could boil it in the car's radiator. The Deux Chevaux, he believes, is air-cooled and doesn't have a radiator.

"Who are you?"

"We're camping, up there."

"Where?"

"Just a little way." He points in the wrong direction.

"We don't have anything to sell."

They stare at each other for an interval.

"That's an interesting structure. Is it a pigeon cote?"

"You'd better clear out of here, or I'll go in the house for my gun."

They go on with their staring match for a little while longer, and then Patrick turns and walks away. Out of the corner of his eye he sees that the peasant is going slowly around behind the house, still watching him. When the peasant is out of sight Patrick hesitates for a moment, then he turns and runs back toward the house. The kitchen door is open; in fact there doesn't seem to be any kitchen door. It is just a hole in the wall. There is a coffeepot on the stove. The coffee isn't fresh but the pot is still warm. He takes it, goes out the door, and starts running.

The coffee is barely tepid, but it tastes good. They have no cups of any kind so they drink it from the pot. They lie down on the bed of leaves, which seems softer now that the sun has warmed things up a little, and pass the coffeepot back and forth. Patrick is surprised to find that it is spring. Because he came up from a warmer Toulouse to the cooler mountains, he has thought of his trip somehow as an autumn. Now he sees that there are sticky buds breaking out on the oak trees and even some wild flowers pushing their way up through the leaves and breaking out in tiny orange and crimson blossoms. It was December when he woke up, and while he was away at the farmhouse the months have unrolled rapidly

194

until now it is April. He lies down on the leaves and props himself on his elbow.

"What happened to Sainte Foy?"

"Sainte Foy," she begins in her schoolteacher voice, "was martyred in the reign of the pagan emperor Diocletian. In the spring the Roman soldiers celebrated the feast of the Lupercalia, which is dedicated to Silenus. They ate watermelon, clashed cymbals, and wore lighted candles attached to a kind of cap of straps which they put on their heads. The governor, whose name was Dacian, had Sainte Foy arrested and invited her to take part in the festivities. She refused. So he had her embraced by Fortinbras, which was a kind of iron maiden, but when it was opened up she was unharmed and all his spikes were bent."

"Fer non serre."

"Yes. At this, Dacian said to her, 'Either you can renounce your Lord Jesus Christ or you can go to bed with me, the one or the other. Whichever you like. It's a matter of indifference to me.' "

"Which did she do?"

"Neither. This enraged Dacian. He stripped her naked and told the soldiers to violate her, but they didn't want to because she was a virgin and they said that wasn't very much fun. So he had her kicked to death by asses."

Marie-Ange lies on her back dozing, her head tilted back and mouth slightly open so she can breathe. Her large hands with their long pale fingers are stretched out on her jeans. A few wild flowers are stuck to her clothing. She looks like Millais's *Ophelia*, half under water, covered with microscopically exact leaves and flowers. Perhaps, he thinks, if he were to communicate these resemblances to someone, for instance to Marie-Ange, they would seem a little less silly. On the other hand it might just make him sound like a professor.

"You look like Millais's *Ophelia*," he tells her.

"I don't know it."

"It's a Pre-Raphaelite painting. It's in the Tate."

"I've never been to London."

"We'll go there some time."

"I don't think we will."

"If we do I'll show you the picture. Elizabeth Siddal posed for it," he plunges on recklessly, unable to stop his lecture. "She was Rossetti's mistress. She posed for it in the bathtub, and caught cold. She almost died, and when they thought she was going to die, Rossetti married her. She didn't die then. Later she died from an overdose of laudanum. Rossetti was grief-stricken and buried all his poems with her. Later he changed his mind and dug them up."

"He sounds rather like you."

"I haven't an ounce of talent as a painter."

"Rossetti was a poet," she says.

"I thought you meant Millais."

In this way, they pass their time like two children in the forest, telling each other stories.

Perhaps later in the morning they will get back in the car and go on. Well, perhaps about noon. They go on dozing. At one point, Patrick wakes up, goes to the camionette, and gets out the packing case. He lifts it out without much difficulty; it doesn't weigh as much as he thought.

He unscrews the four wing nuts and takes off the plywood top. Inside is the Majesté, staring out at him with all her aplomb of a Roman emperor. "I am Foy," she seems to say, "and I am also Dacian, who put me to death." Because she is lying on her back her forearms, which under ordinary circumstances are thrust out before her to hold the flower tubes, are sticking up vertically, in the pose of a drowned and stiffened body. (Of Millais's *Ophelia*, he tells himself. He is running out of artistic allusions and using the same ones over and over.) For the first time Patrick is able to examine her at his leisure. The kind of crown or helmet she is wearing is thinner than he thought. In front it is fairly thick, but on the side he is able to insert his finger into the fretwork and bend the metal quite easily. There is a dent in the side of the crown, probably from bumping against the packing case in the course of his reckless driving, and he presses it out easily with his finger and repairs it. The gold is hardly thicker than tinfoil. Perhaps it shrinks, or evaporates in some way if exposed to cold.

Still, there is quite a lot of it. The throne seems to be made out of slabs of solid metal. The crown, it now occurs to him, looks something like a motorcycle helmet. In the back it is open and he can see the wood underneath. It is carved to simulate hair.

He replaces the top on the packing case and puts it back in the camionette. Shortly after he has gone back to rejoin Marie-Ange, a French army helicopter comes pot-pot-potting by at an altitude of five hundred meters or so. It is khaki-colored, and they can clearly make out the red-white-and-blue band painted around its tail. It pot-pots in a large circle, somewhere near the farmhouse where Patrick found the coffee, and then heads off in the direction of Rodez.

"He couldn't see us under the oak trees."

"It's a good thing you didn't have the Majesté out, or he might have seen it gleam through the branches."

"Yes," he says, "that was lucky. I put it away just in time. You know, we aren't going to be able to drive in the daytime. I don't know why that didn't occur to me before. We're going to have to travel at night and hide in the daytime."

"That's what we're doing."

"Like the Perfects."

"The Inquisition," she says, "didn't have helicopters."

In the late afternoon she goes on with her story.

"The felon Roman," she says, "didn't want to bury her, so he made a nest for her above ground, as the ostriches do in Africa. And there Father Caprus came along and found her. He built a shrine on the spot, and a hut where he could sleep and take shelter from the wild animals. Her flesh smelled good, like a ripe fruit. The worm didn't penetrate it. After several weeks she was still just the same as the day she died. This made him impatient. He told her, 'Get along now, my girl. You can't stay here forever. This isn't your place.' He set her

197

out in the hot sun, and got a couple of maggots from a nearby refuse pile and put them on her. After that she corrupted quite quickly, and in a few days there was nothing there but the bones. Father Caprus, who knew the trade of stonemason, made a marble sarcophagus for her, and he had two monks carry it secretly to the church at Agen, where they put it in the vault. Father Caprus settled down nearby and took the name of Father Gardefoy."

All this folderol makes a pleasant noise, like the wind in the leaves or a babbling brook. Patrick finds that he is quite happy, sitting in the shade under the trees with Marie-Ange. He feels a good place in the center of him. It is possible that there never really was a Sainte Foy, he thinks. She is so far back in history that everything is blurred and we can see shapes only indistinctly. It may be that she is only a kind of coagulation or personification of the notion of the Holy Faith, which in the early years was violated (so to speak) by the Roman Empire. No, he doesn't really believe that. There really was a Sainte Foy.

"Now, in those days there was a knight named Parladuz, who wandered about the countryside and found his keep as he could. He had fallen in love with Sainte Foy while she was still in the life of this world. After she died, he was put in prison because he seduced a countess while her husband was away in the Crusades, and he put up a poem on the town walls in which he described all her private parts. Parladuz lay in the dungeon for many years, but then in despair he breathed a prayer to Sainte Foy. In an instant his fetters fell off and the door of his prison turned to rust. Parladuz went to the place where her bones were and stole them. He took them out of the sarcophagus, and made a bundle out of them which he carried on his back, pretending to be a woodcutter. When night came he took shelter in the very place where Father Gardefoy was living along with the two good monks. Father Gardefoy recognized Sainte Foy immediately and gave thanks to God that her bones had been rendered to him after being

198

stolen by the felon knight. Father Gardefoy, who was also a woodcarver, made an oaken statue and put the bones in it. He and the monks built an oratory for it in the woods, and the monks founded an order to praise her and venerate her name. It was called the Ornithite Order. It no longer exists because the two monks died long ago. They asked Father Gardefoy if he wanted to be an Ornithite too, but he said he couldn't because he was a Caninite. He went on living in a hut in the woods. Shortly after that, Parladuz died of the mange."

"She seems," says Patrick, "to be the special patron of rascals and criminals."

"Well, they're God's children too. It doesn't matter who you are, you can always pray. The Legend says:

> *Si la prie muet ou aveugle,*
> *Ou tourmenté de mal cruel,*
> *Ou s'il est en prison tenu,*
> *Ou bien par la guerre déchu,*
> *Quand vers elle a les mains tendues,*
> *Il peut être jeune ou chenu,*
> *Tôt lui viendront joie et salut.*"

Patrick gets a stub of pencil and writes it down, then he sets about trying to translate it. When he is done he reads it to her.

> "*If blind or dumb shall pray to her,*
> *Or he whose flesh is sore tormented,*
> *Or held in prison long lamented,*
> *Or hurt in war in distant lands,*
> *Let him stretch out to her his hands,*
> *Be he young or bent in limb,*
> *His health and joy return to him.*"

She says, "*Chenu* means hairy, not bent in limb."

"Well, I'm trying to make it rhyme."

Since they have no flashlight, and since there is no dash light in the car, Patrick is careful to memorize the map before nightfall. There they go—he runs his finger along the twisting yellow line—out of the hills at Decazeville—no, there's a side road that comes out a little below Decazeville so they won't have to go through the town—and so, carefully avoiding the main highways, on south to a point near Aubin where they can turn and start working their way eastward toward the Cévennes. This is a good route, only a little out of the way, and anyhow if they went farther south they would run off the map and have to beg, borrow, or steal a copy of Michelin 83. There are two reasons for taking the route he has planned. It follows the back roads, and it stays entirely on the map they have. He folds up the map and puts it in the glove compartment.

They have no possessions and nothing to pack, except for the peasant's coffeepot which they put in the back of the camionette along with the packing case, the MAT 49, and the magazines for the gun. They get in and Patrick presses the starter. The car groans for a while, slower and slower, and then the battery gives out completely. They have to push it to start it. Pushing the car makes Marie-Ange dizzy. She gets back in and rests her head against the seat, her eyes closed, breathing through her mouth.

They come out of the rough trail onto the highway just at nightfall, like a ship stealing out to attack its enemy. The little engine runs raggedly and seems to lack power, but it keeps going. The bushes and rocks slide by on either side in the yellow glow of the headlights.

Marie-Ange coughs, putting her fist to her mouth. She says, "In a novel by Vian there's a girl who is sick because she has a water lily growing in her chest. A nenuphar," she says. "I think that's what I may have."

"Millais's Ophelia may have caught a nenuphar," he says. "In your case, I think it's more likely that you caught a virus."

"You know, Patrick," she says, "you keep asking me if I love you, but you've never told me if you love me."

He thinks, I knew she would ask me that sooner or later. He says, "I do love you."

200

"That's nice, because at times I wonder whether you're just taking advantage of me."

"What advantage have I taken of you?"

She thinks and then says, "No particular advantage, I suppose."

They skirt around Decazeville, come out onto Nationale 662 and cross it cautiously, and continue on down to the south on a two-lane country road, which is however important enough to have a center stripe painted on it in dots and dashes. The ribbon of pavement goes on more or less endlessly through broken country : hills, then a flat valley with some farms in it, then more hills, then another valley. It is quite dark now. A kilometer or so ahead something is happening in the center of the road. A blue light is pulsing, and there are shadowy shapes silhouetted in headlights. As he comes closer Patrick is able to make out a blue police sedan and at least two other cars. A motorcycle is parked in the beam of the headlights. He wonders whether it would have been better to have the gun in the front, under his feet, rather than in the back with the Majesté and the peasant's coffeepot. But if the gun were in front, what would he do with it? He goes on driving, cautiously, peering to see out the dusty windshield.

The blue light is going round and round on top of the police car. There are figures around the cars, some of them only shadows, and others half visible in the headlights. One man is standing in the middle of the road, almost blocking it, holding a long sticklike thing in his hands. Patrick hears Marie-Ange coughing, and another intermittent bump which he finally recognizes as his heart pounding. He goes slower and slower; the camionette has now come almost to a stop.

Impossible to turn around without backing and filling several times. The pavement is narrow. Patrick shifts into first gear and creeps on. The figure ahead in the road looks like a man from Mars. He is wearing tight-fitting black breeches, a black leather jacket, and a helmet with a plastic shield to cover his face. The shield is turned up now and sticks out from his forehead like an insect's antenna. He is extending the thing in his hand out toward the oncoming car. He and Patrick, from a gradually closing range, examine each other.

The motorcyclist is silhouetted in the headlights and it is difficult to see anything beyond him. When Patrick comes closer he sees that there is a small car in the ditch at the side of the road, tipped over at an angle. A little beyond it is another car lying on its side, with broken glass all around it. There is some blood on the pavement, or perhaps it is only water from the radiator of the overturned car.

Patrick has now come to a stop. The yellow headlights pulse in the rhythm of the engine. The motorcyclist stares at them for a few seconds, then he waves them impatiently on. The thing he is holding in his hand is a wand with a red-white-and-blue circle on the end of it, used for directing traffic.

Patrick, still bent forward to see out the windshield, drives carefully around the motorcyclist, the blue police car, the car in the ditch, and the overturned car with the broken glass around it. In the darkness beyond he shifts into second and accelerates. He watches in the rear-vision mirror as the lights behind dwindle away.

Marie-Ange says, "Was that blood on the road?"

"I don't think so. It was water."

"It looked red."

"It was just the reflection from the light on the police car."

"The light was blue."

"Well, I think," he says, "that sometimes water, in a blue light, looks red."

"It was blood," she says.

Somewhere south of Aubin Patrick becomes aware that the car is not running very well. It never runs very well, but now it is running worse. It runs fairly well on the level, but when it is asked to climb even a gentle slope it develops a violent lurch and loses power. It goes *ugh, ugh, ugh* trying to force them up the hill, but

202

gradually slows down. One cylinder is evidently missing. Patrick tries giving it less accelerator on the hills. This way he is able to keep both cylinders firing, but he has somewhat less power than he does with only one cylinder running.

"The car isn't running very well." He says, "We can't go on this way."

"It runs, doesn't it?"

'"It won't climb hills."

"Maybe somebody has put sugar in the gas tank."

"No, it's the ignition." He says, "We have to climb hills, because in order to get from here over to the Vaucluse we have to cross the Cévennes. The roads aren't very steep, but they're too steep to climb with the car running the way it is." He says, "We're going to have to stop on the edge of a town and wait until morning, and get the car repaired."

"Do you think it will be very hard to fix?"

"It's a very simple engine and nothing much can go wrong with it. It's like an outboard motor. Probably it just needs a spark plug or something. But," he says, "it is not going to get us to the Vaucluse running like this."

"I don't know very much about cars."

"I thought you had a Mini-Cooper."

"It's a nice car. But I don't think we could get the packing case into it."

"In any case," he says, "it's back in Conques. We're here now."

They finally decide to stop a few kilometers north of Albi. This time there is no dell under the oaks for them to take shelter in. It is farm country, fairly heavily settled, and there are no woods except small copses that are part of farms and inaccessible behind fences. On a long hill leading down through the wheat fields they find some trees at the side of the road. It is a kind of turnout or rest station provided for tourists; there is a barrel to put wastepaper in and even a makeshift toilet. Patrick drives the camionette under the overhanging branches and stops it. The headlights expire, and he quickly turns them off. It is very quiet. The car can hardly be seen from the road.

The surface they are parked on is pavement, then there is a fence, and beyond that the wheat fields. There is no place for them to sleep. Patrick opens the back of the camionette and stares into it ruminatively.

"Let's try it."

They climb in. The small sheet-metal cabin on the back of the vehicle is perhaps a meter and a half long. It is pitch dark inside and hard to tell what they are doing. The crawl in and feel over each other like two moles in a burrow. On one side is the packing case. It is a meter long to start with, so it pretty well dominates that side of the floor. On the other side, it is possible to lie down, facing away from the packing case, with your feet bent into the fifty centimeters of floor on the other side after the packing case ends. However, this space is also occupied by the MAT 49 and eight or ten magazines full of bullets. The coffeepot is no problem; it can be put on top of the packing case.

They arrange themselves and lie down. In spoon fashion, as some people call it—that is, both facing the same way and their bodies bent at identical angles, nestling into each other—they can manage it. But only a short time later they sit up again and begin taking off their clothes.

Naked, it is even worse. Patrick remembers with regret how soft the dell in the oaks was. The MAT 49 presses into his side, and there are several magazines under him, as hard as penises and evidently determined to prevent him from putting his where he wants to. They shift around several ways but it is no use. They have discovered that it is impossible to make love while lying on top of guns.

204

SEVENTEEN

In the morning they have to push the car to start it again. This accomplished, they drive down the hill into Albi, coasting in places where the slope allows. Under these conditions the Deux Chevaux is able to keep moving at least. But one of the two cylinders, Patrick can tell, is hardly working at all. Marie-Ange too is not in very good condition. She slumps back in the seat, her mouth slightly open. He doesn't need to feel her forehead now, either with his arm or with his palm. She seems to radiate heat like a warm stove.

"How do you feel?"

"You asked me that yesterday."

"Now I'm asking you again."

"I feel terrible. Except for that I'm fine."

"Maybe we'd better get you a doctor."

"Well," she says, "I don't have much faith in doctors."

They enter the city by the Avenue Dembourg and the five-arched bridge over the river. Albi is a good-sized town. It has a cathedral, and its ecclesiastic authority extends all the way up into the mountains; in the Middle Ages Conques was in the diocese of Albi. The cathedral and the episcopal palace, which is called the

Palais de la Berbie, are both built of brick; in the bright morning sunshine they glow with a kind of salmon-colored effulgence. Patrick, trying to interest Marie-Ange in things, says, "Thirteenth century. Not quite as old as Conques, but almost." The cathedral is immense. It resembles a medieval fortress more than a church. The thick walls rise straight up with turrets every few meters or so. There are hardly any windows. A good distance above the ground are some narrow openings that are hardly more than arrow slits. Even higher up there are some windows between the turrets, but these too are long and narrow and seem to resemble defense mechanisms more than openings to let in light. In fact, this church was built by Bernard de Castenet as a fortress against the Cathars. These heretics are more often called Albigensians. They flourished in this part of France. In 1228 a dozen of them were burned in the place Sainte-Cécile, which is just passing by the car window to the left.

Patrick knows Albi well. He has often come here to take notes on the cathedral, and also to look at the Toulouse-Lautrec Museum in the episcopal palace. Toulouse-Lautrec isn't his favorite painter, but it is an important collection. "You look," he tells Marie-Ange, "something like Jane Avril." She would probably not be capable of a cancan right now, however. She is lying back in the seat with her eyes closed, smiling only faintly at his touristical remarks.

He winds his way through the narrow streets to the tree-lined esplanade and back again to the cathedral, looking for a place to get the car fixed. It is running worse and worse. Once when he tries to shift it stalls, but since it is still rolling he is able to get it started again by jamming it into gear. It barely manages to crawl around the cathedral, down to the river, and back up the boulevard to the palace. There it quits quite definitely. Luckily Patrick has managed to roll it to the curb.

They are just under the walls of the palace, which rises up like a cliff over their heads. Across the street is a gas station with a sign: "Esso. Essolube. Service. Réparations."

Patrick says, "Reparations are what we need all right."

It is about nine o'clock in the morning. There are some tourists high up on the ramparts of the palace, looking down at the street below. Most of them are apparently French. There aren't many foreign tourists at this time of the year. They are out for the holiday, and they have come to look at the palace, even though most of them have probably seen it before. Some of them are more interested in what is going on down in the street below. They watch as Patrick gets out of the car, opens the hood, and peers into it.

Patrick walks across the street to the gas station. It is modern and clean and has strings of colored plastic flags running from the building to the light fixtures out in front. There is only one attendant on duty, a tall blond young man with a distant manner. He is dressed in spotless Esso overalls and is wearing a beret.

"Could you fix a Deux Chevaux?" says Patrick. "I don't think there's very much the matter. It's just the ignition."

"Where is the Deux Chevaux?"

Patrick points. "Over there."

"I certainly can't fix it over there."

"Could you fix it if I bought it over here?"

"As a matter of fact, no. It's a holiday."

"It says, 'Réparations.' "

"Yes, but the garage is closed today. It's Easter Sunday." He points out to Patrick that the steel door of the garage part of the service station is shut. "There's nobody here but me. The mechanic is off today. It's a holiday," he explains once more, since Patrick is evidently a foreigner.

"Yes. Thanks."

Patrick goes back to the car, the hood of which is still standing open. A number of people are looking down now from the palace ramparts. He thinks, this is too conspicuous. We should never have got into this situation. This is not going to work. He looks at the engine of the car.

When you have a two-cylinder engine and one cylinder isn't firing, it is easy enough to tell which cylinder it is. You simply short out one spark plug and then the other with a screwdriver. When the engine stops, that is the cylinder that is working.

First he has to start the car. He does this by pushing it. Then he backs it back to its previous position, still with the hood open. He gets out again and bends over into the open maw of the car. The engine is shuddering and barking. He has no screwdriver, so he has to short out the spark plugs with his hand. Each time this causes a sharp jolt that runs up his arm and makes his head snap. The second time he does this, the car stops. This is the plug that is working. The other one is faulty.

He goes back across the street to the gas station.

"May I borrow a wrench?"

"Yes, if you leave a deposit. Ten francs."

Patrick gives him the ten francs and returns to the car with the wrench. It isn't really the right kind of a wrench; it's a spanner and not a spark plug wrench. He decides not to go back across the street again. He adjusts the wrench and fits it to the plug. It is a bad angle and it is hard for him to apply very much force. Everything is rusty and the plug won't come loose. He puts his hand around the other side so that he can push instead of pulling. The wrench slips and the porcelain top of the plug breaks cleanly off. It falls through to the pavement; he can see it gleaming down there.

Patrick straightens up and looks through the windshield at Marie-Ange. Her eyes are open now and she is watching him with a placid expression. Her face is flushed.

He goes back across the street to the service station.

"A spark plug for a Deux Chevaux," he says, "and a fever thermometer."

The blond young man says that he is not a pharmacy. He is not even a garage, on Easter Sunday. He is a service station.

"So you don't have spark plugs?"

208

"Not on Easter Sunday."

"What am I going to do then?"

"Go into the church and pray to the Good Lord for one, if you want. That's the only thing that's open on Easter Sunday."

"Don't be a smart aleck."

"Go bugger yourself then, if you prefer. Hey! where's my wrench? Give it back."

"Give me back my ten francs," says Patrick.

A car has pulled to the curb in front of the camionette. It is a Citroën CX very similar to Madame's, except that it is a slightly later model. A man gets out stiffly from the driver's position, feeling for the fly of his pants. Between the avenue and the palace above, there is a kind of moat or canyon filled with thick vegetation. The man walks around the car and heads for this topographical feature. He is evidently a person of some social pretension; he wears a foulard which he tucks into his shirt, red pants, and suede shoes.

His wife in the car has a flowered nylon dress. She rolls down the window. "Henri, ne le fais pas."

"Where then? I told you I can't wait."

"Henri, don't do it. People can see you. There are people up above."

The husband doesn't listen. He staggers wide-legged down the slope, unbuttoning his pants as he goes.

"Henri!"

Patrick gets into the car and sits beside Marie-Ange watching this drama. A number of people are looking down from the ramparts above now. They wouldn't have noticed the husband in the bushes, if it weren't for the wife calling out to him. The bushes are not as high or as thick as they looked from the avenue above. The husband is unable to find a place where he is sufficiently out of sight. He thrashes around, one hand on his pants and the other pushing aside the bushes.

The wife calls out, "Henri! Tout le monde te regarde!"

She is at the point of exasperation. She half opens the door of the car, undecided. The husband partly disappears under a bush the height of his shoulders, then appears again. He goes on toward the bottom of the moat where there are even fewer bushes.

"Henri! Everyone is looking at you!"

She abandons the car and starts down the slope in pursuit of Henri.

"Here we go," says Patrick.

He gets out of the car with Marie-Ange. They open the rear of the camionette and Patrick takes out the packing case. The trunk of the Citroën is locked, so he puts it in the back seat. He also transfers the gun, the collection of magazines, and the peasant's coffeepot into the Citroën. Everybody is watching Henri so no one pays any attention to what he is doing.

He and Marie-Ange get into the Citroën, and he drives away smoothly. Marie-Ange fastens her seat belt. He leaves his off for the moment. It is more important to get out of town. The big car glides along like a dream, making hardly a sound. Full of fuel too. The needle is resting on P for "Plein." He accelerates and watches the speedometer climb up to eighty kilometers. They leave the town by rue de la Republique and the avenue de Lattre de Tassigny, which outside the city limits turns into Route Nationale 99. There is no traffic because of the holiday and Patrick pushes the car up to a hundred.

Marie-Ange seems a little better now. Perhaps because the car is more comfortable, and because they don't have to worry about it not running. It is a beautiful car. It has a radio, air conditioning, and automatic shift. Madame's car had manual shift, which Patrick personally prefers, but still this is a beautiful car. Marie-Ange spots a box of kleenex propped up against the windshield. "Ah mon dieu, that's what I need," she says. She blows her nose, and tucks the kleenex away under her seat. Then she takes another one which she holds in her lap. From time to time she coughs into it. A yellowish stuff is now coming up, not very healthy looking at all.

Patrick glances at his watch. It is just ten o'clock.

"Let's turn on the radio."

"Why?"

210

"We may be on the news."

"I don't think so," she says.

He turns on the radio. They hear a voice saying, "Ici Paris," then it begins reading a weekly summary of quotations from the Bourse. He turns it off.

"Instead I'll tell you stories," she says. "Now, in those days there were some monks who lived in a place called Conca, or the Town of Shells. In that part of the world the pilgrims came by on their way to the shrine of Saint Yago, near Lands End in Spain, and they stayed the night with the monks."

"Are you sure you're well enough to tell stories?"

"I have to tell you all this. The monks were hard put to feed themselves and also the pilgrims. They tried to raise millet, but the millet wouldn't prosper. They planted fruit trees, but the fruit was eaten by the birds. They got some geese and kept them in iron cages, but as soon as the geese learned to say, 'Foy, Foy,' the cages would open. It was necessary to make wooden cages for them. In this way, the monks learned of the miracles of Sainte Foy.

"Now, as it happened, at this time there came by an Irishman named Padraic, who was an assassin by trade. But he repented of his sinful ways and wished to join the order. The monks told him that first he would have to go to the oratory in the woods, near Agen, and steal the relics of Sainte Foy and bring them back."

"What did you say his name was?"

"Padraic. It's an old Irish name."

She takes another kleenex. Her face is still flushed but she seems calm. The car is floating without a sound down a long country road lined with poplars.

"Padraic went to Agen and passed ten years pretending to be a faithful follower of Sainte Foy, in order to steal the relics. When the time came he had no difficulty stealing them, because of his felon skill, as the Legend says. Padraic took the wooden statue and put it on a donkey, and presently he came with it to Conques, where there was great rejoicing among the monks. Shortly after that a priest arrived, tired and weary and with his garments in tatters. It was Father Gardefoy. He knew the trade of goldsmith, and he began making garments for Sainte Foy out of gold and precious stones. When the monks saw the golden garments they were in awe, and they began raising a great church made of blocks of stone to shelter the Saint in. Gardefoy, who was also a stonemason, showed them how to cut the blocks of stone and fit them together."

"You've already said he was a stonemason."

"When?"

"When he made the sarcophagus."

"The Legend often repeats itself."

Here Marie-Ange seems tired and she stops. Patrick glances at his watch. It's exactly ten thirty. He turns on the radio again. The voice says, "Ici Paris. The news. The President of the Republic has received a visit from Monsieur Sadat, who discussed with him certain aspects of the situation in the Middle East. An important new source of uranium has been discovered in Zaïre. Near Lyon, a motorcylist and his young female companion were killed when their machine left the road. Police are still searching for the bandits who, on Friday, stole at gunpoint some relics and other objects of value from the church at Conques in the Rouergue. A pursuit has been organized and all roads are blocked. The bandits are traveling in a Deux Chevaux camionette, license 3013-RS-31. Monsieur Jacques Delvaux, Deputy Underminister of Agriculture, has announced that wine harvests in the Department of Côte-d'Or for the season just passed amount to one million four hundred thousand hectoliters, an increase of four percent over the previous season."

Patrick turns off the radio. After a while he says, "I don't think the situation in the Middle East is going to change very much."

She says, "I wonder what they're going to do with the uranium from Zaïre. I hope they're not going to make atomic bombs out of it."

He says, "I'm glad they're going to have plenty of wine in the Côte-d'Or."

They have left the Route Nationale now and they are driving on deserted back roads somewhere in the valley

212

of the Tarn. They go through a town called Saint-Affrique, which Patrick has never heard of, even though he thought he knew this part of France fairly well. It is a curious name. The town doesn't amount to much and they are in and out of it in five minutes.

On the other side of it there is another long straight country road, this one lined with plane trees, the leaves of which in April are a pale, almost luminous green, throwing a curious lime-colored light onto the pavement. Patrick checks the rear-vision mirror occasionally. There is nobody behind. In the mirror he can catch a glimpse of the top of the packing case on the rear seat, and he doesn't care for the effect. Lying there all by itself, in a place of state so to speak, it resembles a coffin. He stops the car, gets out in the pale greenish light, and opens the rear door. Without moving the packing case from its position he takes off the top and sets the Majesté upright in it. Then he gets back in and starts the car up again. Since no one can see the packing case from the outside, the Majesté now looks like a rear-seat passenger, perhaps the Golden Owner of the car, which is being driven by two minions.

Marie-Ange says, "This is a fine madness, Patrick."

He decides to take it as a compliment.

By noon they are well up into the Cévennes. It is a national park, for the most part beautiful mountain country with only a few farms and villages scattered about. At one time these mountains were thickly forested, but the forests were destroyed by glassmakers, who cut the trees for charcoal, a great deal of which is necessary in their trade. Now the land is good for little except raising sheep. There are wide expanses of pastureland exposed to the sky, at this time of the year covered with gentian, saxifrage, and adonis printanière or pheasant's-eye.

"Stevenson," says Patrick, "traveled through here with a donkey."

"Who is Stevenson?"

"He wrote *Treasure Island*."

"Oh. I thought perhaps he was a friend of yours. I

read *Treasure Island* when I was a child." She says, "When I was a child I always read boys' books. I never read girls' books."

He says, "Look for the characteristic beehives. They're called ruches cévenoles. They look like mushrooms."

They don't find any characteristic beehives, but after an hour or so of driving through the treeless mountains they come across an unpaved road that leads off into a grove of chestnut trees. There is grass under the trees, and some square rocks just about the right height for sitting on. Great square blocks of granite are scattered all about in this part of the mountains. Patrick stops the car. The grove is a thick one, cutting off the sky overhead entirely. Evidently chestnut wood is no good for making charcoal, or perhaps the glassmakers didn't discover this particular grove. They get out of the car, Marie-Ange with her box of kleenex. Then they notice that they are not alone. A short distance down the road a peasant is working at a curious structure that resembles some medieval instrument of torture, but an immense one. Four pillars of granite are driven into the ground, a half-meter or so thick and as high as a man. Two heavy iron bars or pipes run horizontally between the two pairs of pillars. Something is suspended from the pipes, and it is this that the peasant is working on.

They walk down the road to look at it. The horizontal pipes are very strong, as thick as a man's thigh. Two broad leather slings are attached to them, and in the slings is suspended an ox. The ox's hooves can barely touch the ground. In fact it is a machine for torturing an ox. He is wearing a heavy yoke, so gnarled and weather-beaten that it looks primeval, and this is lashed to the pillars so that he can move neither forward nor backward. On the two forward pillars a pair of short stone beams are driven in horizontally, a half-meter or so off the ground. The ox's knee, if that is what it is called, is lashed to one of these, and the peasant is shoeing him by driving nails into his hoof with a hammer. Patrick finds that he empathizes with the animal much more than he does with the man. First he has been castrated and now

214

a man is driving nails into his hooves. The ox seems to find difficulty understanding the reasons for all this, but he is phlegmatic and not much given to deep thought. A silver rope of saliva drapes from his mouth and slides onto the ground. Patrick doesn't know much about farm animals, but this may mean that he is hungry. Perhaps when the peasant is done torturing him he will give him something to eat.

The peasant doesn't look up as they approach. He takes a nail from his mouth, fixes it into the hoof, and drives it in.

"Bonjour," says Patrick.

Marie-Ange says, "Parlas occitan?"

The peasant says, "Non."

His farm, they now see, is a little farther down the road. Probably the car is parked on his land, but he seems to prefer not having any communication with them at all to raising any objection. They give up trying to elicit some response from him. He and the ox, Patrick thinks, perhaps understand each other. It is a sadomasochistic relation. They are necessary to each other.

As they leave, the peasant glances up at the car down the road, where the Majesté is clearly visible gleaming in the back seat. Then he goes on shoeing his ox. He has the right hoof finished now, and he unlashes it and goes around to tie up the other one.

Patrick says, "There's no feeling in a hoof."

"Yes."

He says, "It's like fingernails. It's like you or me cutting our fingernails. He can't feel it at all."

"Yes."

He says, "You have to have something to hold the ox up. Otherwise, as soon as you start shoeing him he will sit down. You can't shoe an ox while he's sitting down."

"Yes. How do you know all this, Patrick?"

He says, "I'm making it up."

The square blocks of stone are arranged almost like a table and chairs. Marie-Ange sits down on one of them, and Patrick goes to inspect the car more carefully. He looks in the glove compartment and immediately finds what he is looking for, a Michelin map number 80. He left the other one in the Deux Chevaux parked in Albi. He spreads the map out on the dashboard in front of the steering wheel. There is also a Michelin restaurant guide in the glove compartment, but this is of less interest to him. He takes the keys out of the ignition and goes around to the back to unlock the trunk. In the trunk is a folded plaid tourist robe and also a picnic lunch. The lunch is packed in an expensive basket of the kind available in better department stores. There is champagne, then a bottle of Montrachet, cold chicken, cold french-fried artichokes and zucchini, matchstick potatoes in a can, and pastries. The paper napkins are of the better kind that almost resembles linen. They spread all of this out onto the plaid robe which they arrange on one of the square stones. It is pleasantly warm. They sit on the grass with the picnic spread out between them. Manet, *Le déjeuner sur l'herbe*. Another artistic allusion. Patrick pours the champagne.

"They were rich bastards. Although," he adds, "that didn't prevent Henri from having rather bad manners."

"Yes," says Marie-Ange in a muffled tone. "You know, it isn't right to steal people's cars."

"They can probably afford another one." The car, he now notices, has a license number that ends in 31; Henri and his wife are from Toulouse. They went to Albi to see the palace, and later they were going to have a picnic lunch. He wonders where they will eat now, since, according to the blond young man, everything except the church is closed on Easter Sunday.

He opens the Montrachet and takes a piece of chicken.

"Henri," he says, "will have to eat God. He can go to Communion."

"What?" she says. "I don't know what you're talking about. Besides," she says, "you shouldn't say things like that. One can have respect for certain things, even though one doesn't believe."

Probably it was the Toulouse-Lautrec collection they had come to see, Patrick decides. To judge from their clothes, they looked like people who would be more interested in modern art than in medieval architecture. Probably they have a Van Gogh reproduction in their flat. Henri came to Albi to regard Jane Avril, but instead everyone regarded Henri.

Patrick looks at the car again. It was spotless when they took it, although now it is a little dusty from the country roads.

"You know," he says, "I don't believe Gaspar had anything to do with the Front de la Jeunesse."

"What difference does it make?"

"It makes all the difference. If he did it for the Front de la Jeunesse, he did it for a different motive than if he did it for himself."

She says, "There are no motives. Just acts."

"That's just lycée existentialism. Why do you talk like that? If you feel that way," he says, "you shouldn't have done what you did."

"Now what are you talking about?"

"You said it isn't right to steal people's cars."

"It isn't."

"Well then, is it all right to steal relics from churches?"

She is almost ready to say that it depends on the motive, then she stops herself. "I don't know," she says. "You're the one that said it was all right."

After lunch, to end the quarrel, they make love on the grass. This time it is somewhat more successful than it was in the back of the camionette. The peasant looks down the road at them once and then goes back to shoeing his ox.

Marie-Ange is propped on her elbow with the box of Kleenex by her side, and Patrick is lying on his back as usual. She has put her shirt back on but not her jeans, and she has left the shirt unbuttoned. The Cross of Twelve Pearls dangles between her pale, slight, perfectly formed breasts. It is still midafternoon and it is warm under the trees. Everything is much as in the picture. The gentlemen clothed, the ladies not. A ray of sunlight over here please, Monsieur Manet.

He is almost asleep, but he manages to say, "That was nice."

"You are better, Patrick," she says, "when you have wine with your lunch."

"There's more." He gets up drowsily to get it, but he is mistaken; the bottle is empty. He lies down again.

"Because of the relics of Foy," she says without any particular transition, but in her storytelling voice, "many thousands of pilgrims now stopped at Conques on their way to the shrine of Saint Yago. The pilgrims left gifts, and on their way back they left shells to show that they had been all the way to the sea. So the monks became rich. Many of the pilgrims were former prisoners, who had prayed to the Holy Martyr Foy so that their shackles and chains fell from them. They brought their chains with them when they came to Conques, and they laid them in offering by the altar. Father Gardefoy, who knew the trade of blacksmith, set up a forge just behind the church, and he beat the chains into iron grilles which were put around the altar so that felon thieves wouldn't steal the relics and the treasures of gold and jewels that had been gathered in the church in honor of the Saint. People came from all over to see these things, and Conques became famous."

She says, "Now in those days there was a troubadour in the Land of Poitou named Golo. He fell in love with a lady named Mabelle who lived in a castle on the Loire. Her husband, hearing of this traitorous passion, contrived for her a pair of iron drawers with sturdy locks. They fitted her front and rear, covering her female parts, and allowed her only a hole to pee through."

"It's just an ordinary chastity belt. There are lots of them in old engravings."

"But Golo fell down on his knees and prayed to Sainte Foy, promising to compose a ballad in honor of her. He also swore a vow that he would never roger Mabelle on Friday, because that was the day on which Our Lord was put to death. And when he did this, the iron drawers fell off Mabelle, and the two lovers ran away and embarked

218

on a boat that took them down the Loire to Angers. But Golo did not compose a ballad in honor of Sainte Foy, and also he rogered Mabelle on a Friday. So he was stricken with a flux and his bowels fell out of him and he died. But Mabelle did not return to her felon husband, instead she went into a convent in the Land of Tours, and later she became very holy."

"I suppose that Gardefoy beat the chastity belt into a grille."

"The Legend doesn't say. Now, in those days in the Land of Rodez there was a priest named Bélibaste. His godson, Vuitbert, managed his goods for him. One day Vuitbert went to Conques—"

She breaks off, takes a Kleenex, and coughs into it.

"You'd better put your jeans on."

"It doesn't matter. One day Vuitbert went to Conques to pray to the Saint, and on the way back he met Bélibaste, who accused him of being a vagabond and not paying attention to business. Vuitbert said he had only gone for the day to the Feast of Sainte Foy. But the priest lost his temper and ordered his men to tear out Vuitbert's eyes. None of his men would do it, so he got down off his horse and tore out the eyes with his own fingers, which ought to have been devoted to the Body of Christ, as the Legend puts it. But those present saw a dove pick up the bloody eyes and carry them off through the sky toward Conques."

"Are you sure you're all right?"

"I have to tell you all this. When Vuitbert was cured, he took up the trade of jongleur or wandering mountebank. A year went by. On the anniversary of the Feast of Sainte Foy, he was falling off to sleep when he seemed to see near him a young woman of perfect beauty. Her aspect was that of an angel. Her stature was that of an adolescent, but she wore majestic raiments, embroidered with gold and color. On her head was a diadem with four gems that threw off extraordinary fires—so the Legend puts it. She said, 'Vuitbert, are you asleep?' 'Who is it?' 'I am Sainte Foy.' 'Lady, why do you come to me?' 'Tell me, how are you, and how do your affairs

go?' 'Very well, Mistress, and my affairs are going well.'
'How can you be well,' she said, 'and how can your
affairs go well, when your eyes have been torn out by a
brutal and unjust master, so that you cannot see the
light of Heaven? This felon priest,' she said, 'has much
offended God and irritated the wrath of the Creator, by
damaging you gravely in your body without your de-
serving it; but if tomorrow, the vigil of my martyrdom,
you will come to Conques, if you buy two candles and
place one before the altar of the Holy Savior, and the
other before the altar where my statue all in gold is displayed, you will receive the gift of again being able to
use your eyes.' He did so, and in the church about midnight he seemed to see two little spots of light, no larger
than grapes, descending from above into his empty eye
sockets. He fell asleep, but at the hour of Lauds he was
awakened by the sound of singing. He seemed to see
shadows and shapes of people, but he had a terrible
headache and he believed he must be dreaming. Coming little by little out of his torpor, he gradually made
out forms and his vision returned to him. The most as-
tonished over this were those who had long known
Vuitbert, whom they had not considered a very important person."

Patrick is almost asleep. He wakes up and says, "Is all
this in Occitan?"

"It's in the Langue d'Oc. I'm translating for you."

"Is there very much more?"

"There's a whole book of it." She says, "In the Land
of Cahors there was a noble matron, Doda, suzerain of
Castelnau on the Dordogne. She had unjustly occupied
a domain of the monks of Conques. On her deathbed she
restored this land to the abbey of Conques, but her
grandson Bodo, who succeeded her, reoccupied the land."

"Isn't he the knight who died of a flux?"

"No, that was Golo. The monks, to regain their prop-
erty, decided to go to the place in grand procession carrying the statue of Foy, as was the custom. When they got
there, they found Bodo in a boisterous mood because he
had been drinking wine to celebrate Christmas. He
hurled insults against the monks, called them manure,

and said that their statue was a ridiculous masquerade. He proposed to knock it over and trample on it. He also said some other things which it would be a shame to report. Suddenly, a storm burst out overhead with a terrible fracas. The house was wrecked, and the roof fell in. Of all those present, the only to perish were the blasphemer, his wife, and six of his family."

"I don't care very much for that last one."

"Maybe you'd like this one better. In those days, the image was once taken to a territory called Molompise, in the Land of Auvergne, where the abbey had some domains. The monks, as was their custom, sounded oliphants and clashed cymbals, as they went along in procession, to cure the sick. A man called Othon, who was deaf and mute from birth, was helping to carry the litter that bore the image of the Saint. A sudden sensation caused him to put his hands to his ears and rub them vigorously. A triple hemorrhage burst out, from his mouth and both ears, and he cried, 'Sainte Foy, help me!' No one had ever heard him speak before; it was patently a miracle. Meanwhile, bewildered by the sounds of singing and by the oliphants and cymbals, he took to his heels and ran off over the hill, escaping from the hands that sought to retain him. He had lost his wits completely, and people felt that it would have been better for him to remain deaf and mute and keep his reason. However, so God would have it."

"That one is worse."

"Well, it's very primitive material. These are stories told by peasants."

"Most peasants," he says, "are brutes."

Then he realizes that he is more or less quoting Sara on this subject. He is uncomfortable lying on the hard ground. He gets up and walks away drowsily down the road to the four granite pillars. The peasant and his ox are gone now. The two broad leather slings are hanging down from the iron pipes, at their lowest point about waisthigh from the ground. Patrick lies down prone on the slings. One of them supports him under the chest, and the other approximately at his knees. He can't stretch out his leg far enough to imagine how it would feel being shoed. However it is very comfortable being suspended in this way. It is something like a hammock. There is a little manure on the ground, but most of it is toward the rear where it is out of his frame of vision. In this position he falls asleep and wakes up only about an hour later. He glances at his watch, extricates himself rather stiffly, and walks back down the road toward the car.

Marie-Ange has put her jeans back on now and is coughing into a kleenex. She puts the kleenex away in her pocket. She says, "Emil, you don't have very much talent as an ox."

EIGHTEEN

At nightfall they load everything into the car: the plaid robe, the picnic basket, and the two empty bottles. They leave nothing behind. Patrick even smooths out the depression in the grass where they have lain in each other's arms. Then he gets in behind the wheel and, with some difficulty, turns the car around and gets it going back down the dirt road to the highway. Marie-Ange, mastering the lever down at the side that controls the seat, inclines it to a shallow angle and lies back on it with her eyes closed. She is feverish again. A warm and sweet-smelling effulgence, like that from a baby, seems to radiate from her and fill the dark enclosed space of the car. Patrick turns the headlights on. The yellow beams bore down into the darkness, illuminating the road ahead for half a kilometer or more. They are really too bright and he wishes he had some way of dimming them.

He has carefully planned his route from the map while it was still light. There are no large towns in these parts, but there will be as soon as he comes down out of the mountains into the Rhone valley. The proper way to come down out of the Cévennes would be to take Nationale 107 through Florac and Alès. But Alès is a

223

good-sized town, and furthermore the roads down from Alès are all important ones and there are bound to be a good many tourists on them on Easter weekend, which in France includes the day after Easter. Instead, shortly beyond Florac, he turns left onto Départmentale 9, which is exactly the kind of road that suits him : a twisting mountain road so unimportant that it doesn't even have a center stripe. The yellow headlight beams climb up into cols and then soar off across shallow valleys. He leaves the car in top gear and makes good time, accelerating with a rush when he comes to an occasional straight stretch. There is no traffic. From Florac to Anduze, a matter of fifty kilometers or so, he doesn't meet a single car.

There isn't much to Anduze. It is a pretty little place, even in the dark. There is a square with a romanesque tower, and some picturesque narrow streets. It was here that Stevenson came out of the mountains with his donkey. Patrick clearly remembers his copy of *Travels with a Donkey*; he stole it from the library in South Pasadena, California, when he was fourteen and kept it on the shelf in his room until he went away to college. He wonders where it is now; it's odd how the objects of your childhood have a way of going astray as you get older. There was a picture of the donkey on the cover; her name was Modestine. Patrick little thought, in those days, that there would come a time when he would not only be able to pronounce the difficult place-names in the book, like Fouzilhac and Cheylard l'Evêque, but would actually visit the Cévennes himself, in his own car, so to speak. Stevenson, he remembers, liked the people he met in the Cévennes because most of them were Protestants. They have a different kind of heretics on this side of the mountains. There are always heretics in the mountains in France, but these are Huguenots and not Cathars.

Patrick stops the car to look at the romanesque tower. The town is asleep; everything is black against the dark-gray sky. The tower dates from the fourteenth century, about the same time as the bridge in Conques. Later, in the time of the religious wars, it was part of the fortifications that held out for a long time against the Catholic armies of Louis XIII and Richelieu. In fact Anduze was never taken, although the fortifications were demolished after the wars, leaving only the medieval tower. It has some arches at the bottom and an interesting crenelation at the top. He would like to communicate all this touristical information to Marie-Ange, but she seems to be asleep. It is a rather troubled sleep, however, and she wakes up now and then and mumbles to herself. He catches, ". . . in those days . . ." and ". . . thief." Probably she is reciting Legends of Sainte Foy to herself. He reaches over to push the hair out of her face and pulls his hand away, almost as though he were burned, from the hot skin. Her mouth is partly open and there is a frown on her forehead, visible in the light from the instruments. This same glow, filtering back through the dark, faintly illuminates the Majesté in the back seat.

"The leader of the Huguenots in Anduze," he tells the Majesté, "was the Duc de Rohan. He was the highest member of the French nobility ever to declare himself as an Protestant. He was a descendant of the Duc de Rohan who owned the *Grandes Heures de Rohan,* which I once wrote a book about. Actually it was not a book, it was only a small monograph. Marie-Ange," he goes on to tell the Majesté, "is not very well. She ought to be in a hospital, although under the circumstances that's rather difficult. If we went to a hospital we would both be arrested, and it's a question whether she would be better off in the car with me or in jail." He says, "You probably imagine this is hypocritical of me, since what I am really concerned about is being arrested myself. There is some truth in this, but actually what I am concerned about is being separated from Marie-Ange. If we were arrested we would be separated, because they don't put men and women in the same jail in France. Or anywhere else," he adds. "I believe in Mexico they allow conjugal visits. But Marie-Ange and I are not married."

The Majesté probably knows all this. She goes on staring out through the windshield, not changing her expression one iota. Patrick starts the car up, winds his way out of town through the narrow streets, and sets off through the night on the lonely country road.

After driving for some time—his watch has stopped, but to judge from the stars wheeling around overhead it is after midnight—he finally comes out of the hills into relatively flat country, in the valley of the Rhone. According to the map, which he examines in the light from the instruments, he is on Départmentale 982, which ought to take him through Uzès and then across the Rhone somewhere north of Avignon. He will have to work out the exact roads later. Uzès is a fair-sized town but at this time of night no one is likely to be about.

As he slows down to go through Uzès the change in the sound of the car awakens Marie-Ange. She pulls the lever to bring the seat upright, and looks around her as though she isn't quite sure where she is.

"My chest hurts," she says.

"Well, you probably have a little bronchitis. When we get to Les Bouilladoires," he says, "I'll go out and buy you some Ampicillin."

"What's Les Bouilladoires?"

"It's the farm we're going to, in the Vaucluse."

"Why are we going to a farm?"

"It seems the best place to go. There's no one around, and you can rest there and get well."

"I don't know what Ampicillin is. I don't like to take medicine. Where are we anyhow?"

"This is Uzès. It's a Protestant town. Most of the towns in this part of France are Protestant. André Gide was born here. There's a cathedral, but it's bad baroque. It's not worth stopping to look at. I believe there's also a tower, dating from the fourteenth century. For some reason all the towers in this part of the world are fourteenth century. Ampicillin," he says, "is a broad-spectrum antibiotic. It's one of the so-called miracle drugs. It will fix you up in no time."

"Let's not stop to look at the cathedral."

"All right." He sets the car in motion and drives on down the main street, which seems to be called the Boulevard Charles Gide. Then he sees an illuminated sign saying "Pharmacie." He james on the brakes violently.

He gets out and bangs on the glass door of the pharmacy. Then he identifies a doorbell, and works this instead for a while. The pharmacy is dark except for a night light. But someone evidently lives in the apartment overhead, and there is no other way to get there except through the pharmacy. He is up there all right. Patrick goes on ringing the bell.

Finally the pharmacist appears on the stairway, in the gloomy half-light of the shop, and comes to the door. Instead of opening it he slides back a glass panel so he can talk to Patrick. He is actually wearing a nightshirt. Patrick didn't know people wore nightshirts anymore.

Patrick says, "Ampicillin."

"We're closed. The duty pharmacy is in rue des Carmélites, on the other side of town."

"Just a minute, will you please? Stay right there. Don't go away."

The pharmacist waits by the door while Patrick goes back to the car. He opens the rear door and takes the MAT 49, which is lying on the floor of the back seat. He is not sure how to fit a magazine onto it, but probably the pharmacist is not an expert on such things. The pharmacist watches all this. The car, the gun, and the Majesté in the back seat are clearly visible in the thin light of the street lamps.

Patrick goes back to the door of the pharmacy. "Now give us some Ampicillin or I'll blast down everything. I've never shot anybody in a nightshirt, but it'll be a new experience."

"Well, you don't have to get emotional," says the pharmacist. "It's clear you've got the upper hand. You can have whatever you want."

He opens the door, and Patrick goes in. With a professional calm and dexterity, in spite of his costume, the pharmacist pulls open a drawer and slides an oblong box across the counter to Patrick.

"And a glass of water."

The pharmacist looks at him sideways. He goes to the rear of the shop, Patrick following, and draws some

227

water from the tap into a not very clean glass. He hands this to Patrick. Patrick, after a moment of hesitation, puts the medicine in his pocket and takes the glass in his left hand, still holding the gun in his right hand. The pharmacist says nothing more. He accompanies Patrick to the door, and locks it once he is outside. On the street Patrick goes to the car, sets the gun on top, and breaks open the box. He takes out a capsule and passes it through the window to Marie-Ange, then gives her the glass of water. He looks around. The pharmacist is still watching through his glass door.

"I really don't like taking medicine," says Marie-Ange.

"I know you don't. This is a miracle drug. It will have you well in no time."

He puts the rest of the Ampicillin in his pocket and replaces the gun in the back seat. He would prefer not to steal the glass from the pharmacist, but he doesn't know what to do with it. It would be awkward asking to have the door opened again to pass it in. In the end he simply sets it on the sidewalk and leaves it. The pharmacist watches them drive away.

Patrick drives down the road, a kilometer or two east of Uzès, studying the map by the dim glow of the instruments. No chance of avoiding towns now, or main highways. The whole Rhone valley from Nîmes up to Orange is a tangle of red lines, with Avignon sprawled in the middle of it. There are two big autoroutes from the Côte d'Azur roaring up the valley—first the A9, then the A7 on the other side of the river. Still—he slows down a little to look at the map more carefully— suppose he left the highway here and went off across these back roads. There are only some tiny hamlets— Saint-Maximin, Saint-Siffret, Flaux, Valliguières. Then he could duck under the A9 at Tavel, which isn't much of a place either, and work his way across the river somehow into the Vaucluse. It ought to work, as near as he can tell by looking at the map in bad light while driving down the road with one hand.

He finds the junction, leaves the highway, and rattles

along on an unpaved dirt road with some gravel scattered on it. On this road it is *really* dark. There isn't even a farmhouse light showing to break the inky blackness stretched out under the stars. He passes through the four hamlets, one after the other. Everything is dark and there is no sign of life. Then he comes over the top of a rise and the whole valley bursts out in front of him, like a moving and crawling Christmas tree. First there is the A9, consisting of a stream of red lights going one way and pale yellow lights the other, then the lights from Avignon and the other towns along the Rhone, then another stream of red-and-yellow lights from the A7 across the river. The A7 is twice as big at the A9; it is an immense artery filled with cars hurtling incessantly back and forth from Paris to the Côte d'Azur. Where the blazes are all these people driving at three o'clock in the morning! He feels suddenly naked, as though all the red, yellow, and white lights are watching the Citroën as it makes its way down the road. He goes on looking fixedly at them out of the windshield, hoping, perhaps, that he may be able to stare them down.

He goes on through the small town of Tavel—this is where Tavel rosé comes from, he explains to Marie-Ange, who seems to be asleep again—and under the A9 in a concrete tunnel that echoes like a bass drum with the sound of traffic overhead. No sooner has he crossed the river—on a rickety iron bridge that he would hardly believe to exist if he hadn't seen it on the map—than he comes up behind a police car. He slows down. It is a kind of van, painted gray, with the usual blue light on top and POLICE in large black letters on the back. A long antenna is sticking up from the rear. The effing thing is only going about thirty kilometers an hour. He can't go on crawling along behind it in this way. There is no place to turn around, and this would be conspicuous anyhow. He hesitates for a moment longer. Then he kicks the pedal to downshift and pulls out around it.

He watches it go by in the dusty window to his right. Then he catches a glimpse of it again in the rear-vision mirror as he pulls ahead in front of it. It dwindles away behind, still keeping to its snail's pace. It is only a small blocky spot in the mirror, growing constantly smaller. Then the blue light on the top comes on and begins flashing. The gray spot grows in size again as it comes up behind. The yellow headlights of the van glint on the Majesté in the back seat. The klaxon goes on, blaring its two notes a musical third apart.

beep bop

BEEP BOP

BEEP BOP

This is it, he thinks. He feels very odd. He feels disembodied. Someone else is driving the car, and he is watching the whole thing. Should he awaken Marie-Ange? No, better not to. He goes on driving at the same speed, hunching his head into his shoulders like a tortoise. The blue light comes swaying up behind, pulls out, and goes by to the left of him with the klaxon beep-bopping deafeningly in his left ear. The van gathers speed and pulls away rapidly down the road ahead. The beep-bop of the klaxon gradually grows fainter. Then he can see only the flashing blue light. It winks away down the road, goes around a curve, and ascends a ramp to the autoroute. He can follow the flashing light for a long time as it gathers speed up the A7 to the north.

Marie-Ange is awake now and sits up in the seat. "What was that?"

"They seem," he says, "to have heard something on their radio."

Patrick drives into the pasture, turns to the right with the headlights flashing across the rough stone wall, and shuts off the engine and the lights. He has been here before and can find his way pretty well even in the dark. It is almost daylight now anyhow. He gets out, leaving Marie-Ange in the car. On the right is a small stone shed with a tiled roof, and on the left the wall of rough squared stones. Between them is an opening that leads to the courtyard, and at the bottom of the courtyard is the house. It is a big two-story farmhouse with a cluster of outbuildings around it. Everything is built of the flinty

230

fieldstone that is found in this part of the world, a kind of rubble piled up more or less at random. There are frames of finished white stone around the doors and windows. It is a prosperous farmhouse, almost a kind of rustic chateau. Patrick reaches up to the top of the door frame, standing on his toes, and finds the key.

Inside he gropes around for a candle, then a match, and strikes a light. Everything is much as he remembers it. He takes a deep breath and relaxes his muscles one after the other. He hadn't realized how tense he was. He goes back to the car for Marie-Ange.

When he opens the door she turns to get out, then she just sits there.

"It's funny, I can't walk. I know how, but the legs don't work."

He slips his arm under her shoulders. She touches the ground with her feet now and then, but for the most part he carries her into the house. It is like carrying a rag doll that has been heated in an oven. Her breath comes slowly, in little tropic gusts that feel warm in his ear. He sets her down in a chair at the kitchen table.

"First I'll give you another Ampicillin."

"I don't—"

"I know. Take it anyhow."

He gets out the box and extracts a capsule, and she opens her mouth like an obedient child. He sets the capsule on her tongue and she closes her mouth. It is all a kind of parody of a communion; perhaps, because she is feverish, this is what she thinks she is doing.

He goes to the sink for a glass of water, and with this she is able to swallow it.

There are bedrooms upstairs but there is no furniture in them. After some thought he decides to lay her on a kind of stone ledge at one side of the room, which is the usual whitewashed kitchen-cum-living-room of a Provençal farmhouse. The ledge is a kind of seat built into the wall, long enough so that she can lie down on it, and wide enough for her body. It has a smelly old blanket on it. He folds up the plaid robe from the car and puts it under her head as a pillow.

"Are you all right?"

"I'm fine. Except for the nenuphar in my chest."

Feeling a little floaty himself, perhaps because of the sleepless night, he goes back out to the car and brings in the Majesté. He carries the packing case easily in his outspread arms, with the Saint sitting upright in it on her throne. She seems as light as air now; he could almost hold her on his finger. Gold in Latin is *aurum*, he thinks; perhaps it is the same word as air. Professor Lohengrin would probably know. Looking around for a place to put the Majesté, he takes her out of the packing case and sets the packing case up against the wall at the end of the room. Then he puts the gold statue on top of the packing case. Since the packing case is one meter high and the Majesté eighty-five centimeters, the whole affair is about as high as he is so that the two of them can look at each other eye-to-eye. Over on the ledge Marie-Ange has her eyes closed but she isn't asleep; she is mumbling to herself again.

He goes back out to the car and brings in the MAT 49 and the collection of loaded magazines. He puts the gun on the kitchen table, with the magazines in a neat row beside it, like an exhibition in a museum. Then he looks around to see what there is to eat. There isn't very much. There is a wine bottle with a little something red in the bottom of it, but it smells like vinegar. The bread, half of a baguette, is fossilized. He finds some cornmeal and sets about trying to make some porridge, feeling like the young and incompetent heroine of a fairy tale. He gets some water boiling, and shakes in a few handfuls of the meal. Some salt. After a while the mixture thickens, then it begins going blop blop. Fine; as he understands it this is what it is supposed to do. While it is blopping he examines the picture on the Farine de Maïs box. Fleur de Provence, it says. Farine de Maïs de Haute Qualité. Suitable for Children and for Those Who Are Unwell. It will do, he thinks, both for me and for her.

A grayish light is coming in through the door, which he has left open. With a rag he wipes some muck out of a couple of bowls and fills them with the porridge, but Marie-Ange isn't able to eat any. Her throat is too swollen, and besides she says she isn't hungry. However, she slept a good deal in the car, so she isn't sleepy. When she closes her eyes it is only to rest them. As for Patrick, he *is* sleepy. He walks around the kitchen, rubbing his eyes to keep them open. Then he takes a chair over and sits down to look at her.

She is still mumbling to herself in a vague way. He wonders if delirium is a serious symptom. Probably it is more or less normal with a fever. But she isn't mumbling to herself, she is trying to say something to him.

"I want to tell you the rest of the Legend," she breathes in a whisper.

"You shouldn't."

"In those days," she says, "in the Land of Rodez, there was a strange fire that burned under the ground. If men put it out in one place, it would come up in another. It crept through the roots of trees and vines, which it consumed, so that the land was wasted and there was famine everywhere."

"Don't talk."

"Because of the fire, men in Rodez and in the whole Land of Oc became mad. They took off their breeches and put on pants instead. They were called sans-culottes. In the church in Rodez, they tore down the image of the Virgin and in its place they put up a statue called Liberty. Instead of going to church they shouted in the square and made speeches, and also they violated the nuns and put the priests to death. All the men in the Land of Oc had lost their senses, because of the fire that was burning underground."

"It sounds to me," he says, "as though some intellectuals have been working on this material. It doesn't sound like peasant material to me. It sounds like fake peasant material."

"When the men in Rodez had desecrated the church, and torn down the Virgin and put up the statue of Liberty in her place, and violated all the nuns, they looked around for more infamy to commit. They took their sharpened pikes and came to Conques, shouting and jeering in their long pants. Now, in the church in Conques was the sacred image of Foy, which they knew, and they coveted it for its gold. When the monks heard them coming they were seized with fear and began to pray. The sans-culottes crowded into the church and put a red cap on the image which was called the Cap of Liberty. Then they seized it and attempted to carry it off, but suddenly it became so heavy they couldn't lift it. At this they became enraged and set about to slay the monks. But the blades of their pikes became as soft as wax, and drooped down and melted onto the floor of the church. In this way they knew the power of the Saint. And so they turned and went back to Rodez."

"It was probably Catholic university students who worked the material over," he says. "It's highly tendentious. You ought to be able to see that. I thought you were supposed to be a radical."

"Radical means root," she says. "The fire that came to the Land of Oc spread through the roots of the trees."

"You'd better get some rest."

"I have to tell you all this."

It is later in the morning and the sun is warming things up. A beam of sunlight comes in through the open door and creeps its way slowly across the room, with motes of dust floating in it. It is very quiet. Occasionally there is the sound of a car passing on the highway a kilometer or so away, and now and then there are caws from a pair of crows who are quarreling over a grain of corn out in the field. Then Patrick hears the burr of a small car coming up the road from the highway. At the entrance to the farm the sound drops to a lower note as the car idles, then there is a whine as it shifts into low gear and pulls up the slope into the pasture. The small blue car goes by the opening between the shed and the end of the wall. Then the noise of the engine stops. In the silence Patrick can hear it clicking faintly, as an engine sometimes will after it is shut off.

"Hello," he hears Anstruc's voice, "this looks like the Citroën that was stolen in Albi."

Patrick takes the MAT 49 from the table and examines it, turning it over in his hands. It seems that the magazine sticks up into the bottom. He takes a magazine, tries it first upside down, and finally gets it to go into the gun. Now what? He pulls back the cocking handle on the left side. Pointing the thing out the open door, he tries the trigger tentatively. The trigger goes back with his finger, but nothing happens. He sees now that the cocking handle has to go forward again for the bolt to be freed. He pushes and it goes forward into position with an oily click.

Anstruc appears in the opening between the wall and the shed. He looks around at everything out of his tanned face, turning his bull-like torso to one side and the other. The gold on his epaulets glints in the sunshine.

Patrick levels the MAT 49 and pulls the trigger. Immediately he thinks the universe has blown up. The reports seem to bang in rapid succession against his skull like hammer blows, bouncing back and forth inside his head. The muzzle of the gun flies up wildly and a round or two goes into the door frame. The noise knocks the dust off the walls and sends it floating around in the room. Anstruc turns on his heel, like a doll in a shooting gallery, and disappears behind the rustic stone wall.

There is a certain interval in which nothing happens. Patrick waits. There is a treble singing in his ears that sounds something like the Boys' Choir of the Vatican. He becomes aware that, in his lack of experience with the gun, he has fired off the whole magazine. He figures out how to remove the magazine by pushing the catch and fits in another one. There are brass cartridges lying all over the floor to his right.

Patrick can see the gilded képi showing over the top of the wall. He yells out the door, "I DON'T WANT TO HURT YOU, ANSTRUC!"

Anstruc shouts back, "I KNOW YOU DON'T, BUT YOU MAY ANYHOW IF YOU'RE NOT CAREFUL WITH THAT THING!"

There is another silence. Anstruc is evidently thinking, as he usually does before he makes some statement.

"HELLO, PROFESSOR?"

"WHAT?"

"MAY I CALL YOU PATRICK?"

"ALL RIGHT!"

There is another pause. Then Anstruc yells, "WHY DON'T YOU COME OUT OF THERE?"

This isn't a threat or even an order. It is just a proposal for Patrick's consideration, even though Anstruc has to shout it because of the distance between them.

"MARIE-ANGE ISN'T VERY WELL!" Patrick shouts back.

"ALL THE MORE REASON TO COME OUT THEN!"

When Patrick doesn't respond to this, Anstruc steps out into the opening between the shed and the wall. He seems to be unarmed. His square tanned face is expressionless. Patrick lets fly with the gun again. This time he manages to keep the muzzle down. Dust and chips of stone fly up from the wall. Anstruc moves sideways, as though he were executing a figure in a dance, and disappears behind the wall again.

After a while he shouts, "WATCH OUT FOR THAT THING! IT HAS PARABELLUM NINES IN IT! THEY CAN CAUSE A LOT OF DAMAGE!"

The two crows, who seem to be unmoved by gunfire, are still quarreling out in the field. Patrick touches the barrel of the gun and burns himself. He moves his hand farther back, near the stock.

"LISTEN, PATRICK! WHY DON'T YOU COME OUT!" yells Anstruc. "YOU'RE NOT REALLY IN SERIOUS TROUBLE! I'VE KNOWN PEOPLE WHO WERE IN A LOT MORE SERIOUS TROUBLE THAN YOU!"

Still in shouts, they launch into a discussion of Patrick's legal problems.

"DON'T THEY STILL HAVE THE GUILLOTINE IN FRANCE?"

"YES, BUT IT'S ONLY FOR CAPITAL CRIMES!"

"I KILLED FATHER DION!"

"NONSENSE! HE WAS AN OLD MAN! HE HAD A HEART ATTACK! IT WAS A COINCIDENCE!"

Patrick yells, "I WISH I COULD BELIEVE THAT!"

"YOU CAN! I'VE JUST TOLD YOU!"

"WHAT ABOUT GASPAR?"

"YOU'RE AN ACCESSORY! HE DIED IN THE COURSE

236

OF A FELONY IN WHICH YOU WERE A PARTICIPANT! BUT THAT'S NOT SERIOUS!"

"ISN'T IT?"

"NO! YOUR TWO FRIENDS ALSO KILLED A GUN DEALER!"

"I DIDN'T KNOW THAT! THEY DID?"

"YES! HE WAS AN ILLEGAL GUN DEALER, BUT IT'S STILL A CRIME!"

"I WISH THEY HADN'T DONE THAT!"

"I WOULDN'T WORRY ABOUT IT!" Anstruc shouts back. "YOU WEREN'T THERE, AND IT'S CLEAR THAT YOU DIDN'T KNOW ABOUT IT! YOU MIGHT BE AN AC-COMPLICE AFTER THE FACT, BUT THAT'S NOT SERIOUS EITHER!"

Patrick glances around behind him. He can't see Marie-Ange very clearly because the table is in the way. He levels the gun a little to the right of the képi which is showing over the top of the wall, and pulls the trigger. This time the gun only fires two rounds. He has come to the end of the magazine.

"ANSTRUC!" he shouts. "YOU STAY WHERE YOU ARE BEHIND THAT WALL! DAMN IT! DON'T COME CLOSER! I'M CAPABLE OF HURTING YOU!"

"YOU'RE CAPABLE OF IT!" Anstruc shouts back. "BUT I DON'T THINK YOU WILL!"

Patrick fits in another magazine, and then goes over to see how Marie-Ange is. He kneels down beside her. Her eyes are closed. She is frowning and there is a little tremor at the corner of her mouth.

She says, "That's awfully loud, Patrick. It hurts in my ears. It also hurts my chest."

"It hurts my ears too."

"Then why do you do it?"

"Because I don't want to be separated from you."

"You will though."

At this, something hurts in *his* chest. The gun still in his right hand, he stretches out his left and touches her face. Her long hair is disarranged on the folded robe. He slips his hand under her head, smooths out the hair, and straightens it along her cheek. Her eyes remain closed. She doesn't seem so hot now, but perhaps it is because he himself is warm from shouting at Anstruc and shooting the gun at him.

"Patrick," she whispers.

"What?"

"Listen. After the sans-culottes went away, Father Gardefoy came to the church of Conques with a donkey."

"Don't. Just be quiet."

"He loaded the image of the Saint and all the relics onto the donkey, and went away into the wilderness. The donkey was very humble and contrite, because he knew that other donkeys like himself had kicked the Holy Virgin and Martyr Foy to death under orders of the felon Dacian. It is for this that donkeys even today are so docile and obedient." Her voice is very faint and he has to bend low over her to hear it. A strand of hair has worked its way loose from her cheek and curled up to the edge of her mouth. As she speaks the strand is moved very slightly by her breath. "Father Gardefoy went away into the wilderness, where he became a recluse and hairy hermit. He stayed there for many years, until there was no more danger from the sans-culottes. During this time he kept the relics and the image of the Saint buried in the dirt under his hut."

Patrick says, "Just a minute."

He goes to the door, levels the MAT 49 again, and fires a half-dozen rounds at the wall.

"ARE YOU STILL THERE?" he shouts.

There is a pause, and then Anstruc yells back, "YES I AM!"

"WELL, STAY THERE!"

There is no answer to this. He goes back and kneels beside Marie-Ange.

She says, "Don't do that."

"I'm sorry."

"If you're sorry for doing things, why do you do them?"

"Listen. I just want to tell you that I love you."

"That's nice. Father Gardefoy grew old only very gradually, but he did grow old. When his hair was white and his limbs were shrunken away to sticks, he

238

dug up the relics and the image of the Saint and put them on the donkey again."

"The same donkey?"

He has to put his ear almost to her mouth. The strand of hair pulses in and out.

"No, it was a different donkey. He carried the relics and the image back to Conques, and put them in the church again. Later he became a Dominican and took the name of Father Dion. He knew the trade of watchman, and he became the guard and watchman for the sacristy."

"He was a Caninite before. Caninite is the same as Dominican."

"What?"

"Domini canes. The Hounds of the Lord."

"Well, I don't know about that. As for the donkey, it was later killed by a speeding automobile on the road which was built from Conques to Rodez."

"Is that all?"

"Yes."

Patrick says, "Well, I'm glad to hear how it all turned out."

"I'm glad I finished," she says faintly.

He remains kneeling beside her for a long while after that. There is no sound from the wall outside where Anstruc is waiting. Marie-Ange mumbles once in a while, but it is hard to make out what she is saying. At one point she seems to say, "I'm fine, except that I can't breathe." He bends over her, trying to catch the words. It's something about "païs." He makes out, "Vòli viure al païs." *I want to live in the land;* but which land? Whichever land it is, it probably isn't this one. He goes on watching, listening to a faint ticking that seems to come from the walls and the bawk, bawk of the two crows quarreling in the pasture. After a while he notices that the strand of hair by her mouth is not moving anymore.

He gets up from the floor in a rage, seizes the gun from the table, and rushes to the door with it. He blasts away, first at the wall across the courtyard so that chips of stone fly up in a shower, then into the sky. When he comes to the end of the magazine he puts in another one and fires it off too. He gets down on the floor for another magazine and finds that it is empty. He looks at the rest of them. They are all empty.

A water fills his eyes, making the external world wobble. The square doorway, the courtyard, Anstruc's képi over the wall, everything wavers in a liquid film. He goes back to look at Marie-Ange again. Her mouth is open and he closes it. Then he takes her hands and lays them together on her chest, the fingers just touching the Cross of Twelve Pearls. Now she resembles one of those medieval queens who lie chastely on top of their sepulchers, hands folded in prayer, dreaming stone thoughts inside their cold heads of stone. His eyes are still watering, but after this thought he is comforted and feels better.

He goes back to the doorway. "MARIE-ANGE IS DEAD!" he shouts.

Anstruc yells back, "DID YOU HARM HER SOME WAY?"

"NO! SHE DIED OF PNEUMONIA!"

"WHY DON'T YOU COME OUT THEN?"

"I'M AFRAID TO!"

"WHY?"

"I'VE SINNED A LOT SINCE MY LAST CONFESSION!"

"WE ALL HAVE!" Anstruc shouts at the top of his voice. "THESE THINGS HAPPEN," he yells, "BECAUSE PEOPLE ARE CONSUMED WITH LUST AND AVARICE. IT'S LOVE THAT'S NEEDED, PATRICK! MORE LOVE! INSTEAD OF PEOPLE COVETING THINGS, AND INFLICTING VIOLENCE ON EACH OTHER!"

"THAT'S RIGHT!"

"THAT'S WHY IT'S SO HARD TO BE A POLICEMAN!" Anstruc shouts. "BECAUSE PEOPLE ARE CONSUMED WITH PASSION!"

Patrick looks at the gun on the table, and then remembers that the magazines are all empty. He goes through the kitchen drawers, finds a paring knife and a somewhat longer knife which is evidently used for peeling vegetables, both rather rusty, and a pair of scissors. He puts them away in the drawer again.

"ANSTRUC!"

240

Silence. Over the wall he can see a spark of gold on the top of the képi.

"I THINK I'M GOING TO COME OUT OF HERE!"

"FINE! BETTER COME OUT WITHOUT THE GUN!"

"I'M OUT OF AMMUNITION ANYHOW!"

"THAT'S GOOD! JUST PUT THE GUN AWAY, AND COME OUT WITH YOUR HANDS UP AS THOUGH YOU WERE REACHING FOR SOMETHING ON A SHELF!"

Patrick turns and goes back into the room. His glance is caught by the Majesté, which is now receiving a ray of sunlight from the open door. It is a rather theatrical effect. One would think that a modern God could do better, in an age of advanced stagecraft. He opens the drawer again and takes out the knives and the scissors. He looks for a screwdriver but he can't find one. He goes to the door again.

"ANSTRUC!"

"HELLO!"

"WAIT A MINUTE!" he shouts. "I'LL BE OUT IN FIVE MINUTES!"

"ALL RIGHT!"

"TEN MINUTES AT THE LATEST!"

"ALL RIGHT!"

He goes to Marie-Ange. Pretending to caress her hair, he surreptitiously cuts off the lock by her mouth with the scissors. He also clips her fingernails, replacing the hands in their position on the cross when he is finished. He puts the hair and the clippings on the table. Then he goes over to have a look at the Majesté.

The head is definitely from the Roman period. It is too large for the rest of the body, and when examined carefully it doesn't even fit very well. He tries to pull it off as one might unscrew the head of a doll, but it is too tight. He tries to force it up with the two knives, and then with the scissors, but they are too sharp and begin to damage the gold. He goes back to the drawer again, rummages around, and finds a drink opener of the kind with a sharp point on one end and a prong to pry off caps on the other. With this he prizes up the head without damaging it very much.

241

The first thing he sees is that the gilding is much thinner than he expected. It is hardly more than gold leaf. The alabaster-and-onyx eyes are slightly loose and vibrate a little when he shakes the head. He turns it upside down. The carved wooden head under the gold is hollow; a hole the size of a person's thumb is drilled up into it for a distance, and then it widens out into a round chamber. There is some stuff up in there, but he can't tell what it is. He puts the fingernail clippings and the hair into the opening and rams them farther up with the handle of a spoon. Then he fits the head back onto the statue again. It is slightly askew, as though the saint were looking at something a little to her left, but once he has fixed it in place he can't straighten it. He hopes he hasn't damaged the head. He pats it, to be sure it is firmly in place. The head, he thinks, is perhaps a portrait of Diocletian, or possibly even something earlier from the Aurelian period.

He goes to the door and shouts. "ANSTRUC!"

"WHAT?"

"I'M COMING OUT NOW!"

"ALL RIGHT!"

Patrick, forgetting to lift his arms, walks out into the sunlight, which is so dazzling that it seems gilded. Anstruc comes out from behind the wall. He still doesn't seem to be armed.

"This is better," says Anstruc. "My voice was about to give out."

"Mine too."

Anstruc takes something out of his back pocket. "Would you like to put these on?"

"What are they?"

"They're handcuffs. It's just regulations. I know you're not a violent person. Although you did blast away at me an awful lot with that MAT 49."

"It was just a form of communication," says Patrick.

Anstruc says, "It's against the law even to own a gun like that."

MacDonald Harris is the author of seven novels before this one, including *The Balloonist*, which was nominated for the National Book Award in fiction, *Yukiko*, and *Pandora's Galley*. His award-winning short fiction has appeared in *Harper's*, *Atlantic Monthly*, and many other magazines. He has taught in the Writing Program at the University of California, Irvine. Except for frequent stays in Europe, he lives in Southern California.